CARIBBEAN MAGIC

JULY, 1665

TUPPENCE VAN DE VAARST

CARIBBEAN MAGIC

ISBN-10: 1-945994-02-9
ISBN-13: 978-1-945994-02-9

First Edition: March 2017

Cover Art: Charlotte Hayes
Editor: Erin Foster

This book was published by Tannhauser Press.
www.tannhauserpress.com
info@tannhauserpress.com

DEDICATION

To Cambria

Caribbean Magic

July, 1665

*****Chapter 1*****

I knew something was different the moment I stepped into the plantation house. The front patio was freshly scrubbed and the windows and doors were flung open, allowing a refreshing breeze to pass through the front room. I was just coming in from the garden, and was in a cheerful mood.

"Are we expecting visitors?" I called as I stepped across the threshold.

Ma entered the room, a vase of yellow lilies in her hands. I suspected the vase was the only reason she didn't throw her hands into the air at the sight of me.

"Josephine! Your dress! And your hair! And with Mr. Reddings arriving soon... Oh dear Lord, where is Mary? We must get you presentable!"

I glanced down reflexively. My dress and apron were streaked with dirt from being in the garden, and they hadn't been in the best condition to begin with. My black, stringy hair was bound back in a tight braid, the only way I could keep it under control. Ma said the women in her old village would sometimes crop their hair as short as the men, but that would never pass here in Jamaica. Especially not for the legitimate daughter of a white plantation owner, regardless of her skin color. I was nearly as dark as any African, despite the fact that Ma's relatives never left the Caribbean. Ma was Taino, native to one of the islands in the north. She had left her village to marry my father.

"Who's Mr. Reddings?"

Ma wasn't listening to me anymore. "Mary!" she cried, setting the vase of flowers on the table. "Mary!"

Our maid came running at the sound of Ma's voice. "Yes ma'am?" she asked calmly. Dear Mary. She never let anything fluster her. As black as black came, straight from a village in Africa. She never told me her story.

"Oh Mary... Just look at the state Josephine is in! And with Mr. Reddings coming. How are we to get her ready in time?"

I took an instinctive step backwards. "Get me ready? For what? And who the bloody hell is this Mr. Reddings?"

Mary gave me a disapproving look. She always did that when I cursed. "No worries, ma'am. I'll get her straightened out."

I withheld a groan. I knew what was coming. Mr. Reddings was a rich white man coming to visit, and I would be expected to dine with him. Properly. With the rich white woman's dress to match.

I cursed under my breath. Mary narrowed her eyes at me. "Come along then, Josephine. My, it will take a bit of work to get you sorted, won't it?"

I glared at her, but I knew I couldn't win a battle of wills when both Ma and Mary were united. Like it or not, I was getting dressed up for this Mr. Reddings. But I was not going to enjoy it.

I was right. Mary fished out one of the more elaborate dresses in my wardrobe and pushed, poked, and prodded me into it. It was a gorgeous thing, all blue silk and lace, but I kept a scowl on my face the entire time. The rich, white woman's dress might fit me, but it did nothing to make me look feminine. My hips were still skinny as a beanpole, my chest still flat, and my face... Well, at least I wasn't ugly. I could say that much.

Rosa came into the room just as Mary was putting the finishing touches on my hair. I saw the ghost of a smile cross her face.

"Don't even think it," I snapped at my sister. I knew she could read my emotions and I was in no mood for it.

Rosa must have noticed even more than I realized; she pursed her lips and looked at me. I glared at her until she spoke.

"Can you do anything with 'it?'" she asked delicately.

My head jerked up, startled. There was only one thing Rosa could be talking about, but in what context?

"'It?'" I asked sharply. "What would I be using 'it' for?"

"To make yourself look more womanly," Rosa said. "You look like a boy in a dress right now."

I ground my teeth. Rosa was trying to help, she truly was. And she was right. I could use 'it.' But to make myself more attractive to a white man? The only thing that I used 'it' for right now was to disguise my spider medallion as a crucifix. It wouldn't do for a plantation owner's daughter to be seen with an African pagan symbol around her neck. But my Nana had given it to me before she died, and it was the only thing I had left of her.

"Why?" I demanded. "What's so special about this visitor that I should look more womanly?"

Rosa blinked, surprised. "They didn't tell you?" she asked.

I narrowed my eyes, immediately suspicious. "Tell me what?" I asked.

She hesitated, but only for a brief instant. "He's thinking about marrying you."

I stared at her. "Mr. Reddings?"

She nodded. "And the womanlier you look, the more likely he is to ask for your hand."

I continued to stare at her. Finally, the only thing I could get to come out of my mouth was, "The bloody hell."

"It would help if you didn't curse in front of him, either," she said serenely.

There were several things wrong with this picture. I shook my head, trying to clear it. "Are you serious?" I asked.

"About cursing? Definitely," she said.

I glared at her. "You're evading the question," I snapped. "Me? Marry?"

"It's not that odd of a concept," she said, her voice tinged with exasperation. "I'm engaged to be married, after all. It's only logical that you should be next."

I clamped down hard on what threatened to come out of my mouth next, namely more curses.

"And just who is this Mr. Reddings they're threatening to give me to?" I asked, trying to keep my voice level.

"He's a rich, English plantation owner." Rosa said calmly.

I couldn't help it. I started laughing.

Rosa glared at me. "It's not that much out of the question," she snapped.

Slowly, it dawned on me that she was serious. I stared at her. "Me, marry a plantation owner?" I exclaimed.

"Father's a plantation owner, Jo," Rosa said.

I looked at Rosa, my mouth opening and closing like a fish. This wasn't happening to me. It really wasn't. I wasn't ready for this marriage thing. Especially not to a white man.

I thought things would be different when we moved to Jamaica. I grew up in St. Kitts, to the north. Three years ago, we moved here, hoping that my brother, sister, and I would be more welcome. We were wrong.

Rosa sighed. "Well, are you going to use 'it' when you meet Mr. Reddings or not?" she asked.

I felt the anger flare up inside of me. As if I were somehow not good enough for him the way I was.

"He'll see me the way I am," I snapped. "It's not worth doing anything else."

I could see Rosa's exasperation. "Have it your way, Jo," she said, pausing." At least try to be polite to him, won't you?"

I glared at her again.

She rolled her eyes and walked out of the room.

Why was she so damn insistent on me making a good impression on Mr. Reddings, anyway?

This wasn't going to work. Me, marry a rich, white plantation owner? Hell would surely freeze over before that happened.

Tuppence Van de Vaarst

*****Chapter 2*****

Hell had not reckoned with the strength of Ma's determination. I walked into the sitting room straight into one of the longest lectures about 'proper behavior' that I'd ever received. As if I gave a damn.

I did try to curb my tongue for Ma's sake. 'Try' was the operative word.

"You've said that already, Ma," I snapped as she told me for the thousandth time to mind my manners.

"And you haven't listened! What will he think?"

I glared at her. "Well, maybe if you'd told me about him before the day of the meeting!"

Ma raised her eyebrows. "Would that have improved your behavior? Or merely given you a chance to run off?"

The nerve! She was right, of course, but really!

The sound of a carriage driving up cut off anything else I might have said. Ma gave me one last warning look before Mary came into the room.

"Mr. Reddings is here, mum."

Ma nodded. "Show him in."

I did manage to follow proper manners and rise to my feet as Mary ushered the white man into the sitting room. He bowed smartly before walking forward to greet Ma. "It's a pleasure to see you again, madam."

It was likely prejudice, but I disliked the man on the spot. Oh, there was nothing about his physical appearance that was wrong. He was tall, moderately handsome, with dark, slicked back hair and nondescript brown eyes. His cheekbones were neither too fat nor too sharp, and a glance at his hands showed that he probably had never done physical labor in his life. And yet, there was something about him I couldn't place.

"Mr. Edward Reddings," Ma said warmly as she took his hand. "Please allow me to introduce my daughter, Josephine."

I was clumsy as I curtsied, but at least I tried.

"A pleasure to make your acquaintance, Miss Josephine." Mr. Reddings took one of my hands in his and bowed over it.

I froze. There was an electricity to his touch that I did not like. It was like the energy from the plants, but much stronger, with a fierceness and fire I did not care for in the least.

Ma would've had a fit if I were unpleasant to the man. Even though every bone in my body was screaming, Get away! I merely withdrew my hand.

"Yours as well," I said, my voice cracking slightly.

I shot a glance at Ma. She had touched him as well. How could she not feel it? Everything I was taught screamed that this man couldn't be trusted. But then, Ma was a devout Catholic. Any hint of what Nana had taught me would have been deemed witchcraft. If Ma had ever found out Nana taught me about the pagan religions of Africa, as well as my talent, there would have been hell to pay.

I must've been decent company the rest of the afternoon. My mind was in turmoil, trying to decide what about Mr. Reddings set me off. Ma was completely enamored by him, acting all welcoming and friendly. Even Mary was being extra nice. Probably because they wanted me married.

Like hell!

"Oh, my plantation is quite vast, madam." His voice was like silk. Dirty, soiled silk.

I couldn't help myself. "How many workers do you have?"

Mr. Reddings raised an eyebrow. I heard Ma gasp. It wasn't seemly for a woman to be interested in the running of a plantation.

I met his eyes without flinching. I knew the most common practices for running a plantation. Most were run with large quantities of slaves. Though I had no African blood myself, I looked black, and I knew it. Mr. Reddings hadn't said whether his plantation was coffee or sugar, but if it was sugar, I knew he was thinking of slaves.

We had no slaves on our plantation, contrary to the popular custom. I don't think Ma would have let Father forgive himself if he started buying people. We paid them a wage. Not much of one, but at least they were free.

"Currently I employ around one hundred and fifty men and women," Mr. Reddings said finally. "Sugar does not come without labor, you understand."

Sugar. Of course.

The conversation was stilted after that, at least on my part. Mr. Reddings continued to be as charming as possible. At least, that was how Ma reacted to him. We had tea, in proper English style. I hated tea.

If I was Mr. Reddings wife, I would be expected to have tea with every visitor he had. I shuddered.

Ma knew what my thoughts were. After Mr. Reddings had left, she told me "He won't make a slave of you, Josephine. You're not black. You're Taino."

"As if that makes a difference to him." I turned away. I couldn't explain to her what I felt. She wouldn't understand.

"Mr. Reddings is one of the richest Englishmen here," Ma said gently. "He will make a fine match for you. It's a compliment that he's willing to look at a Taino girl, even one who is half English."

I felt my fists clench. And there was the crux. I was supposed to feel flattered that an Englishman would look at me. As if I were somehow lesser than an Englishwoman.

"He'll be calling again in two days' time. I trust you will maintain your manners."

****

Reddings kept calling on me, and I kept trying to avoid him. I remained civil during his visits, but I was trying to make it plain I had no interest in him.

Of course, Ma and Rosa kept badgering me. They wanted to see me married, and in their minds, Reddings was the best thing that could have happened to me. I nearly came to blows with Rosa during one conversation, after which I was summoned to Father's office.

I still didn't know how I truly felt about Father. He was a white Englishman, but one who consented to marry a native woman and treat her, Rosa, my brother Miguel, and me as equals. Or as near to equals as the English came, anyway. Even though I had all the privileges he gave me, I rarely saw him. I couldn't believe he actually cared.

This feeling was emphasized by the way he stared at me from across his desk. He wore high-class clothes, as always. I always felt underdressed around him, but I gave up on dressing up long ago. His eyes were stern and, try as I might, I could detect no compassion in them.

"What's this I hear about you refusing Mr. Reddings, Josephine?" he asked.

I crossed my arms across my chest. "As far as I know, he ain't asked for my hand yet."

Father rolled his eyes. "Hasn't, Josephine, as you well know. That does not change the fact that you have refused to even entertain the notion of marriage to him."

I knew it irritated him when I spoke like the servants, but I couldn't help provoking him. It annoyed him so.

"I don't like him," I snapped. "He gives me the creeps."

"Do you have any logical basis for your feelings?"

There he was again. Logic. Always logic with him. It was one of the reasons I had never told him about 'it'. He wouldn't have believed in something he couldn't logically define.

"Women's intuition," I said instead, knowing that would lead me nowhere.

Predictably, he shook his head. "You know there's no such thing, Josephine. And if it were women's intuition, don't you think your mother and sister would have the same feeling? Instead, they have each told me they can't think of a better match for you. To be honest, I can't believe he is even showing an interest. My plantation is not that wealthy, and Miguel will inherit the vast majority of it."

That was an interesting question, but one I filed away for future examination. My priority right now was to convince Father I couldn't marry the bastard.

I strode forward and placed both my hands on his desk. I leaned forward so I could look him directly in the eye. He didn't flinch back but I saw the resignation on his face.

"Are you gonna force me to marry a man I dislike, Father?" I said, fighting to keep my voice calm.

"I rather hope you will see reason instead, daughter."

I threw my hands in the air. "Reason!" I exclaimed. "Is that all you ever think about? What about the feelings of your youngest daughter? You let Rosa marry who she chose, why not me?"

"Because Rosa is an obedient daughter," I blinked at the harshness of Father's tone. "You are headstrong and willful, Josephine, and have been a trial to me for far too long. This conversation would have never happened with Rosa. She would have been an obedient daughter were there a suitable suitor for her at the time."

I was surprised and angry to feel tears stinging my eyes. I shouldn't be surprised Father preferred Rosa over me. She always was the more feminine of the two of us. And she was much subtler in her disobedience than me.

"Is that the end of it, then?" I asked, trying to keep my voice from trembling. "You'll sell me to the highest bidder, like I was your slave instead of your daughter?"

Father got to his feet. "It's not the same, and you know it, Josephine Crawford. You'll be doing this for your own good. Are you going to behave or not?"

I felt my hands curl into fists, and I couldn't conceal my trembling anymore. "Not if that means obeying your ridiculous orders as to who I marry!" I yelled.

Father's hand slammed down on the desk, and I jumped.

"To your room, Josephine!" he shouted. "I'll hear no more of your insubordination."

I spun on my heels, more than ready to flee his presence. His voice followed me out of the door.

"And you will marry the man, Josephine! Whether you like it or not!"

I slammed the door behind me without replying. I stopped in the hallway, trembling. My hands were clenched in the folds of my dress, causing the brown muslin to wrinkle. I couldn't quite take in what I just heard. Father was going to force me into marriage with that man, no matter what my feelings were. Because I was the disobedient daughter.

For a moment, I tried to picture what marriage to Mr. Reddings might be like. I would live on a plantation much like this one, like Ma, with run of the house. It wouldn't be so bad, would it?

Then I pictured Mr. Reddings' face. The affable mask he always wore faded away to become hard and cold, with dark eyes that bored into me and stripped away at my soul. I shivered. I couldn't let myself fall into his power.

I shook again. What the blazes was I thinking? I never saw anything to indicate Mr. Reddings was anything but stuffy, arrogant, and uncaring. And that he probably owned slaves. Nevertheless, I wouldn't marry him. If Father saw me as a disobedient daughter, then by God I would be one. He hadn't seen anything yet.

"Jo?"

Rosa's hesitant voice made me straighten up in surprise. She was pale underneath her dark skin, and her eyes were filled with worry as she looked at me. Worry for me.

"Were you listening?" I demanded.

Rosa flushed. "I could hardly help hear you two," she snapped. "You were shouting so loud at each other, it's a wonder the roof didn't blow off."

I sighed. I didn't want to argue with Rosa. Not so soon after fighting with Father.

"Leave me alone, won't you?"

"Not until you answer me one question." Rosa stepped close and looked around. I felt my eyes narrow. What did she want?

She leaned close and whispered, "Jo, are you just being stubborn, or is there something else telling you not to trust Reddings? Like 'it?'"

I tensed. I wasn't certain, but it was as good of a reason as any. "He gives me the creeps," I said. "I hate being in his presence."

Rosa nodded. "Then I won't badger you anymore," she said. "Nana always said we had to trust our feelings. And if yours are this strong..." She shrugged.

I felt a flash of guilt. I wasn't sure my dislike of Mr. Reddings was based on 'it' or not. But if Rosa believed that 'it' was the source of my dislike, she was more likely to help me avoid marrying him.

"Rosa, will you help me?"

Her eyes widened in alarm, and I hastened to reassure her. "Not against Father. No, I want you to find something out for me. Ask your sewing circle. Someone has to know something about Mr. Reddings. Find out if he has slaves. Find out what his plans are, anything. Find out why he'd be willing to marry me, of all people. I'm hardly a good catch."

Rosa nodded slowly. "I can do that. You're right, it is strange he should be courting you."

I breathed a sigh of relief. "Thank you, Rosa," I said. I meant it, too.

Rosa smiled at me. "What are sisters for?"

That got a laugh out of me. We had rarely worked together during the seventeen years of my life, but occasionally it did happen. "I'd better get to my room before Father orders locked up," I said. "Good hunting."

I made sure my posture and stride were confident on my way to my room. If anyone told Father what I was acting like, I wanted to make sure he got a defiant report.

I had no idea if Rosa would actually find anything out, and whether or not it would make a difference if she did. Even if he did own slaves, it was hardly against the law. And as long as he swore he wouldn't make me a slave, I doubt Father would see that fact as abhorrent as I did. Then again, he wasn't the one with dark skin. I was.

I shut the door behind me quietly as I entered my room. If my suspicions were true, I could never marry Mr. Reddings, no matter how much Father tried to force me. In which case, I had better make other plans. As drastic as it was, I was going to have to run away. The only question was, to where?

Tuppence Van de Vaarst

*****Chapter 3*****

I wasn't confined to my room for long. The very next day, Mary told me Mr. Reddings was coming to dinner and I was ordered to be on my best behavior. Better news to me, however, was that Miguel was coming home from Port Royal.

"He's coming back?" I exclaimed, standing up in delight.

"Aye, that he is, the scoundrel." Mary's voice was disapproving, but I wasn't fooled. Mary might disapprove of Miguel while he was absent, but as soon as he showed his face, he'd be charming her again, same as always. He could do that to everyone. I often suspected his charm was his own version of the gift I had. If it was, it was a pity it didn't last while he wasn't around.

My gift. 'It.' I wished Nana had told me more about 'it' before she passed on. All I could do was make people see what I wanted them to see. Not to any major extent, and it was easier if they expected to see my tricks. I knew had to be able to do more. Using different plants helped, but it was trial and error for the most part as to which ones worked the best. If Miguel knew more...

And if he didn't, he might think me crazed and a witch, much as he loved me. As far as I knew, Rosa was the only one who knew about 'it,' and that was only because I was incapable of keeping secrets from her.

Mary cleared her throat and I abruptly came back to reality. I raised my eyebrow at her.

"What else, Mary?"

I knew my tone was insubordinate, and Mary's face flushed in response. But really, what else could she expect?

"Don't take that tone with me, young lady," Mary said. "I know all about your dealings with your father. If I were him, I'd have taken a switch to you long before it came to this."

I managed a smile. "But you're not him, are you?" I asked sweetly.

Mary's face darkened even more and I felt a flash of guilt. Why was I baiting her? It wasn't like she did anything to me. I quickly repressed the thought. She was trying to sell me to Mr. Reddings, same as the rest of them.

"If I wasn't a good, proper woman-"

The sound of the door opening cut Mary off as Rosa stepped into the room. She looked from me, to Mary, and back again. Her face remained calm, but she raised an inquisitive eyebrow at me.

I rolled my eyes at her.

"I'll take care of Jo, Mary," Rosa said. "Ma wants you downstairs."

Mary sniffed haughtily. "I wish you joy of your sister. Thank the Lord your father has one well-behaved daughter." She turned and marched out of the room, her back as stiff as a board. She probably had a stick up her ass.

Rosa remained silent until Mary closed the door behind her. "Not so obedient as all that," she remarked. "I doubt Father would have appreciated the inquiries I made on your behalf."

I straightened. "Why?"

"Because everything I learned is going to make you more determined not to marry him. Father would hate any information that prevented you from going willingly to the bonds of matrimony."

"What did you find out?" My excitement was showing.

Rosa's expression darkened. "You're not going to like it," she warned.

I put my hands on my hips. "Any more than I already dislike him?"

Rosa shrugged. "Word is Mr. Reddings isn't just a planter," she said. "He also owns a great deal of capital in the shipping business. Specifically, the slave shipping business."

I felt certainty flare like a large fire inside of me. "And what is the word on the street about his interest in a Taino wife?" I asked.

Rosa shook her head. "No word about that yet," she said. "Although it's said it's not just you he's courting."

A knot of suspicion coiled inside me. "Not just me?"

"Eleanor Fitzgerald, to be precise," Rosa said. "Her father's wealthy, and she has no brothers."

My brow furrowed. "Then why's he wasting his time on me?"

It didn't make sense. This Eleanor Fitzgerald sounded like the perfect girl for a man like Reddings. I would be a hindrance to him, like Ma was to Father. What use was I to him?

I paced up the room. I was plain, outspoken, looked more native than white, and I didn't think that Reddings could be unaware of my distaste of him. He had to have a powerful reason to marry me.

Or not...

"Rosa, he doesn't intend to marry me."

"What do you mean?" Rosa was clearly taken aback by that.

I nodded. "He means to make Father think he's married me, but he'll keep me as his slave, saying it's against the law to marry a black woman. Then he'll marry this Fitzgerald girl and get all her money."

Rosa laughed shortly. "Jo, that's preposterous!" Despite her words, there was a flicker of doubt in her eyes.

"No?" I raised my eyebrows. "You're supposed to be the one who's good at reading people, Rosa. Why don't you look at him closely tonight when he comes to dinner? I bet his intentions are plain to see if you look hard enough."

I didn't think Rosa had any abilities like Miguel and me, but she always could see straight through a person's motivations, if she tried hard enough.

"It would cause a scandal," Rosa predicted. "You're no slave. Your father's a plantation owner. Mr. Reddings would have his hands full dealing with lawsuits and Father's attempts to ruin him."

I shook my head. I didn't know why I was so certain about this. "Just look, please?" I begged. "I don't want to end up a slave."

"And what if he is planning to make you one?" Rosa asked. "Father won't believe you. He'll make you marry him anyway. What will you do if it's true?"

"Leave that to me." I couldn't tell her I planned on running away. "Just find out for me, all right? Please?"

To my relief, Rosa nodded slowly. "All right," she said. "I'll try. I think you're crazy, but I'll try to keep an open mind when I talk to him tonight."

I nodded. "Thank you, Rosa."

Rosa straightened. "Well, I'd better do what I told Mary I'd do and help you get ready," she said. "Think you can stand to be polite to Mr. Reddings one more time? Wouldn't do to give the family a bad name."

I sighed. Like I had any bloody choice. I had to get out of this marriage, and fast. The sooner I found out more, the sooner I could make plans.

****

It was extra hard for me to be polite to Mr. Reddings that evening. For once, Father joined us for supper. He kept glaring at me the entire time and I wondered if he wanted Mr. Reddings to know I was being "willful" in the matter of my engagement. As if I bloody cared. If Mr. Reddings thought me unwilling, all the better.

Ma must have sensed my mood, because she was extra nice to Mr. Reddings, exerting her charm in almost every way possible. She stopped just shy of flirting with him. Thankfully.

"Have you seen much of the coffee plantation, Edward?" my Father asked during a lull in the conversation.

Mr. Reddings shook his head. "I have not. Of course, I am intimately acquainted with the running of my sugar plantation, but I assume you do things differently?"

Father nodded. "Perhaps you and Josephine might like to take a stroll together after supper. She can show you around."

My head snapped up at that. He couldn't seriously propose leaving me in the man's company by myself!

"I think that would be an excellent idea," Mr. Reddings said smoothly. "It would allow me to acquaint myself with many things."

If that was supposed to be an attempt at courtship, it failed horribly. But Father, Ma, and Rosa were all giving me warning looks, so it would do no good to cause a scene. I bit my tongue with an effort. I hated being good.

I resolved to be as quiet as possible during the walk. Knowing my temperament, I shouldn't have been surprised how well that worked out for me.

The walk started fine enough. We left the large plantation house, wandering through the house garden.

Although most of our land was acres of coffee plants, there were dozens of other buildings, including a kitchen house, smokehouse, two sheds, and a little village where our workers lived. Reddings and I started towards the village. It was a lovely trail through trees and groves. I usually enjoyed the walk.

A little way down, Mr. Reddings stopped. He smiled at me, which immediately made my skin crawl. "A word with you, Miss Crawford."

I stopped and crossed my arms over my chest instinctively. "Yes?"

Mr. Reddings' smile grew wider. "I'm glad I finally have a chance to talk to you alone. Your mother is so very charming and your father so eager to see you married, but they grow tiresome after a while. I think it will be better for me to talk to you alone."

I felt my brow furrow. "Talk to me about what?"

"Why, about what your deportment will be on my plantation."

I couldn't help myself. "Deportment? You're using fancy words, Englishman."

His eyes narrowed. "You'd best watch your tone. I've heard about your sharp tongue. There'll be none of that when you're living with me. Do I make myself clear?"

I let out a short laugh. So, all pretense of politeness was gone now that we were alone. That was fine by me. "You think we're actually going to live together? You've yet to propose marriage, and then there's the question if I would accept you. The answer's no, if you were wondering."

He seemed unruffled by my words. "I'm sure your Father will disagree with that statement. He seems quite worried you will never be able to marry anyone. I must seem like a godsend to him."

"Not to me you're not," I snapped.

"Ah, ah." He raised a hand. "Your tone, Miss Crawford."

I hardly cared what he wanted. "Why should I moderate my tone?" I demanded. "You've already made it clear you don't care about my feelings."

Mr. Reddings seemed honestly surprised. "What an interesting thing to say, Miss Crawford. Nevertheless, you will moderate your tone. And you will remove that symbol you wear when you come to live with me. We are all good Christians in my household, and I will not have symbols of slave gods paraded about."

I froze. The spider medallion of Anansi felt like a heavy weight around my neck. He shouldn't have known what it was. I disguised it since Nana gave it to me. To the world, it looked like a plain gold crucifix.

Mr. Reddings raised an eyebrow. "At a loss for words, Miss Crawford?"

I took a step backwards. Had I forgotten to shield it? Had the seeming disappeared somehow? I reached a hand to grab it. The energy was as strong as ever. That left only one possibility.

"Oh yes, I can see what it really is," he said. "I don't know what you're trying to disguise it as, but in the end, it really doesn't matter. But it is good for you to know you will never be able to fool me with your tricks."

I found my voice again. "Tricks?" I managed.

The smile on his face was enough to chill my blood. "Tricks," he said calmly. "Now, you will be using those tricks, but only when I tell you to. Do you know how much of an advantage I could have over my competition with your tricks? A wrong notation in a ledger here, a miscounted sum of money there... The damage would be extraordinary. If it were under my control, of course. Which it will be, the moment you are mine."

That did it. "Never, you bastard," I spat. "I will never marry you."

He laughed. He had the gall to laugh. "You have no choice, Miss Crawford. If you don't, I still have the means to bring this entire plantation to ruin. And I'll hunt you down. It will be much easier if you just accept that now."

I backed up from him even further. "Easier for you, or me?"

"Why, both of us, of course. Come now, you won't be unhappy. I'll take very good care of you."

"Go to hell, you arrogant swine." I was shaking inside. All my words were false bravado, but a deep resolve lay underneath them. If he could hold me in his power like he was threatening, I'd kill myself first.

****Chapter 4*****

I made it back to the house all right. Mr. Reddings was unfailingly polite when he left, making sure to tell me he'd be delighted to call again in two days. I fled to my room after that, ignoring Ma's cries that she needed to talk to me. Like hell. I needed to escape. Only problem was, I had no idea where to go.

I paced up and down the room, trying to think. I had to run away. Mr. Reddings could threaten all he liked, but I didn't think he would truly destroy the family finances if I ran. There was too much else at stake for a man like him. Besides, both Ma and Father were in on the conspiracy. Rosa was engaged, and Miguel was smart. Both of them could figure it out. The rest of the plantation could go to hell for all I cared.

I was startled out of my contemplations by a knock on the door. "Jo? It's me."

I relaxed at my brother's voice. "Come in."

Miguel entered and shut the door quickly behind me. The expression on his face was one of the most serious I'd ever seen him wear.

"I need to ask you something, Jo," he said. "Something very important, that could impact both of our futures."

I narrowed my eyes. Why all the seriousness? I trusted Miguel with my life.

Miguel took a deep breath. "Jo, did Nana ever teach you anything? Anything that might make a man like Reddings want to get his hands on you?"

I drew in a quick breath. "You know?"

Miguel closed his eyes. I had just confirmed his suspicions, it seemed.

"You're not the only one Nana taught," he said, opening his eyes again. "I suspect she would have taught

Rosa too, but she was too much of a Catholic girl. I can see the medallion of Anansi, by the way. Anyone with our talents can. That seems to be the drawback. Whatever we can do, it can't affect another one of us."

"Us?" I stepped forward, urgency filling me. If Miguel knew anything more about this, I needed to find out. If it would get me out of Reddings' clutches, I would use it.

"People with power," Miguel said.

I grabbed his shoulders. "Where did you learn this?" I demanded. "How did you learn it? Can you teach me?"

Miguel cracked a smile. "That's my sister," he said. "Always demanding."

I nearly slapped him. "Miguel, I warn you," I took a breath. "If you don't tell me some way to get myself free from a marriage where I wind up a slave, you'll have other things to worry about, brother mine."

Miguel gently removed my hands from his shoulders. "I know," he whispered. "Believe me. I've been trying to think of a way to get you out of here all night. I don't know if it's possible. Reddings will see through any illusion you can make. He'll be unaffected by any charm I can use. And he's got Ma and Father so thoroughly charmed they'll believe anything he says."

"Charm? Is that what you do?"

Miguel nodded. "Why do you think everyone loves a rogue like me?" he smirked, the same one that always endeared him to everyone.

"Not when you're gone," I said, remembering Mary.

"I know. I need more practice. And more power. Which is what I need to tell you. Your power, where do you get it from? The plants?"

I had never really stopped to think about it, but yes. That was one of the reasons I loved the garden.

"That power's nothing, Jo." Miguel's eyes bored into mine. "You should have felt the power in Port Royal. The sea, she holds more than this island ever could. You go there, you'll be safe."

Not just safe. Miguel's words lit the smoldering fires that had burned inside me forever. Power. The plants were never enough, I knew that. But if I could get to the sea, if he was right... I had an image of myself sailing the high seas, the wind in my face. I knew it wasn't the romantic life, but if the power was there, then it would be worth it.

"Miguel..." I paused. "Would you help me run away?"

Miguel shook his head and laughed. "I can get you to Port Royal. You can hide there. I'll try and keep Reddings distracted here so he doesn't find out where you've gone."

It was a good plan for now. I debated telling Miguel about my vision, but decided against it. If he knew the thought festering in my mind, he'd likely try to dissuade me. I needed more time to flesh out the idea. Getting to Port Royal was a good start.

****

I always knew my brother had a way of getting things done. This time was no different. I hadn't expected to leave for Port Royal that very night, but I had no objections to the fact.

Rosa was the only one I said goodbye to. When Miguel and I knocked on her door, understanding was writ across her face.

"You're leaving."

I felt myself relax. At least I didn't have to explain myself to her.

Rosa embraced me and I buried my face in her shoulder one last time. For all of our disagreements, I truly did love my sister. I hoped she'd be happy.

I blinked, startled, as a thought occurred to me. I had no idea when I'd even see my sister again.

Rosa thought of that before me, apparently. She drew back and took a deep breath. "Good luck, Jo," she said. "May God go with you in your travels. May you have plenty of adventures, and may we meet again one day."

I bowed my head. Heretic and heathen I may have been, but at that moment I couldn't deny Rosa her beliefs.

There wasn't much else to say. We embraced a final time, then I resolutely turned aside as she closed the door.

I raised my eyebrow at Miguel. "Same as always?"

Miguel grinned, and I felt myself responding. Even with all the stress, this felt exactly like old times.

"Get your breeches, little sister. I trust you still know your way around men's clothing?"

I laughed. It had been a few years since Miguel last snuck me off the plantation, but my memories were still just as clear as ever. The only difference this time was that I had him help me cut my hair off first. It felt so wonderful and free to be rid of the stringy tangles that always followed me around.

Miguel and I could barely keep from laughing as we made our way first to my room to change, then down to the kitchen for provisions. I didn't tell Miguel I stole a kitchen knife and slipped it into my boot as well, but I suspected he noticed anyway.

Before we went to the stables, Miguel stopped me. "Question, little brother."

I grinned. That had always been our private joke. "What, big brother?"

"You mess with perceptions, correct?"

I stilled. It was still very awkward to talk about 'it', even though I knew Miguel had the same ability. It wasn't something I could shout to the world, after all. Nana warned me there were still those who would happily burn me as a witch, even on this side of the ocean.

"As far as I can tell," I said slowly.

"Sound as well as sight?" Miguel persisted.

To my shame, that never occurred to me to try before. Most of what Nana taught me was to manipulate sight and touch. I could make an apple feel and look like a piece of eight, but to manipulate sound never occurred to me.

"Try it," Miguel suggested when I admitted my ignorance. "It could come in useful. See if you can't muffle the horses."

I swallowed. I never used 'it' with someone actively watching me before.

I tried to ignore Miguel as best I could as I closed my eyes. I felt my mental fingers, and I reached down into the earth and drew on the power within it. Every plant had its own unique signature, and I could feel all of them deep in my bones. Without consciously being aware, I automatically sorted out the feelings and drew up the one most useful for manipulating the sounds around me.

There was a drawback to working with others who shared the same power. There was no way to tell if 'it' worked or not. Both Miguel and I could still hear the horses and we had to take it on faith that 'it' worked.

Miguel grimaced. "Reddings won't be fooled by anything you do, remember," he said.

I bit my lip. Damn the man. If he hadn't smashed his way into my life, I wouldn't have to flee my home in the middle of the night.

"He has the same ability as you, correct?"

Miguel nodded. "As far as I've seen," he said. "Charm seems to be his primary ability, anyway. He's got both Ma and Father completely wrapped around his finger."

I scowled as we mounted our horses. "Couldn't you uncharm them, since you have the same ability?" I wished I knew more about it. I wished Nana were still alive so I could ask her more questions.

Miguel shook his head. "He's more powerful than me, little brother," he said. "Be careful in Port Royal. Anyone there could be charmed into telling Reddings about your whereabouts, whether they're normally trustworthy or not. And people in Port Royal aren't generally that trustworthy anyway."

My lips quirked at that one. Even I knew the reputation of Port Royal. Debauchery, thievery, prostitutes, pirates...

And legitimate sailing ships. If my luck served, I would be testing Miguel's claim about the power of the sea for myself fairly soon.

"How far will you ride with me?" I asked. "Our parents might miss you."

Miguel laughed. "Father barely notices when I'm around. I doubt he'll notice when I'm gone."

I frowned. That didn't seem right. "But you're the son. You've been doing business for him."

Miguel shook his head. "I think Father regretted marrying Ma as soon as I was born. He has to live with the skin color of his children for the rest of his life."

I felt my anger coiling in my gut again. It wasn't our fault we were born the way we were. And why should it matter, anyway? Miguel was just as smart as any Englishman. Why should we have to pay a price for the color of our skin?

Miguel must have known what I was thinking. "It's not all bad," he said. "We don't burn in this climate, after all."

His words forced me to laugh. But my anger and resentment still rested in the pit of my stomach, ready to lash out any time it was awakened.

I turned my face towards the road. I could focus on my anger later. Now, I had to focus on getting to Port Royal, and then, getting to the sea.

Tuppence Van de Vaarst

*****Chapter 5*****

I had only been to Port Royal once, three years ago when we first moved to Jamaica. During that time, I had visited a few of the other plantations, but had never been back to the town. Father said it was dangerous for women.

It was early morning when we rode into Port Royal, and I had to admit I was not impressed by the sight. At the plantation, everyone would already be hard at work. Not here. Oh, there were the beggars and drunks staggering through the street, but for the most part, the streets were silent, as well as covered in filth and muck.

Miguel must have caught part of my thoughts in my expression. "Not to your taste, little brother?" he laughed.

I glared at him. Where was this power he spoke of? Right now, I couldn't even find many plants to work with.

Miguel didn't pause the horses, and we continued down the street. I wrinkled my nose. The smell of fish was starting to permeate the air.

"Where are we going?" I finally asked.

Miguel raised his eyebrow. "To the docks, of course. Where else are you going to find the ocean?"

True enough. I stifled my impatience.

My first sight of the docks was not that impressive. We rounded the corner of a building and suddenly there they were, in all their filthy splendor. I couldn't count how many ships lay in the harbor. The docks themselves were rotting in a number of places, and barrels of all sizes lay scattered about. I saw a few women walking around and their clothing, or lack of it, led me to assume they were the whores. They made no move to proposition Miguel or myself, however. It must have been the time of day.

I couldn't quite believe Miguel had spoken of this place so fondly. When I looked around, I saw a broken-down wreck where everything was dead.

Before I could say anything, Miguel sighed happily. "Can you feel it, Jo?" he asked.

I furrowed my brow and took a second glance at the water. I started. Through the deep, dark spirals that swirled around the ships ran a current so deep and powerful. It was like nothing I'd ever seen before. It drew me deeper and deeper, pulling me closer. I looked out towards the horizon and felt the same call, much more distant, but much stronger. I had to get out there. I had to feel it. If this was what the sea felt like, then how could Miguel ever bear to leave?

"How did you come home?" I managed.

Miguel chuckled. "It wasn't easy," he said.

I gazed at it for another long moment. When we had made the crossing from St. Kitt's, I had spent almost the entire voyage corralled below decks with Ma and Rosa. Father hadn't wanted any of us getting in the way of the sailors.

I dismounted my horse and led him all the way up to the edge of the dock almost without noticing. It was hypnotizing.

"Let's find you an inn, Jo," Miguel said. "The sooner the better. The ocean will still be there."

I tore my gaze away reluctantly. I knew he was right. But the sea was calling.

Once again, Miguel knew exactly where he was going: down a little side street, where things were a bit cleaner than they had been on the pier. Signs hung above most of the buildings here, proclaiming them either shops, ale houses, or other areas of interest. Most of them had pictures rather than words.

Miguel went into an ale house with a mermaid on its sign. Unlike many of the other places on the street, there was already activity going on, and there was even a boy outside for us to give our horses to.

I glanced around as Miguel led us inside. It seemed clean enough. And it was close to the docks. There would be someone here who could direct me to where to sign aboard a ship.

A rather lovely woman waited inside. She gave my brother a bright smile.

"Miguel! You're back already! Dare I think it's on my account?"

I kept my expression neutral as Miguel laughed and smiled at her. "I'm afraid not, dearest Liz. I'm going to have to leave again shortly."

Liz pouted briefly, revealing full, red lips. "Ah well," she said. "I knew you were too much to hope for. What can I do for you instead?"

"My brother needs a room."

Right. I was supposed to be a boy. A boy would not be unaffected by a beautiful woman. I mustered a smile. Somehow I didn't think I was very convincing.

Liz raised her eyebrow at me. "Your brother, hmm?"

"Jo Crawford, miss," I said, managing a slight bow.

She smiled at me, a brilliant smile that showed off all her teeth. "He has your manners, Miguel. I'm Liz, the mistress of this establishment. You'll be well taken care of here, Mr. Crawford."

"Just Jo, please," I said, more than a little flustered now. She was flirting with me. She had to be.

I caught Miguel's smirk out of the corner of my eye and fought the urge to glare at him. I dearly wanted to find out how flustered he would be if he dressed as a woman and a man started flirting with him.

"Have a seat, gentlemen. I'll get you some refreshments." Liz went bustling towards the back, saying something to a serving wench as she passed.

Miguel looked at me carefully as we sat down. "Will you be all right?" he asked.

I nodded. What else was there to say? I had to manage if I didn't want to be sold off. At least no one had taken a second glance at my skin tone yet.

"Do you have a plan, Jo?" Miguel asked. "I should have asked before, but is there something you can do now? Or was running the only plan?"

I bit my lip. "I have an idea," I said.

Miguel narrowed his eyes. "I know that tone," he said. "You don't want to tell me because you think I'll talk you out of it. Spill the beans, little brother. I'll offer advice if I can."

I weighed my options. Miguel couldn't really prevent me in any case, not at this point. I knew he wouldn't take me back home, and that was all I cared about at this point.

"I want to sign aboard a ship," I said.

Miguel's eyes nearly popped out of his head. "You what?"

I suppressed a laugh. It wasn't often I had the chance to surprise my older brother.

"You realize how much work that'll be for you?" he asked. "It's not an easy life, from what I've heard. Don't let the romance fool you."

I nodded. I knew that. Despite the truth in his words, my determination was only strengthened.

He shook his head. "I knew I had a crazy sister," he muttered. "Don't tell me it was the power out there that drew you to this."

"What else?" I demanded. "I have to learn how to use this. And out there will be the best chance."

"Jo." he looked at my expression and stopped. He sighed. "All right. Advice, then. Don't sign aboard immediately. Learn to act like a man first. Use 'it' to disguise yourself as well. You do a good job, but you'll want to look even more manly onboard. And there isn't much privacy, so you'll have to disguise other things as well." He looked at me closely to make sure I understood.

I suppressed a smile. I knew what a naked man looked like. I wasn't supposed to, but I did.

He continued. "Don't just go for the first ship, either. Learn where it's going, talk to some of the crew, make sure you'll get along with them. Find out how the captain treats them, if you can. Try not to do a long voyage first, if you can. You might get seasick."

Somehow I knew I wouldn't, but I let his comment slide. He meant well, and he wasn't trying to persuade me to change my mind.

"Thank you, brother," I said quietly.

This was it. It was time to say farewell.

"I hope you find happiness, sister," Miguel took my hand.

I bit my lip. "I hope you do too, brother." I met his eyes. "I hope Father treats you more like his son than his servant. I hope you find what you want."

Miguel nodded. "Anansi protect you."

I took a deep breath as he rose and left the ale house. I forced myself not to look as he exited. I was on my own now.

Liz came bustling over, surprising me out of my thoughts. "Is your brother already leaving, Jo? I'm sorry. He's such a charmer, do you know that? I hope he comes again soon. Are you planning on staying for long?"

I blinked, confused as to which question I should answer. I settled for the last one. "A few days at least. I have some business to conduct here in Port Royal."

Liz smiled at me. "Well, if you have any questions or need directions, be sure to ask me. I'm more than willing to help in whatever way you desire."

Was I imagining the sultry tone, or was she really flirting with me? "Thank you, Liz," I managed. "Could you show me where my room is?"

"Of course. Just this way." She beckoned me towards the back of the ale house, through a small, door almost hidden behind the bar and up the back stairs. "First one on the right. Just yell if you need anything." She disappeared down the stairs.

I took a deep breath to steady myself. I was on my own now. Miguel would not be coming back to check on me. I couldn't go home. But there was power on the ocean, and I was determined to feel it.

I followed Miguel's advice for the rest of the day. I wandered around the streets of Port Royal a bit, seeing what I could see. The town woke up closer to midday. Soon, there were people everywhere, shouting, hawking their wares, greeting friends, insulting random passersby, begging for handouts. The streets, not clean to begin with, became even filthier. How could people stand to live in a place like this?

As I thought that, I gazed out towards the ocean. Could others feel it? Was that why the towns tended to congregate so close to the sea?

Logically, of course, I knew that wasn't the answer. I overheard Father and Miguel talk about it before. Towns were near the ocean because that's where the ships could land and carry on cargo. It was all economics. Such a fancy word.

I used 'it' to cement my disguise as a young man. I even gave myself a stubble of a beard. So far it seemed to be holding up. No one had commented on me being a girl, anyway.

It was almost evening when I finally returned to the inn. My eyes widened. People were crowded in the common room, and serving girls were bustling here and there with plates and mugs. Luckily for me, Liz saw me almost immediately.

"Jo! Have a seat by the fire!"

I glanced over towards the fireplace. There wasn't much room on the bench, but I was small. I could fit.

I nodded my thanks to the girl when she brought me a plate and a mug of ale. I smiled to myself. This was thick, heavy, common food, the sort that Ma never would have served on her table. Although she probably grew up on something similar in the Taino.

I was halfway through my portion of fish when I felt a huge presence standing beside me. I glanced up into the face of a giant white man, standing over me with his arms crossed.

"Stand up, boy."

I frowned, my anger immediately roused. Despite my actual age, my disguise was that of a young man. I was certainly no boy.

"Are you talking to me?" I kept my voice civil as possible.

Immediately the table quieted, and I tensed. Something was up. Had I just made a terrible mistake?

"Don't mess with me, boy," the man said. "Your kind don't deserve to sit at the table with us."

My temper, which I had kept so carefully banked, surged to the fore. "My kind?" I demanded. "And what kind would that be, Englishman?"

"You know exactly what kind, boy!"

I saw Liz out of the corner of my eye. "Sir, Mr. Crawford is a paying guest. He is as welcome here as you are. More, if you keep saying the things you are."

The man dismissed Liz with no more than a glance. "Keep out of the way, woman." He glared down at me. "You gonna move?"

I kept my seat and raised my fish to my mouth once more.

I barely had time to see the man's hands reach down before he grabbed my collar and picked me up off the bench and threw me to the floor. I hit the ground with a whoosh of air, and I tumbled into another table, knocking into two of the other patrons.

The man strode over to me again. "You need a lesson in manners, negro."

I scrambled into a crouch before the man got too close. "I'm Taino, you fricking bastard!"

I rushed at him without thinking. Miguel and I had wrestled a number of times while I was growing up. And while this man was twice the size of Miguel, I was so worked up I would have taken on four of him without even thinking about it.

I saw the confident grin spread across the man's face, and I knew exactly what to do about it. I ducked low underneath his arms and went for his knees.

I almost evaded him. I ran full strength into his legs just as his arm wrapped around the back of my neck. We both went tumbling to the floor, and he dragged me down underneath him.

I struggled to get free. I kicked and clawed, but the man was solid muscle. I saw his fist raise above my face for a punch, and I took a deep breath as I tried to evade.

He missed my nose, but his fist struck the side of my face. I saw stars for a moment, but the adrenaline had hit me. I managed to get a hand free long enough to poke my fingers towards his eyes. He flinched, and I slithered out from his grip.

My ear was ringing from where he had punched me, but I couldn't stop to feel for blood. He was coming at me again, and it was all I could do to keep him from grabbing my throat and grabbing my shoulder instead.

"Gentlemen! Stop at once!"

I ignored Liz's voice as I was thrown to the ground once again. I felt my shirt catch on a splinter on the floor, and it tore as I rolled, cutting into my arm. Dimly, I heard the roar of the other patrons as they either scrambled out of the way or started moving closer to watch.

"A shilling that the black one wins!"

I hated that man. Instead of helping me out of a tight spot, he decided to place bets on my survival instead.

The giant was back on top of me, leaning down with an evil smile, his fists ready for another punch. For the first time, I began to wonder if it was a good idea to let my temper get me into this. He was much bigger than I was. That gave him quite the advantage.

I never claimed to be the best at thinking ahead. I was in for it now, and there was no way to back out. As he punched towards my face again, instead of scrambling out of the way I lunged towards him.

I still took the punch on my right shoulder and my entire arm screamed in pain. I let loose a shriek, but I hit his most tender parts with my left arm before I collapsed back onto the ground.

I was out. My arm was an entire mass of pain, and I wasn't sure I would be able to stand up in time to defend myself again. Luckily, the giant man was down for the count, too. He was crouched over in an agony of pain, close to joining me on the ground.

I gritted my teeth and attempted to stand up. Suddenly Liz was there with one of the serving girls, helping me to my feet.

"You need to get back to your room before the watch shows up," Liz said briskly. "Not that they'll care, but at least one of you has to disappear from this room."

I glanced once more at the man, who by now had dropped to his knees. Liz followed my eyes.

"We'll throw him out as soon as possible. Now go with Jill, please."

I had no real option but to follow Jill to the back stairs and up to the room. I kept a close grip on my right arm. I had no real knowledge of how to manage injuries, but hopefully Liz knew someone who did.

Jill made sure I was settled, and promised to send somebody up to help me with my arm. I sank down on the bed with a grimace.

I managed a wry smile as I thought about what had just transpired. Of course I got into a bar fight my first night alone in Port Royal. Miguel would not have been surprised. At least I taught that bastard a lesson about what blacks could do. I doubted he learned anything, but I could hope. More likely, I had just increased his hatred.

A knock on the door nearly made me jump out of my skin, but it was Liz's voice that answered my inquiry. She bustled in, followed closely by another of the serving maids.

"Erica's father is a doctor," Liz explained. "She knows some of the basics of medicine. Hopefully she can fix your shoulder for you."

Erica was a pretty girl, dark and sultry looking, although still clearly white. She looked at me with apprehension.

"You... You're going to have to take your shirt off, sir," she said.

I bit my lip. I had never used my gift at such close quarters before. What if she found out I was a girl?

I couldn't hesitate, though. I needed my shoulder fixed if I was going to continue my plan. If she suspected anything, maybe I could buy her off.

I attempted to raise my arms, but was stopped by a flare of pain. I grimaced.

"I'm going to need some help with that," I admitted.

Erica flushed and I realized her apparent shyness had nothing to do with her natural character. Rather, it was brought on by the fact that I was supposedly a young man, and she was asking me to strip.

I nearly smiled at the irony of the notion. If only she knew.

Hesitantly, Erica stepped forward to help me. I noticed Liz stayed unobtrusively in the background, and I wondered if she stayed in case I decided to try and take advantage of Erica.

If I were my brother, perhaps I would have. As it was, I could barely focus on anything other than the pain in my shoulder. The only other distraction I had was holding onto 'it', making me seem as male as possible.

Erica laid her hands gently on my shoulder, feeling around, poking and prodding. I winced as her grip firmed, but she released me almost immediately.

"Just a bad bruise," she said. "You're lucky he didn't dislocate anything, though. I have a salve that should help with the healing, and a drink for the pain."

I didn't ask what was in the bitter drink she handed me. It tasted awful, but the pain dulled almost immediately.

I stared at her in amazement. "You have a wondrous talent, miss."

Erica flushed again, this time in pleasure. She smiled at me under lowered eyebrows. "You are kind to say so, sir."

My tongue failed as I realized she was beginning to flirt with me.

Erica waited a moment, then became all business. "It will be a bit sore for the next few days," she warned. "Try not to overuse it."

Liz snorted, coming out from the back of the room. "He won't listen to that advice, Erica. No young man does."

I smiled to myself. Maybe it was a good thing I wasn't actually a young man. I had no intention of overusing my shoulder. I needed it if I was going to sign aboard a ship.

Miguel was right, though. I needed practice acting like a man. I needed a few more days in the town. But at least I wasn't going to begin acting like a man by acting stupid.

*****Chapter 6*****

I learned to eat those words the next morning. Erica was the one who brought me the news.

"He's who?" I stared at her in disbelief.

"He's the governor's personal assistant." Her lips tightened. "Everyone knows he has a temper and is a mean drunk, but that doesn't mean you'll escape unscathed."

I shook my head, still trying to process the information.

"The man who attacked me yesterday is the governor's assistant?" I asked again.

I saw the impatience in Erica's eyes, but I still couldn't believe it.

"What was an upper-class man like that doing in a low-class ale house like this?"

"Does it matter?" Erica demanded. "Looking for trouble, I expect. The problem is, now he's going to come looking for you again. There's already been people asking questions."

Frick. I sat bolt upright with a start.

"What are they asking about?" I demanded.

Erica shrugged. "Nothing specific for now, just a young black man who doesn't know how to keep his place." She raised her eyebrow meaningfully.

I felt my temper flare again. Of course. He hadn't listened to a word I said in our brief exchange last night. Didn't know the difference between black and Taino. Then again, Ma had always warned me we would be treated the same, no matter what the actual differences.

Maybe there weren't any differences. After all, Mary lived among us my entire life, and there was no obvious difference between her and Ma.

I was getting distracted. "What do you think I should do?"

Erica smiled a little. "You've a head start in that you're asking questions," she said. "Most men don't. As it happens, Liz does have the perfect solution, if what your brother told her is true."

I had to laugh at that. "And what did my brother tell her?" I asked.

"That you're looking to sign aboard a ship," Erica said. "He said to wait a week or so, let you get used to the idea and see if you want to change your mind, but in light of recent events, I don't think that's such a good idea anymore, do you?"

She was right. Bless Miguel. Still looking after me, even when he was gone. Probably the last time he would be able to do so.

I nodded. "I assume you already have a plan?" I was starting to like Erica. Even though she flirted with me, she was still remaining very calm, businesslike, and professional.

"Liz knows a quartermaster," Erica said, shading the word 'know' with subtle meanings. I shrugged the thought aside. None of my business. "If she recommends you to him, then you're sure to get signed on. Even with no experience."

"I learn fast," I offered. "Can read and write, too."

Erica's eyebrows raised. "Might not want to be shouting that one too loudly, mind," she said. "Slaves aren't allowed to know. Not that you're a slave," she raised a hand, "but most will think you escaped somewhere. Still, could be useful."

I kept my temper under control this time. She was trying to help.

"I'll talk to Liz," Erica said. She cocked her head slightly, and the tone of her voice changed. "The ship's due to sail tomorrow," she said. "You'll be gone before I have the chance to know you better."

I flushed and leaned away instinctively, then instantly berated myself. If I was going to pull off the masquerade of a boy, I had to stop doing that.

Erica noticed. "Have you ever had a woman, Jo?" she asked.

How the hell was I supposed to respond to that? It was as good of an explanation for my blushes as any, and it had the added benefit of being the truth.

I didn't even have to answer. She nodded. "Thought as much," she said with satisfaction. "Oh, I wish you were staying longer, Jo. We could have so much fun." She shook her head. "I'll go tell Liz. Good luck to you, Mr. Crawford."

I nodded at her. "Thank you, Erica," I said. "For everything."

Erica looked over her shoulder on her way out and smiled so charmingly that any real man's breath would have been stolen away.

I let my own breath out in a rush as soon as the door was closed. There was definitely another benefit to going away to sea: I wouldn't have to deal with women flirting with me!

I was an idiot, though. Of all the men to have picked a fight with, it had to be with a government official. At least the guards hadn't come charging into the building to arrest me first thing that morning.

Erica had the right idea. I had to sign aboard a ship, and I had to do it soon. I could theoretically use 'it' to change my appearance further, but I had the sneaking suspicion that would take more power than I currently had access to.

I needed to find Liz. I pushed myself off the bed and headed for the door.

I found her downstairs, bustling around, getting everything in the common room ready for the day. She broke off her task immediately when she saw me.

"Jo! I sent a message to the quartermaster. I hope you don't mind the presumption."

I smiled at her. "Of course not," I said. I couldn't help but wonder why she went to the trouble for me, though. Was it Miguel? Did she have a soft spot for him, despite apparently being "connected" with this quartermaster?

Liz smiled a brilliant smile. "Good," she said. "I think you'll have a fine time aboard the ship. I'll let him tell you all about it, though. He does tell wonderful stories."

I had to refrain a laugh at the misty look that came into Liz's eye. Despite Miguel's charm, it was obvious that Liz's heart was elsewhere. Unless there were other men too...

None of my business, I reminded myself. Besides, I had other things to worry about. Like a government official coming to arrest me.

"Is your quartermaster coming here? What's his name? What's the name of the ship?" I had so many questions.

"Richard Freeman, and he sails on The Vixen. If he pays heed to my message, he should be here in an hour or so. Care for some breakfast until then?"

I had nothing else to do, so I accepted. Hopefully this Richard Freeman would let me sign on.

****

My first glimpse of Richard Freeman did not give me much confidence. He was a big, burly man wearing the typical sailor's outfit of breeches and shirt of canvas. His hair was tied back in a short ponytail and he had a scar down the left side of his face that made him look menacing. The fact that he was glaring at me didn't help.

"So you're the one Liz tells me I should give a chance," he said shortly. "Name?"

I straightened my shoulders. "Jo Crawford."

"Hmph," Richard raised his eyebrows. "Any experience at sea, Mr. Crawford?"

"Not yet," I said. "But I'm willing to learn."

"That's what they all say," Richard grumbled. "Well, Liz has been persuasive, so I'll give you a chance. Ship's The Vixen. Find her tenth dock down. We're leaving tomorrow. If your mind's truly set on this, be there tonight. Pay'll be sixteen shillings and eight pence a month. First port of call after here will be Charleston. Any questions?"

I didn't know preciselyhow long it would take to get to Charleston, but I didn't want to make my ignorance apparent, so I shook my head. "I'll be there."

Richard snorted. "Don't make me regret this," he said. "If I do, there'll be hell to pay, and you'll be the one paying it."

I crossed my arms over my chest as Richard walked out the door. Somehow, I did not have a good feeling about this ship, no matter what Liz's feelings towards its quartermaster might be.

*****Chapter 7*****

I arrived at the Vixen shortly before sunrise the day that evening. She wasn't hard to find. I rather wished I had my own choice of ships to choose from. She looked run-down and weather-beaten, and I wasn't entirely certain I trusted her far out to sea. Still, she was the only choice I had right now. Unless I wanted to face the governor's assistant. Or Reddings. I shuddered involuntarily at the thought. That was a man I wanted to leave far behind. The sailors kept me running around until late that night, when I was able to collapse in the berth assigned to me. The next morning, we set sail.

I looked out at the harbor from the deck of the ship, gazing at the far expanse of ocean. Was Miguel right? Was there power out there? Could I use it better than I could the plants? I barely knew anything at all about my talent. I needed to learn and I needed to learn fast.

"Hey! No daydreaming, Mr. Crawford!"

I bit back a curse as someone threw a heavy rope at me. I managed to catch it without staggering, and I glared at the man who had thrown it.

"I do not daydream, Mr. Tanner," I said sharply. "My dreaming is done during sleep, where it belongs."

Tanner snorted. He'd been introduced to me as the ship's bos'n, which generally meant he was in charge of most of the men on deck, which included me and seven other men. Other than that, there was the navigator, the first mate, Richard Freeman, and the captain. 'A small crew to be chancing the seas,' as I overheard one of the other men muttering, but they seemed confident enough to me.

Well, confident about the voyage, at any rate. I already caught a few of them giving me side-long glances. It was either my lack of skills or the color of my skin, and I was willing to bet good money it was a mixture of both.

"Better take that line to the foc'sle, Mr. Crawford. They'll be waiting for it."

Foc'sle? What the hell was the foc'sle?

I stared at Tanner, whose eyes twinkled slightly. I felt my anger start to rise. It had to be standard sailor slang and he was going to make me look a fool by not explaining what it was.

Well, I was not going to give him the chance. "Point me in the direction, Mr. Tanner?" I said with exaggerated politeness. "I would not like to hold the ship's voyage up."

Tanner glared at me, then pointed forward towards the bow of the ship. I knew that term at least. Bow, stern, forward, aft, port, starboard- I was going to have to brush up on my terminology.

The foc'sle proved to be the deck at the very front of the ship. Two men were already running around like mad, securing lines here, loosening ropes there. The first mate stood nearby, and he let loose a curse of exasperation when he saw me.

"Finally! Take that to Mr. Morningwood. He'll show you what to do with it. Move! The wind will only last so long!"

I hastened my way over to the man the first mate indicated.

Morningwood proved to be exceptionally tall and covered in tattoos. He wore his shirt open to display the ones on his chest, mostly nautical symbols and birds. Swiftly, he took the rope from my hand and attached it to the sail. He rigged it through a contraption in the mast and handed the end back to me.

He grinned and I felt my eyes widen. His face was almost maniacal. "Time to get underway, lads!" he roared. "You ready to pull, boy?"

I clenched my jaw. "Whenever the order's given," I managed to say without too much sarcasm.

Morningwood laughed, an obnoxious belly laugh that made his stomach shake as he threw his head back. "You hear that, Linden? It appears we're ready!"

The first mate turned to look at us. He saw me holding the line, raised an eyebrow, but said nothing.

He turned to the other two men he was supervising. "Are you ready, lads?"

They were holding the line at the other side of the sail together. I caught my breath in realization. If the two of them were working together, and Morningwood was just standing there... I snapped my gaze to him and glared. He laughed again.

"Pull!" came the first mate's shout.

I cursed as I strained on the line. It was moving, but only agonizingly slow. I saw the amusement on Morningwood's face, and I redoubled my efforts.

God damn that arrogant bastard for putting me in a pickle like this.

"Something funny, Morningwood?" I growled out as I pulled again.

He widened his eyes in mock innocence. "Funny? Nothing at all, Crawford."

I glared again. "Well maybe you could do your job and help me instead of just standing there!"

He laughed again, but finally came around to join me. I didn't dare show my relief as the burden suddenly grew lighter. The sail went up, and we secured the lines to various cleats in the deck. I paid close attention. I would have to learn how to do this sooner or later if I intended to sail for long.

I glanced at Morningwood. "What next?" I asked unwillingly. I didn't trust the man, but from the way the first mate turned away from us, he was technically in charge of me right now.

He grinned. "Can you feel the wind, boy?" he asked. "We're underway! You know what the rocking does to things unsecured on deck?"

I raised my eyebrows. Almost everything I'd seen had been tied down already. "Looks like you already did that."

He nodded. "But there's always something we missed. Come on, boy, let's get to it. By the time we're done, they'll have the watch schedule sorted out."

I followed him hesitantly down into the hold. I suppose it made sense.

The hold was packed full of cargo, all of it strapped to the deck and pillars by various contraptions of rope. None of it seemed to be shifting around much. Morningwood ignored the cargo and headed straight for the forward part of below decks, where our sleeping area was.

It was a berthing area. I had to remember these terms!

"This is where people always slack," Morningwood told me over his shoulder. "The captain and Freeman get so caught up in the cargo that we end up having to ignore our own stuff. You don't have much, right?"

I shook my head. "Didn't have the money for much," I answered, lying through my teeth. Of course I had brought some of my things. Miguel had given me money, and I used it wisely. It was hidden in plain sight in the small chest that was mine, disguised by whatever power I had to look like a pair of tattered clothes.

"Well, you won't have much after this voyage, it being your first one and all, but you'll have more than what you do now, that's for certain. What, you run away?"

58

I gaped at the bluntness of his question. He was implying I was a former slave.

"From my family, yes," I answered shortly, deciding to use something similar to the truth. "If you're implying something else, Morningwood, I have never been a slave in my life, and I have no intention of ever becoming one."

He laughed again, but to my ears it sounded strained. Or maybe that was just paranoia.

He changed the subject by pointing at one of the other sailor's chests. "See that? Right now, it's not moving, but when the high seas come, it'll be all over the place disturbing everyone. Let's strap Jennings' stuff down for him, shall we?"

I followed, but I kept my eye on Morningwood. Was he being friendly, or did he have another reason for implying I was an escaped slave? I had no real knowledge of what happened to escaped slaves if they were caught. After all, I never had to worry about it. I wasn't of slave blood, damn it! I was Taino!

'Dark enough to not make a difference,' my mother's voice said in my thoughts.

Sternly, I told Ma's voice to shut up. Maybe there wasn't a difference, at least in the eyes of these white men, but I was proud of my heritage. And no bloody white man insinuating I was a slave could take that from me.

It didn't take long to secure the berthing area. I gazed at my rack with a small feeling of dismay. It was tiny. It was a good thing I wasn't near as tall as Morningwood. The mattress was thin and tattered, and I had a feeling that sleeping on it in high seas without falling off was going to be a challenge.

Morningwood saw my look and laughed. "You get used to it," he said. "If you've ever been used to soft beds, you'd better forget them now."

I could see that. For the first time since I ran away, I thought of home. What had Ma and Pa's reactions been? Rosa and Miguel knew, of course, but were they forced to reveal anything to our parents? And what had they told Reddings when he came around? Would they admit their child ran away without a trace rather than marry him? And would Reddings follow through on his threat to ruin them?

I stiffened my spine. It didn't matter what was going on back home. Rosa's wedding was soon, and her bridegroom was willing to take her without a penny. Miguel could manage. He always could. Anyone else, I could have cared less than fig about.

I turned to Morningwood again. "So, you mentioned something about a watch schedule?"

He nodded. "Follow me, boy, and the whole mystical watch will soon be explained."

I rolled my eyes behind his back as we climbed the ladder to the main deck again. Morningwood was proving to have an interesting sense of humor, to say the least.

He waved his hand at Tanner the moment we came out on deck. "Tanner! He shouted. "You got the watch made up yet?"

Tanner looked at the two of us and nodded shortly. "You have the morning watch with Crawford, there," he said. He looked at me. "Don't be late. Morning watch starts at four o'clock."

Morningwood groaned, but didn't complain. I raised my eyebrow inquiringly.

"I hate getting up that early," he explained. "But it's the watch the new sailors always get, and since I suppose I've been nominated your teacher, that's what I get."

Morning watch didn't sound so bad to me. Of course, I'd always been one to get up at the crack of dawn, much to Rosa and Ma's dismay. I might have something different to say once I worked hard a full day and then had to get up in the wee hours of the morning.

"So why are we heading up to the colonies, Tanner?" Morningwood asked. "And stopping by the Spanish ports along the way?"

Tanner shrugged. "From what the captain tells me, the Spanish ports are very interested in our cargo this time of year, and Reddings is willing to risk dealing with the Spanish to get the gold. He's meeting us in Charleston to make sure we come out of it alive."

I felt my blood run cold, and I stared at Tanner. Had he just said the name I thought he had?

Morningwood shuddered theatrically. "I hate dealing with the Spanish," he said. "They're always so fricking formal. And of course they refuse to use English properly."

Tanner cocked his head. "You enjoyed St. Augustine the last time we were there, as I recall. How much did the two whores take off of you?"

Morningwood blushed a fiery red. I would have laughed if my mind wasn't so taken up by the name that Tanner had said.

"Who's Reddings?" I managed to ask. I tried desperately to keep my voice as level as possible.

Tanner shook his head. "The owner," he said. "No one you need to concern yourself with. He normally lives in Jamaica, but apparently he has business in Charleston, so he's going to meet us there. Since we're stopping at St. Augustine, he'll likely beat us."

Every word Tanner spoke had he freezing inside more and more. Reddings was the owner of the Vixen. I escaped him in Jamaica, only to sign on board of a ship that he owned. Could my luck have been any worse?

Tanner shook his head. "As I said, no one you need to worry about. Reddings doesn't trouble himself with common sailors like us. He only ever deals with Freeman and the captain."

That didn't matter to me. I had the distinct feeling that as soon as Reddings stepped onboard the ship, he would know I was there. He had already proved his ability to see through my seemings before. Anything I did to disguise myself was going to prove moot against him.

God had bloody well damn Reddings to hell. How in God's name was I going to escape this bastard?

"Crawford!"

I turned at the first mate's shout. "We need a hand here!"

I clenched my teeth. I was going to have to worry about the problem Reddings presented later. Right now, I had other things to worry about.

****

I was exhausted by the time supper rolled around. It was an informal affair. Jennings proved to be the cook as well as a deckhand, and his food was passable, at least. Nothing like what I'd be eating on the plantation, but I'd be damned if I ever went back there again.

One of the men gave me a sharp look. "Who's the new one?" he asked Tanner.

As if he couldn't ask me himself. Actually, it was kind of odd I hadn't seen this man yet. I made the passing acquaintance of all the deckhands, but this man didn't seem to be one of them. He was better dressed than the rest of us, for one, and he wore thick glasses. He had short brown hair that fell untidily around his face, but behind the glasses, his eyes were as sharp as razors.

"Jo Crawford, meet Eric Nelson, ship's navigator," Tanner said shortly before returning to his meal.

Navigator. I looked at Nelson with more interest. I had seen maps - charts - of the ocean before, and they fascinated me. And this man knew how to navigate them.

"Crawford," Nelson seemed to turn my name over in his mind. "You know how to read, Mr. Crawford?"

Morningwood laughed, and the rest of the men joined in. "You never give up, do you, Nelson?" he asked. "Haven't you learned yet that us sailors don't have time for your reading and figuring?"

Nelson glared at Morningwood. A scowl seemed to be his habitual expression. "I want Crawford to answer, not you, Mr. Morningwood." He turned back to me again. "Well?"

I braced myself. "Actually, I can," I said. "I can figure, as well."

Silence descended on the sailors, and I remembered Erica's warning. Slaves weren't allowed to read and write. Well, maybe this would convince them I hadn't been a slave.

Nelson seemed unperturbed by the sudden silence. "Good," he said. "Then with your permission, Mr. Tanner, I'd like Crawford as my assistant."

I sat in dumb surprise. What did that mean?

Tanner didn't seem to like the idea. "Mr. Nelson, just because we finally hire a deckhand who knows how to read does not mean you can steal him from me at the first opportunity. Mr. Crawford has a job to do, same as the rest of us. I've never heard of any other navigator requiring an assistant."

This had the sound of a long-standing argument. I stayed silent, figuring there wasn't any need for me to be involved at this point.

Nelson shook his head at Tanner. "And I've also told you, Mr. Tanner, that I am not getting any younger. How else do you think navigators learn their trade? And I am not going through the process of teaching someone reading and figuring. At least Mr. Crawford here is already half-trained."

I felt my breath catch in my throat. Was Nelson suggesting training me as a navigator, not merely hiring me as an assistant? Now wouldn't that be a fine thing!

Tanner scowled. "I am not letting you steal a deckhand, Mr. Nelson. It was pure luck we hired Mr. Crawford when we did."

Nelson opened his mouth to protest, but Freeman, the quartermaster, beat him to it.

"Mr. Tanner," he said in a deceptively mild tone. "How many voyages have we done short-handed?"

Tanner glared at Freeman, not backing down an inch. "More than I care to remember. I'm not letting some navigator who can't do his own job turn this into another one."

Freeman smiled. "Remember, this is Mr. Crawford's first voyage," he said. "Any work he does, someone will have to show him. So we might as well be sailing short-handed. Split his time between you and Mr. Nelson. Navigation doesn't take that much time, does it, Mr. Nelson?"

Nelson shook his head. "I'd need him at sunrise, noon, and sunset," he said. "For around an hour each time. And preferably one hour during the afternoon to plot courses."

Freeman turned back to Tanner. "Does that sound agreeable to you, Mr. Tanner?"

Tanner glared. "He still has to stand his watches," he growled. He turned to glare at me. "And don't think you'll get away with slacking because of this!"

I blinked in surprise. How had this decision been made so quickly, without even taking into consideration my opinion? Discarding the fact that I thought learning navigation was a fine idea, I wasn't so sure I liked how this plan was made.

"It's decided, then," Mr. Nelson said. His face finally settled back into a peaceable expression. "I'll see you at sunrise, Mr. Crawford. In the chart room."

"I'll be there, Mr. Nelson." What else was there for me to say?

"You have early morning watch," Tanner growled.

Unexpectedly, Morningwood spoke up. "The only reason you need two people on watch is if something happens, bos'n," he said. "And it's not as if Mr. Crawford here will be out of reach if something does."

I glanced at Morningwood in surprise. What were his motives, here? Was he actually being friendly? I couldn't quite believe it. He had to have an ulterior motive. Something was making my spine tingle, at any rate.

Tanner paused, unwilling to give up the argument, but Freeman took the decision away from him. "It's settled," he said. "Mr. Nelson will train Mr. Crawford, and he will continue working the deck. Nothing more is to be said upon the subject."

Freeman's word seemed to be law, and everyone went back to their meals with varying degrees of satisfaction or unhappiness.

I wasn't sure what to make of this. On the one hand, I was going to be learning navigation. On the other, it had been decided without me. And from looking at everyone's faces, not all of them were happy with this decision. No one was saying anything outright, but occasionally I caught a resentful glance my way.

I thought about that. It seemed I was getting more work this way, not getting out of it. Why would they be resentful?

I looked at Nelson again. Better clothes. Less muscles. Maybe being navigator was considered an easy gig.

If so, I would take it. All I really wanted right now was to be on the ocean and learn about using the power available here. Which I hadn't had a chance to do yet. I wanted some privacy, after all, and so far there'd been precious little of that.

We finished our meal with minimal conversation. One of the men, whose name I thought was Roberts, took out a fiddle, and the rest began clapping with enthusiasm. Apparently it wasn't all work and no play aboard this ship.

Morningwood, however, shook his head at me. "You'd better get sleep if you're going to be up at four in the morning," he told me.

He was right, of course. But there was still something I wanted to do before bed.

I nodded. "I want a breath of fresh air first," I said. "See you in the morning."

Morningwood disappeared towards the berthing area, and I went out onto the main deck.

I took a deep breath as I took in the sight of the ocean. Jamaica had disappeared from view miles ago, and all I could see was water. There wasn't even another ship anywhere on the horizon. We were all alone, out here on the water.

I closed my eyes and felt for the power I knew was there. I had done this with plants, of course, but this was my first time experimenting like this.

My eyes flew open in surprise. I had felt some of this from Port Royal. I had not imagined what it would be like out here. How was I even supposed to use all of this? I couldn't even begin to handle a fraction of what I felt. I would lose it all.

I shook my head at myself. I had to try. And to be smart, I would start by using a fraction of it. I had unlimited power to play with, after all.

I needed to create something that wouldn't seem out of place, though. The last thing I needed was for someone to spot something they shouldn't.

I gazed out at the sea again, remembering seeing some dolphins earlier in the day. That would do, I decided. I would see if I could create the illusion of a dolphin swimming alongside the ship.

I formed the image in my mind, remembering the leaps and bounds that the dolphins I had seen made. I reached for the power, and joined it with my mental image.

What I saw was an odd layering of what was actually there, and what anyone else would have seen. To my inner eye, for lack of a better term, there was nothing but the sea and waves. To my outer eyes, there was suddenly a dolphin breaking the surf and leaping into the air.

I gasped, feeling the power draining out through my hands. Hastily, I visualized the dolphin diving back into the water before grabbing the rail for support.

I had never tried to create something that moved as fast as that dolphin. It took more out of me than I realized, and the power available in the ocean did nothing to replenish me. It all went into the dolphin.

I had to learn how this worked. I wished desperately Nana had been able to tell me more before she passed on. Maybe she knew better.

I wasn't going to discover anything else right now, as exhausted as I was. I stumbled down to the berthing area, noting Morningwood was lying in his bunk, but not yet asleep. He didn't say anything as I slipped into my own bed.

My first day at sea had been eventful, at least. And God only knew what would happen in the morning.

*****Chapter 8*****

Morning came far too early. Watch involved Morningwood sending me up to the crow's nest for two hours, while he did... Something below on the deck. I tried to watch him, but I was supposed to be keeping a watch for ships. Pirates did sail these waters, after all. Although I didn't know what cargo we were carrying, it had to be valuable if Reddings was dealing in it.

At least I knew it wasn't slaves, although I knew he was looking into buying them. Maybe that was why he was going to Charleston. I knew the southern colonies were the center of the slave trade here in the New World.

I stayed in the crow's nest until the sun started peeking over the horizon. Not a single sail disturbed my view of the water, and it was with some reluctance that I climbed down the rigging when Morningwood came up to relieve me.

My reluctance soon vanished when I saw Nelson standing near the navigator's cabin, waving hurriedly at me. He held a large instrument in his hands.

"The sun's about to clear the horizon, and I need to get an accurate measurement. Hold this." He thrust one of the instruments at me, and I got a better look at it. It was a sphere of some sort, with all sorts of different moving metal objects.

The instrument Nelson held was much different. It was a long wooden pole with four shorter poles perpendicular to it at various points. Nelson balanced it for a moment, then raised it to stare where the sun was rising.

"Eighteen, seventeen, thirteen," he said shortly. "Remember that, will you, Mr. Crawford?"

I nodded, though I had no idea what the numbers meant. Nelson gave me the staff and took the globe from my hands.

He did something similar with the globe, then nodded in satisfaction. "Same measurement. Now, come with me, Mr. Crawford, and we'll begin your education in the art of navigation."

Nelson led me into the cabin, where a table covered in charts stood in the center of the room. He took the instruments from me and locked them in a cabinet.

"Captain's policy is the cross-staff and astrolabe must be under lock and key when they're not in use," he said. "They're incredibly valuable. Don't know why any of the men would try to steal them, though. It would rather limit their chances of getting home safely."

I didn't know what to say to this. Nelson frowned at me.

"You do have a tongue, right? I haven't heard you say more than five words altogether."

At that, a sardonic laugh made its way out of my mouth. Apparently I'd been doing a good job at keeping my mouth shut. That was a surprise.

Nelson grinned at me. "What, you have the same difficulty I do?"

I raised my eyebrows. "Keeping my mouth shut?" I asked.

Nelson's grin widened. "Thought so," he said. "Knew Tanner didn't like you for a reason, and it wasn't because of the color of your skin. Now, take a look at this chart here. This," he pointed at a mark, "is where we were at midnight. We've been steady on this course for the entire night since then. Now, with the measurements we took, what were those numbers again?"

"Eighteen, seventeen, thirteen," I said.

"Right. So we should be somewhere along this line, and based on our course," He took a ruler out and started making some marks in pencil. "This is where we are now."

I stared at the chart, trying to see the logic in what had just happened. How had Nelson figured that out?

Nelson must have seen the confusion in my face, and he sighed. "I'm going to have to start at the beginning, aren't I? You know about latitude? longitude? knots? cardinal directions?"

This was getting confusing.

"I know how to use a compass," I said, mentioning the only thing I thought would relate.

Nelson sighed. "Figures. I finally get one who can read and write, and he doesn't know anything about navigation. So, lesson time. You will learn this, boy. Mark my words!"

I didn't argue with him. I didn't really want to. As much as the rest of the men on the ship seemed to dislike me, Nelson seemed to sympathize with me. And he truly wanted to teach. It seemed fascinating enough to me.

The next hour passed with me learning basic navigation terminology, and ended with Nelson drilling me about how many seconds were in a minute, how many minutes were in a degree, and how fast a ship was going if it went two minutes in twenty hours. When Tanner finally stuck his head in the cabin, wondering angrily if Nelson was done with me yet, my head was swimming.

"I'll need him again at noon, remember," Nelson told Tanner. "I'll tell the quartermaster if you try to keep him from me."

Tanner grunted, but made no reply. I kept my mouth shut as I followed him onto the deck. If Tanner didn't like me, as Nelson had observed, I really shouldn't try exacerbate his dislike.

It turned out most of the day's work entailed cleaning. The first thing Tanner did was shove a mop - swab - in my hand and order me to join Roberts in swabbing the deck. Roberts greeted me with a raised eyebrow.

"Was this what you expected when you signed up for a life at sea?" he asked. "I know it wasn't what I expected."

I suppressed a smile as I dunked my swab in the bucket of filthy water that we were using. I had found what I expected. It just wasn't anything anyone else would know to look for.

I shrugged in response to Roberts' question. "Don't know yet," I asked. "Doesn't seem so bad so far."

Roberts shook his head. "Just wait a few more days," he said. "It's seven, maybe eight days to St. Augustine, if the weather's good. If it's not," he shook his head again. "We get restless. And bored. And our dear quartermaster and captain take a dim view of the things we get up to when we're bored."

My eyes narrowed. "What does that mean?" I asked sharply.

Roberts shrugged. "Most of us have cards," he said. He grinned suddenly. "I'm a fair hand myself. But some people don't take too kindly when they lose part of their hard-earned pay. They shouldn't play, is all I say."

I didn't quite follow, but it did bring an idea to my mind. I'd have to learn the rules for the various card games, but if I could make the cards look like other cards... Dangerous thought. But one worth considering. I needed ways to experiment with my power, whatever it was. Gift.

Tanner glared when he saw the two of us talking rather than swabbing. "You remember what the punishment for lollygagging is, Mr. Roberts?" he asked sharply.

I could see Roberts wanted to roll his eyes, but he suppressed it. "Yes, Mr. Tanner. Very well."

Tanner snorted. "You may want to enlighten our new shipmate. It will not be tolerated, you understand me?"

Roberts nodded, and Tanner spun around on his heel and stalked off towards the helm.

Roberts snorted. "Stick up his bum, that one," he said softly.

I cocked my head. "What's the punishment for lollygagging?"

"Ten lashes from the cat," Roberts said shortly. "Must have got it four or five times our last voyage. That bastard loves threatening me with it."

I stopped short. "The cat o' nine tails?"

Roberts gave me a look that clearly said, 'Right, he's a landlubber.'

"That's what I said. It's no fun, believe me."

"Then we'd better get back to work," I said, dunking my swab in the water again and starting to scrub the deck.

Roberts snorted, but followed suit. "It's pointless work," he grumbled. "We do this every bloody day. It gets worse when there's nothing broken."

I could see how swabbing the deck could get monotonous after a while, but I decided I could manage it for another seven days, and then however long it took to get to Charleston. If I got as far as Charleston, with Reddings waiting there for me.

I had to figure this out. Somehow, I needed to escape the ship before we met Reddings in Charleston. I could jump ship in St. Augustine, I supposed. The Spanish had an awful reputation for slavery, though. And not just slavery of Africans. Of the Taino, as well.

It seemed I was boxed into a corner, and it wasn't one I enjoyed, not in the least.

I didn't have much time to ponder it. Swabbing the deck took all morning, after which Nelson commandeered me for another round of measurement taking and plotting. This time, he asked me where I thought we were, which had him shaking his head in disappointment when I estimated our position to be fifteen miles east of where we actually were.

"Precision, boy. That's what matters when it comes to this art. Fifteen miles is another three hours. And what happens if you were fifteen miles west? We'd be that much closer to land, which can be perilous at night."

I could see that. It seemed that the navigator had a lot more responsibility than I originally thought.

"This afternoon, I'll show you how to plot out a course," he said. "I've already done the basic work for the trip to St. Augustine, but I still need to map the best route to Charleston. We need to update our current route based upon where we now are."

I looked at him in confusion, and he shook his head.

"My original route was fine, but you can never account for how the seas take us. We're about ten miles further south than I estimated us being now. It happens all the time. You ever become a navigator, you'll get used to it."

I stared at the charts laid across the table. Tricky, and with perilous consequences. I wasn't sure I liked the idea of that much responsibility, but then again, I could never back down from a challenge. Although Nelson hadn't actually issued me a verbal one, it was clear he meant me to learn, whether I actually wanted to or not. It was Tanner who gave me the challenge, with his attitude at least. Somehow, I knew he wanted me to fail at this. I wouldn't give him the chance to gloat.

*****Chapter 9*****

The next few days passed with the same excitement as the first two. I never had a chance to rest. If we weren't scrubbing the deck, we were doing rigging drills, and I was learning how all the lines on the ship went together. I was kept on the early morning watch, although it wasn't always Morningwood who stood it with me. Nelson kept my head crammed full of figures and equations, as well as logic, maps, and charts. Fascinating, really, and something I would have never learned if I stayed on the plantation. In the evenings, I practiced using my gift.

I decided I would call 'it' that. I couldn't keep calling 'it' 'it', after all. Now that I was using 'it' constantly to keep my disguise as a man, 'it' deserved a better name. And gift was what 'it' was to me so far.

I was still working on mastering the trick to use the power to not only perform whatever seeming I wanted, but also replenish myself afterwards so I wasn't exhausted. I knew there had to be a way to do it, but I kept failing. And after the first failure I was hardly in any shape to try again.

It was on our fourth day out to sea that the routine was broken. I was swabbing the deck again, this time with Jennings, when Tanner marched into the center and called all of us to attention.

This was new. I looked at Jennings, who just rolled his eyes and looked resigned.

Freeman stepped out, followed by the captain. Now this was very odd. I had hardly seen a glimpse or more of the captain during the four days I had spent onboard. Freeman seemed to be very much the one in charge. I couldn't even remember the captain's name.

Freeman was the one who spoke first. "You all know how important discipline is onboard this ship," he said. "We are alone at sea. If any of us slack, then the rest of us have to pay the price, and we may not reach our destination. There are dangers here at sea. If we are less than ready at any time, we may not survive the trip."

There was a shuffling of feet amongst the sailors. Apparently this was a speech that had been made before.

"There are some among you who have tested this theory before," Freeman's voice was raised. He turned to Tanner, who was now standing behind Roberts. My eyes widened as I realized what was going on.

"Mr. Tanner, how many times has our shipmate Mr. Roberts been lashed for failing to do his duty?" he asked.

Tanner had his arms crossed. "Six, at my last count, Mr. Freeman. At least onboard this ship."

Freeman nodded. "Six times under the lash for the same offense. It seems that the lesson has not been brought home, has it, Mr. Roberts?"

Roberts looked angry and defiant, but resigned at the same time. He didn't answer, just glared at Tanner.

Freeman shook his head. "Take your shirt off, Mr. Roberts," he said. "Tanner, tie him to the mast."

Slowly, Roberts complied, folding his shirt neatly and handing it to the sailor next to him. Tanner obeyed with alacrity, tying Roberts' hands together so that they were wrapped around the mast.

Freeman approached Roberts, his stance and face indifferent. For the first time, I saw the whip in his hand. I shivered. It looked wicked.

"Ten lashes," Freeman said calmly. "Ten lashes every time. How many does that make, Mr. Crawford? Since you're so good at figuring and all."

I swallowed hard as every eye turned to look at me. "Sixty," I said. I had to force my voice to speak above a whisper.

I saw Roberts' shoulders shudder.

"Sixty," Freeman looked like he was musing over the number. "Think you can handle sixty lashes, Mr. Roberts? I think that is what it's going to take to drive the lesson home."

Before Roberts had a chance to answer, Freeman pulled his arm back and swung.

The cat o' nine tails made a resounding crack as it swung through the air and landed on Roberts' back. He jumped, but made no sound.

"One!" Tanner shouted.

Freeman shook his head. "I know you always scream after seven, Roberts," he said. "Will you get any louder, now that there's more coming?"

This was getting cruel. I looked at the other sailors, but none of them seemed surprised. Without an answer, Freeman swung the cat again.

Soon enough, Roberts' back was a bloody mess, and he was screaming hoarsely every time the cat cracked down. Freeman never let up during the whipping.

I was almost sick at the sight of so much blood. I had never seen a man whipped before, although I knew it was a common punishment for minor infractions on the plantation at home. And the way Roberts was screaming and writhing...

Some of my disgust and distress must have shown on my face, because Tanner gave me a leer that sent spiders through my skin. He seemed to be enjoying this.

I glared back at him, not caring about the consequences. Any man who could do this to another and enjoy it must be sick and twisted somewhere. I had no desire to make any man like that my friend.

That included Freeman, I realized, as I watched the whip strike home once again. He wasn't showing his pleasure as clearly as Tanner was, but it was there to see. Especially in his eyes, which gleamed every time the whip left another welt and streak of blood on Roberts' back.

I suppressed a shudder, remembering the other man whose eyes had gleamed like that. The man who may have said he wanted to marry me, but instead wanted to keep me as a slave and use my gift for his own purposes. Reddings was like that. Would he have done to me what Freeman was doing to Roberts, had I refused to serve him?

I couldn't bring myself to believe otherwise. I had to get away from that man. And more than that, I wasn't sure if I could stand being on this ship much longer. Not with men like this in charge.

At last, the whipping was over. Roberts sagged against his bonds, leaning against the mast for support. Freeman coiled up the cat and handed it to Tanner.

"Cut him free," Freeman ordered, nodding to Jennings. Jennings rushed forward to cut the rope holding Roberts' wrists, and he slumped to the deck.

"Treat those cuts," Freeman said. "He needs to be back at work tomorrow morning."

My eyes widened. I couldn't imagine how a man so injured could stand to work the next day.

I wasn't the only one thinking that. The thought was mirrored in the eyes of every other sailor, including Tanner's. Except Tanner was smiling.

"Good work, Mr. Freeman."

I jumped and stared at the captain. I almost forgot about him standing there. He hadn't moved or said a word the entire time.

Freeman nodded, and the captain turned to stare at me. I stared back, startled. I had done nothing to gain his attention. At least, I thought I hadn't.

"Come with me, Mr. Freeman," the captain said without taking his eyes off of me. "We have some matters to discuss."

Freeman looked at me, then back to the captain. What the hell was going on between those two? He nodded. "Aye, aye, Captain," he said. He stared at the rest of us. "Well? Back to work, you lot, unless you want a set of scars like Roberts is going to have!"

I turned to go back to swabbing he deck. Jennings looked like he was taking care of Roberts. It wasn't like I could do anything for him that Jennings couldn't.

Morningwood picked up Jennings' discarded swab. "You never see a whipping before?" he asked. "I would have thought you'd have seen plenty."

I stared at him. "Why would I have seen plenty of whippings?" I managed.

He shook his head. "Must have been mistaken."

I tried to figure out what he meant while we continued swabbing. I eventually put the question aside. There were better things I could be trying to figure out. "Do they do that sort of thing often?" I asked.

Morningwood shrugged. "At least once a voyage," he said. "More if anyone commits a severe offence. They say it keeps us on our toes, knowing we might have to face the cat at any time."

I shook my head in disgust. Morningwood laughed at me. "Best not let our bos'n and quartermaster see that opinion, Mr. Crawford," he said. "You might end up tied to the mast yourself."

My blood turned cold at the thought. I had heard Roberts' screams. I had no desire to face the same pain. But more than that, I wasn't sure if I could maintain my disguise while being flogged like that. What would happen if this crew found out I was a woman? They didn't seem to be the type of men to forgive deception easily.

I was in trouble. I should have listened to Miguel. I should have looked around and seen which ships were better and tried to sign on with one that I liked. But no, I had to go lose my temper with a government official, and now I was here. On a ship run by bastards and owned by Reddings. God damn it.

It was in that frame of mind that I reported to Nelson at noon for measurement taking and lessons. He looked at me sharply.

"Not happy with the demonstration the captain and quartermaster gave, are you?" he said.

I frowned at him. "Is it that obvious?" I asked.

Nelson snorted. "No one's happy with it. The sailors would be a fool to like it. That's kind of the point."

I shook my head. "I'm not happy with the idea they can randomly decide to do that."

"Oh, they can't flog everyone because they feel like it," Nelson said casually. "To do that would run the risk of mutiny, and there's far too few officers here to risk that. But what Roberts did? It's harsh, but at least there was some kind of offence. Just enough to keep everyone on their toes."

His voice was too casual for me.

"It's barbaric," I snapped. "How is Roberts supposed to work tomorrow? I bet he'll barely have the strength to get out of his rack."

I wasn't prepared for what Nelson did next. He grabbed my arm and shoved me against the wall, his face inches from mine. He wasn't a tall man, but his wiry body held a surprising amount of strength.

"You keep those opinions to yourself, Mr. Crawford," Nelson said in a low voice. "Mr. Tanner hears what you just said, you'll be the next one tied to the mast. I'd hate to lose my assistant so soon after finding one."

Angrily, I shoved Nelson away from me. "I'm not an idiot," I snapped. "I can keep my mouth shut."

Nelson raised his eyebrows, and I glared back at him defiantly. I had, hadn't I? I hadn't said anything mutinous or disrespectful the entire time I'd been onboard this ship. Ma wouldn't have believed it. She always said I couldn't hold my tongue to save my life.

"See that you do," was all Nelson said. "You have more against you already than the rest of the men here."

My temper rose again. "If that's because of the color of my skin-"

"Shut up, Joseph," Nelson said, startling me. He'd used my assumed first name, the first time someone onboard this ship had actually done so. "You can't change the bias people here have. You're lucky I'm here and I don't share their prejudices. You're lucky they didn't just decide to sell you in Port Royal when Mr. Freeman first found you. I know you've said you're not an escaped slave, but do you really think anyone would care a fig about what you say? I know our captain and I know he cares only for profit. If you make an enemy out of the rest of the men here because of their prejudice, he can sell you next port call, no questions asked."

I stared at him, dumbfounded. It had never been laid out to me in such bald terms how my words meant nothing to white men. That I was a tool and commodity, nothing more.

I could feel myself start to shake. "I'm not even African," I said, glaring at Nelson again. I couldn't seem to help it. "I'm Taino. My people were here long before you white men."

Nelson laughed softly. "The white men are here now," he said. "And I think we're here to stay. You'd better get used to it. Not all white men are kind like me."

My glare hardened. "No white man is kind," I snapped. "I've learned that lesson."

"Then learn how to work around it," Nelson said. He nodded sharply. "Ready to learn how to use the cross-staff?"

I wanted to continue the argument, but I bottled up my feelings. For all his harsh words, Nelson did seem to be trying to help me. I couldn't guess why, but he didn't seem to have any ulterior motives.

We spent the next hour as we normally did, with me learning even more about the art of navigation. It was truly an art, I learned. It relied a lot more on guesswork than most people would care to know. Everything relied on us knowing where we were last. If for some reason the markings were wrong even once, every position after that was wrong. If we couldn't get readings for some reason, say, during a storm, there could be hours during which we would have no idea where we were. If we were blown off course during a storm, it would take sighting land for Nelson to figure out where we were. Definitely an art.

We finished the hour by measuring the speed at which the boat was sailing. We did this with a much simpler contraption, merely a long spool of rope that ran out for a set length of time. We were going five knots, much the same speed we had been going the entire voyage.

Nelson grabbed my arm before I headed back to the deck. "Remember what I said," he cautioned. "Don't get in trouble."

I narrowed my eyes. I could take a hint the first time. I didn't need to be reminded. "I won't."

Nelson didn't seem to be convinced, but he let me go. I felt his eyes watching me as I walked back towards the deck.

Why did people seem to believe I wouldn't keep my mouth shut? Hadn't I proved I could in the last four days? I had plenty of opportunities to lose my temper.

Tuppence Van de Vaarst

*****Chapter 10*****

I should have known keeping my mouth shut wouldn't last long.

It was right after my sunset shift with Nelson the next day. It had gone well. Nelson had even let me plot our position on the chart, along with my prediction of where we would be the following morning. We were still three days from St Augustine, but that shouldn't be an issue. We had plenty of provisions on board, after all.

The other sailors typically played card games in the galley before lights out. I normally didn't join them, because of early watch, but for some reason I decided to poke my head in today.

I was glad I did, and even gladder the men didn't notice me at first.

"He says he's never been a slave," Morningwood said. "How has a man that black lived in Jamaica and never been a slave?"

"Spanish were there until recently," Jennings said. "They were strange people. Maybe he's the bastard son of one of them?"

Roberts snorted. "Whether or not it's true, why are we hiring him instead of making a side profit?"

I froze and backed up into the shadows. Without thinking, I drew on my gift. I had never tried this before, but if I could look like the wall behind me...

I let my breath out in a quiet sigh as I felt the seeming settle over me, and my knees nearly buckled. Apparently, changing more than just a few superficial things took power.

"Nelson seems friendly with him," one of the other men said. I didn't know who. Green?

Roberts snorted. "Too friendly. Why would he take him as his assistant, when he could have any of us?"

"As if you'd want to be Nelson's assistant, Roberts," Jennings said sardonically. The rest of the men laughed before returning to the topic of their conversation, namely me.

"Do you think the captain's got something in mind?" Green asked.

Morningwood laughed. "Captain's always got something in mind. In this case, though, I would say Freeman has the plan. He's the one who brought him onboard, anyway."

There was my proof, at least. Morningwood, however friendly he might appear, did not have my best interests at heart. Then again, none of these bastards did.

"Do you know anything?" Jennings asked. "You talk to Tanner more than the rest of us, after all. He tell you anything about this Crawford?"

Morningwood shrugged. "He's looking for an excuse to do what he did to Roberts. More than that, I can't tell you, although he's hinted something's going to happen in St. Augustine."

God damn it.

"Well, good," Roberts said. "If that bastard hadn't said sixty, maybe my back wouldn't hurt so much right now!"

"If you guys played cards, maybe you'd all have your money!" The fifth man, another one I hadn't talked to much, drew their conversation back to the cards in their hands, and the conversation shifted. I walked out of the galley and back to the berthing, trying to catch my breath.

Well. I knew the men were prejudiced, but I never thought they'd go as far as willingly selling me into slavery. I hadn't alienated them that much.

I jumped when Morningwood walked into the berthing. He gave me an inquisitive look. I couldn't hold back my glare.

He laughed. "What's wrong?"

I shook my head. I couldn't risk letting him know what I overheard. Not until I knew what I was going to do about it.

"You heard." It wasn't a question so much as a statement.

I couldn't hide my reaction. "So what's the plan when we get to St. Augustine?" I asked, my voice hard. "Sell me to the Spanish?"

Morningwood held up his hands. "I never said that," he said.

"But you implied it." I was shaking with rage at this point. "You think that just because my skin is darker than yours, you can decide my life and force me into lifelong servitude with a cruel master. Except I'm the one studying navigation, and not any of you lot. Are you guys scared because I'm smarter than you? Do you not want to admit that a black man can be just as smart as a white one?"

Morningwood's eyes darkened. "I'd watch your tongue, Mr. Crawford," he said, his tone hard.

"And I'd watch your actions, Mr. Morningwood," I said. "I tell you right now, you, or any of this crew, try to sell me into slavery, you'll regret it for the rest of your life."

I had no idea how I was going to follow through on that threat, and apparently Morningwood had the same thought. He shook his head.

"I suppose we'll find out at St. Augustine, won't we?" he asked.

I laughed bitterly. I wasn't even sure I was going to make it to St. Augustine.

Tuppence Van de Vaarst

*****Chapter 11*****

I had to go to sleep after that. Disguising myself as a wall had drained me more than I realized. But on watch the next morning, I brooded. Was it possible for me to jump ship in St. Augustine? Could I learn enough about using my gift to disguise myself as a white man for the length of time I spent there?

My stomach nearly revolted at the thought. Why should I have to cater to other people's prejudices? Why couldn't they look at my abilities and actions, rather than my appearance?

I was lucky that there wasn't anything to report, because I don't think I would have seen it, as preoccupied with my things as I was.

Nelson was waiting for me when I climbed down the rigging. "Ready to plot our position?" he asked.

I nodded, but before I could take the sextant from him Tanner's voice rang across the deck. "Boy! Get over here!"

I jumped and glanced over to where Tanner was standing. His expression did not look friendly.

I looked at Nelson for support, but he just shrugged. I rolled my eyes and started towards Tanner.

Tanner glared at me. "Where are you from, boy?" he asked.

I folded my arms across my chest. "Jamaica," I said shortly.

"Who was your master?"

My eyes widened, and I felt my fists clench. "I was not a slave!" I snapped.

"Liar," Tanner was clearly enjoying himself. "No man like you could walk through an English colony and not be taken into slavery. Who was your master?"

I couldn't stand it. "I had no master, you son of a bitch! What's so hard to understand about that?"

Tanner's eyes narrowed in satisfaction, and I got an uneasy feeling in the pit of my stomach.

"That's it," he said. "Flogging for insubordination. And lying."

I gaped at him, but Tanner was already calling for Morningwood and Jenner to restrain me.

This could not be bloody happening to me. I tried to shrug Morningwood's hands off my shoulders, but his grip was firm.

"What did you do, boy?" Morningwood asked.

I glared at him. "Nothing," I snapped. "This is all your fault."

"Mine?" There was so much mock innocence in his face I wanted to spit. "How could this be mine?"

Tanner smiled, the same cruel smile I remembered from Roberts' flogging. "Hold him while I get Freeman and the captain," he said. "How many lashes are there for insubordination? Fifty?"

Jenner nodded, his iron grip on my arms never loosening. "That sounds right."

My blood was like ice in my veins. Fifty. Not as many as Roberts had to endure, but still far too many for me to be certain of my disguise.

"Tanner! Sail!"

Tanner cursed and drew his spyglass. Moments later, Freeman and the Captain came running out, each with their own spyglasses.

I heard muttered curses from them soon later.

"Armed," the captain said. "What's a French flag doing so close to Spanish property?"

It was as if the word they were all thinking was written clear in the air. I swallowed. Pirates.

I had heard my fair share of stories about pirates. Even on the plantation, we heard about pirates and privateers and the atrocities they committed. Someone always tried to make it sound exciting, but now that the reality was facing me, I could have done without it.

Tanner went running below decks, presumable to muster the crew. Freeman glanced at Morningwood, Jenner, and me.

"Let him go," he said. "He can't go anywhere, and we have bigger problems."

I sighed in relief as Morningwood and Jenner released their grip. I felt like I was going to have bruises.

"Crawford, get up to the crow's nest," Freeman ordered. "Send Roberts down. Let us know if the ship gets closer."

I nodded without saying anything. I climbed quickly up the rigging again. I didn't want to be anywhere near the rest of the crew right now.

The next few hours passed in suspense. Long, tiring suspense. The captain and Freeman stood on the deck, yelling harsh orders about trimming this sail, and letting out more sail on that one. Tanner ran around, relaying those orders and yelling at everyone to get a move on. I caught Roberts' resentful glance towards the crow's nest, and anger surged up. It wasn't my fault Freeman had ordered me to take his watch, was it?

Whatever tactics the captain was trying to employ, however, were failing. The ship was gradually getting closer and closer. I reported this to Nelson, who said nothing, only nodded grimly.

The ship finally drew into view so I could see her clearly. It was at least twice the size of the Vixen, and more than five times the men scurried around on deck. I couldn't tell who was below deck, of course, but they had cannon holes in the side, although none of them were open yet. If there were cannons, someone had to be manning them.

They did fly a French flag, which was confusing. As far as I knew, England and France weren't at war, although with the hostilities between the countries, that really didn't matter. And if these were pirates, there was no telling if that was their actual flag or not.

"Get down from there, Mr. Crawford!"

I looked down to see Tanner shouting up at me.

He shook his head. "We can't outrun them. We need all hands."

He seemed resigned and I swallowed. Well, I was onboard a ship that was about to be attacked by pirates. Wasn't this great?

I climbed down and Tanner directed me to help Morningwood and Jennings in securing their sail. We were all distracted. Every few seconds, we would cast glances back at the ship that was determinedly pursuing us.

"Damn pirates," Morningwood muttered.

I looked at him. "What will happen?"

He shook his head. "We won't fight, most likely. Hopefully they put up the black flag soon. You don't want to see the red one."

I frowned. "What does that mean?" I demanded.

"Red means no quarter given," Morningwood said shortly.

I sighed in exasperation, but Morningwood seemed disinclined to answer any more of my questions. I didn't relish the thought of just waiting for things to happen, but I didn't seem to have any other choice.

Finally, Tanner came to us and ordered us all to the main deck. We were offering no struggle, it seemed. At least the captain was smart in that regard. I saw no way we could fight against a ship that size and win.

The men and I stood in silence on the deck as the ship drew closer and closer. There was a collective intake of breath as the French colors came down, followed by the hoisting of a black flag. At the same time, the covers for the cannon holes came out, and we saw the flash of power. A boom followed shortly afterwards. A warning shot.

I looked up to where the captain stood. We didn't carry a white flag, apparently, but he had improvised with what looked like a sheet. His face was a blank mask, and I shivered at the rage hiding beneath it.

The captain gave no orders as the ship drew up alongside us. From the pirate ship came a loud voice, echoing across the water.

"Thank you for your courtesy, Captain!" he shouted. "You're saving both of us a great deal of trouble, here!"

It cost the captain to answer, I could see that. "You do not make it easy on us, pirate," he said. "Stop your gloating and get on with it."

A laugh echoed across the water. "But I wouldn't be a proper pirate if I didn't gloat, now would I? Board her, lads!"

A cheer came up from the other ship, and I felt some of the men around me shiver. I wasn't doing much better myself. What in God's name was going to happen to us?

We were only two days out of St. Augustine. We almost made it. Well, they almost made it. I might have had a different welcome waiting for me there than the rest of the crew.

With loud cries, the pirates threw grappling hooks and started hauling the ships closer together. A few of them swung across on ropes, weapons ready in their belts, teeth, or free hands.

I stared at one of them. There was a black man onboard the pirate ship. A huge man, with muscles that defied reality. He was naked from the waist up, and he was definitely enjoying himself. He caught my eye and laughed.

I continued staring at him. I couldn't help myself. Was he an equal onboard that ship, or was he a slave? He couldn't be a slave. He was carrying weapons, for God's sake!

I glanced at the other men to see if they noticed. Roberts had, for sure. He was giving the man an uneasy look, which he then turned in my direction.

For Christ's sake. I glared at Roberts. Did he really think that just because the man was black, the two of us would stick together? Even if he did feel sympathy towards me, he was a pirate. And if he found out I was Taino rather than African, any sympathy he might have felt would be gone. Roberts was an idiot.

Soon enough, there were at least twenty pirates marching around the decks of the Vixen. Surprisingly enough, it seemed to be the black man that was in charge.

"This all the men you have, Captain?" he asked.

The captain nodded, his face still set. The black man grinned at him. "Well, we'll soon be seeing about that, but thank you for your answer. Men! Start searching below decks! Carefully! And tell me what cargo you find!"

Loud shouts came in reply and the black man started making his way over to where Tanner and us eight sailors stood. I watched him approaching, apprehension building. He kept looking at me, a sardonic smile on his face. It wasn't a friendly expression.

"Who's in charge of you lot?"

As one, we all turned to Tanner, who flushed red. Apparently he hadn't expected to be put on the spot.

"I am," he blustered, stepping forward. "Who are you to be asking?"

The man grinned. "One of the pirates who's about to take your cargo from you," he said. "Name?"

Tanner scowled. "Why don't you tell me your name first, you thieving bastard?"

It happened so quickly that I could barely see the motions. One moment Tanner was insulting the black man, and the next he was lying on the deck, stunned by the man's punch to the jaw. In one swift motion, the man had a sword to Tanner's neck.

"You may want to rephrase that," he said mildly. "Or I won't be responsible for what happens to you. Now, your name?"

Apparently Tanner was stupider than I realized, for he spat.

The man shrugged and drove his sword home.

I had heard stories of the cruelty of pirates, but this wasn't a story. This was happening right before my eyes. Much as I disliked Tanner, he was murdered. Right in front of me. His blood was soaking into the deck of the ship.

The man turned to us and smiled. "Now, would anyone like to answer my question, or would you like to share the same fate as your misguided leader?"

For a long moment, no one spoke. After all, who was going to speak up after that?

The man tapped his sword on the deck. "I'm waiting."

God damn these men. Apparently they were not only stupid and prejudiced, they were cowards as well.

"I'm Joseph Crawford," I said, stepping forward. "The man you just killed was Tanner, the ship's bos'n."

I regretted my decision when the man turned fully to stare at me. His eyes were hard, and they seemed to pierce right through me. I strengthened my hold on my seeming.

"Joseph Crawford, hmm?" the man said. "This all the men from the ship?"

I looked around, counting again to make sure. "'cept the quartermaster, navigator, and Captain," I said.

I heard Roberts hiss, and I looked at him in surprise. There was no harm answering his questions. The captain himself had said we weren't to resist. And after the way this man had killed Tanner in cold blood, I had no inclinations to make things difficult for him. At least, not yet.

The man nodded in satisfaction. "Any idea what cargo you're carrying, Joseph?"

I blinked. I was so used to people calling me Mr. Crawford. "No," I said. "I actually have no idea."

Morningwood snorted. I turned to look at him at the same time the man did, and he blanched.

"Care to enlighten me to the joke?" The man's tone was friendly, but the hold he had on his sword was not.

Morningwood swallowed, his face suddenly pale. "It's Mr. Crawford's first voyage, so of course he doesn't know. We're carrying coffee beans. Not much use for you."

The man grinned, showing two lines of perfect white teeth. "Let us be the judge of what is and isn't useful," he said. "Your name?"

"William Morningwood."

"Good." The man looked at the rest of the men. "Everyone else?"

One by one, the other men gave their names, however reluctantly.

"Well done," the man said. "Now, this is the way it's going to work. You're going to help us transfer the cargo onto our ship. Then, we'll interview each of you one by one. If you feel like joining, we're always looking for able-bodied hands. Hands that are loyal, do their work, and treat each other fairly." His eyes snapped to each of us in turn. "Now get to the hold, and start unloading the cargo."

I moved to join the rest of the men, but was stopped by the man's voice. "You, Joseph," he snapped. "You come with me."

I froze, not knowing what to expect. The rest of the men continued on, none of them giving me a second glance. I turned to follow the man.

He led me to, of all places, the captain's cabin. I had never actually been in there before, and I looked around with interest as we entered. There was a bit more room than our ten-man berthing area, but the rack was still made of the same hard stuff.

My attention snapped fully back to the man as he stared at me and chuckled. I stared at him, trying to decide what I should do.

"Joseph, hmm?" he shook his head. "What's your real name?"

I blanched. What the hell was this man talking about? He couldn't have been able to tell I was lying. I had been Joseph as often as Josephine.

"What do you mean?" I asked, fighting to keep my voice level.

The man laughed. "Come on," he said. "I know very few women who are christened Joseph at birth. So what's your real name?"

I felt all the blood in me turn to ice. How the hell? I stared at him, then looked instinctively at the door.

Instantly, he was almost on top of me. "Don't think you can escape," he said. "Not even by turning invisible or whatever else you do. There's not a lot of room on this ship. I'll be certain to find you."

My eyes snapped back to him again. "How do you-" I couldn't finish the question. I felt my tongue cleave to the roof of my mouth. I was in trouble.

The man laughed. "Can't you recognize a fellow when you see one, girl?" he asked. "I can see your true form, no matter what it is you're projecting to everyone else. Now, will you answer my question, or shall I give you a taste of what Tanner suffered?"

I swallowed hard. "Josephine Crawford," I said. Apparently there was no point in hiding it from him.

"Josephine." The man turned my name over his mouth, like he was savoring it. "I won't ask how you came onboard this ship. That's your own business, but since you did, here's what you're going to do."

My temper flared, but I clamped down hard on my tongue. He was armed and I wasn't. It wasn't a good idea to start a confrontation that I had no hope of winning.

"When we do the interviews, you are going to express your interest and enthusiasm in joining the pirate crew. I'll make sure the captain takes you. Once you're ours, you will learn to hone those abilities of yours to make our attacks easier. How does that sound?"

For a moment, I couldn't speak. What the hell was he thinking?

Then it came to me. He was going to try to use me, just like Reddings had tried to. He didn't see me at all, just my gift. I was a tool for him, nothing more.

"What if I don't?" I asked.

The man's eyes darkened and I instinctively backed up a step. He followed.

"If you don't, then we will set sail without you. But not before every man on this ship has found out you're a woman. Women are considered bad luck onboard ships like this Did you know that? Everyone will be certain it's because of your presence they were attacked, and they're going to take it out on you."

I backed up again, but my back hit the wall of the cabin. I couldn't deny the man's words.

He continued. "You know what that will mean for you, right?" he said.

I couldn't answer. I knew.

He said it anyway. "Rape, at the very least. Then torture and beatings. And then, once they get to wherever they were going, they'll likely sell you. And they'll make sure that whoever buys you knows you're a woman."

I bit my lip and said the only thing that came to my mind. "I'm not bloody African. I'm Taino."

The man's smile grew wider. "Even better. The Spanish love having native slaves, didn't you know that? You'll likely fetch a higher price for them that way."

He stayed silent for a moment while that played out in my mind. I shuddered.

He cocked his head. "Belay that. If you don't join us, I'll tell your old crew about you, let them have their revenge, and then we'll sell you. Hate to see that profit go to waste."

I stared at him, open mouthed. He would sell me into slavery? He was darker than me! What kind of man did that?

"On the other hand, you could sign onboard a pirate ship. I'd teach you some more about using that talent of yours. You're woefully ill-trained. And all you'd have to do is exactly what I tell you to. You wouldn't want the rest of us pirates to find out you're a woman. Many of us are just as superstitious."

I let his words sink in. "What kind of things would you be telling me to do?"

He smiled. "Anything I want you to. You're not exactly my type, and I doubt you have the kind of experience I'd require, so you don't have to worry about sleeping with me, but anything else would be fair game."

I froze. "You lay one finger on me, and you'll regret it."

The man's eyes narrowed, and he stepped forward again, crowding me against the wall. "You have quite the mouth, don't you?" he said. "You watch that tongue when you're around me, you understand?"

I swallowed hard and nodded. Somehow, I didn't doubt this man's ability to do whatever he threatened.

"Let me make one thing clear. I'm offering you a much better life if you join us. You know the fate that awaits you if you don't. But if you talk back to me, or disobey me in any way, I'll let everyone know you're a woman and what they should do to you."

"Why?" My voice came out as a whisper.

"Someone has to make use of those talents of yours. I can get good money out of you, but if you're too much trouble, I have no difficulty discarding you."

He stepped back, and suddenly his face was back to pleasantness. "I'll let you decide what option to pick. Stay in here. Someone will come get you for the interview."

Without a further word, he stalked out the door. I heard the click of the lock behind him.

A quiet, hysterical, laugh bubbled out of me. Stay in here. I had no chance to leave!

I stared down at my hands. Dimly, I realized they were shaking. Of all the things I thought would happen to me when I ran away, this was not one of them.

That man, whatever his name was, had the same gift I did. More, he knew how to use it. He said he would teach me. He also threatened me with torture and rape if I didn't give him what he wanted. And from what I had seen, he was entirely capable of following through with that without regard for me. I had seen him murder Tanner.

If I stayed... I shivered. There was no point contemplating that possibility. The man was right about what this crew would do to me. Even if they didn't rape and beat me, they'd definitely sell me when they got to St. Augustine. They'd have to make up their profits somehow. And if they waited until Charleston for some reason, and Reddings saw me there...

I swallowed again as a cold knot of fear built in me. I had only met two men with the same type of talents as mine outside of my family. And both of them wanted to use me.

There wasn't really a choice. Reddings would use me, and hold me in virtual slavery. This crew would sell me into actual slavery. On the pirate ship, I might actually stand a chance. The black man would be the only one with a hold over me, and I might find allies among the crew.

I couldn't believe that of the three options, my best one was joining with a pirate crew. In that moment, I hated everyone here. Everyone who thought to use me because of my talent, who disrespected me because of the color of my skin, and who threatened me because of my sex. I hated the fact that I could be threatened just because I was female. Most of all, I hated Reddings for putting me in this situation to begin with.

It was rather illogical of me, but I didn't care. Reddings was the reason for all this trouble, at least in my mind. I didn't stop to think about what would be happening to me if Reddings had never showed up.

I paid no attention to the passing of time as I started pacing up and down the length of the cabin. I was worrying over my situation, when in reality there was very little I could do about it. I trusted the man when he said that he would find me if I tried to escape. And anyway, I couldn't get out of this room to try.

I nearly flew out of my skin when I heard the key turn in the lock. I stared at the boy who opened the door.

He was a boy, too. He couldn't have been more than eleven or twelve. He grinned at my dumbfounded expression.

"Capt'n's ready to see you," he said.

I snapped my mouth shut. "Care to lead the way?" I fought to keep my tone civil. There was no sense taking my anger out on a child. Though if I ever ran into the person who thought a pirate ship was a good place for a child, they were going to get a piece of my mind.

"Course! Bos'n said I wasn't to take my eyes off you, anyway."

Bos'n. That must have been the man who threatened me. I was careful to keep my expression neutral. "Does this bos'n have a name?" I asked. "And does your captain?"

"Course they do!" the boy exclaimed. "Bos'n is Hades. Captain is Captain Victor Abrams. I'll sure they'll be pleased to meet you!"

"Will they now?" I kept my tone curious. "And why would that be?"

"Because you'll be joining us! Bos'n said so!"

I felt my temper flare up in me again. So. This Hades had already seen fit to tell his captain I would be signing on? He had seen fit to make my decision for me, without even having the courtesy to let me make the decision myself?

I sternly told my temper to hush. It wasn't as if I had another choice.

My temper told me that wasn't the point. The point was that this man, this Hades, took every decision and choice out of my hands, and decided my life for me without regard to my own wishes. What kind of name was Hades, anyway? I knew my classics. Who named their child after a Greek god? The god of death, of all things? And he was talking about me having a false name?

My temper was winning.

The boy led me out onto the main deck again, towards the helm. Around the rudder stood four men, including Hades. The boy saluted one of them, a young fellow, with a beard that almost covered his face and a hat with the plumage of at least three birds in it. He returned the salute, and the boy nodded to Hades before he spun around on his heel and headed back towards the pirate ship.

"So, Joseph Crawford," the man with the hat said. I assumed he must be the captain. No one else would wear such a garish costume. Aside from that, though, he was quite handsome. His hair was tied back into a neat tail, and his sharp eyes bored into me. "I hear you want to join our crew."

I felt my spine stiffen. "I would," I said, "on one condition."

Every single muscle in my body tensed as Hades glared at me. I didn't dare look at him. I kept my eyes fixed on the captain.

The captain laughed openly. "Oh, really?" he asked. "And what condition would that be?"

I took a deep breath. "Don't take anyone else from this crew. Except the navigator, if he wants to come."

There was silence among the four men for a moment. Then, as one, they all burst into laughter.

I stood stock-still, trying not to tremble with rage. What right did these men have to laugh at me?

"I think that's a request we can accommodate," the captain said. He wiped his face with his hand. "Considering that none of your other shipmates showed the slightest inclination to abandon this ship for a life of piracy. Quite strange, considering the scars the one man had on his back. Freshly given too, I'd say. Was he a troublemaker?"

Roberts. I could care less about him. "He was for me."

The captain laughed again. "Fair enough," he said. He turned to one of the other men. "Harry, would you be so good as to make sure the articles are ready when we return to the ship?"

The man addressed as Harry nodded amiably. "Sure thing, Captain," he said. He gave me a considering look. "Can you read?"

I nodded, and his eyes widened with both surprise and respect. "Good. Then you can look at the articles yourself. What was your job on the Vixen?"

The captain held up his hands before I could answer. "Harry, before you start interrogating our newest shipmate, we have the business of sorting the cargo. Hades, you take him back to the Reliance and show him about, will you? I'll send Derry to come find you when I'm ready."

I stared at Hades warily. Him, show me around the pirate ship? After what he had just threatened to do to me?

I didn't seem to have a choice, though. The captain and the other two men disappeared towards the line of cargo being transferred, and Hades raised his eyebrow at me.

"You picked the right choice, Josephine," he said softly.

I nearly jumped out of my skin. I knew my eyes were burning as they glared at him. "Don't call me that," I snapped.

Hades laughed. "But Joseph is a lie," he said. "You wouldn't want me to lie, now would you?"

It was on the tip of my tongue to suggest that he was already lying to everyone on the pirate ship by concealing my gender, but I managed to hold my tongue. What if he decided those words were a suggestion to tell everyone what sex I was? Whatever my fate would have been on the Vixen, I thought that somehow the pirate ship would be worse.

"Jo, then," I forced out. "It's what I've always been called."

Hades nodded, his smile affable. I hated that man. How dare he act so friendly and nice after threatening and murdering?

"Jo. A nice name, if a bit too short. You should really reconsider Josephine at some point. You might find it suits you."

I couldn't take it anymore. I crossed my arms and redoubled my glare. "If you're done making personal comments about names, Hades, then perhaps you might actually do your job and show me around your ship?"

Despite my tone, his only reaction was a quirked eyebrow. I felt my cheeks start to heat. He had warned me about my tone. But God damn it, he wasn't making it easy to shut up.

"If you really want to," he said. "Follow me."

I followed him across to the pirate ship, dodging sailors carrying sacks and crates across the gangplank that stretched between the ships. Morningwood, Roberts, Jennings, and Linden all glared at me as I crossed. I glared back, especially at Morningwood. What did he expect, especially after what I overheard the previous night?

Not that this seemed to be much better. Although at least now I knew who was actually out to get me.

I caught a glimpse of the ship's name, the Reliance, painted on the hull as we crossed. It sat right behind the figurehead, which was a gloriously carved statue of a mermaid holding a lyre. The way her hair was carved was so realistic, I had to double check to make sure no wind was actually blowing.

I realized quickly how much worse it would be if the pirates discovered I was a woman. For one thing, there were a lot more of them. I tried to count as we passed, but it was impossible. There had to be at least fifty, though.

The Reliance was a gorgeous ship. Even I had to admit that. It boasted four masts, each rigged with a complicated array of sails, and it had an actual wheel for the helm, rather than the rudder post the Vixen had. There were multiple cabins above deck, including the navigator's own personal chart room. I glanced at it wistfully as we passed. I was going to miss my lessons with Nelson. That was perhaps the only part of the Vixen I would miss.

Surprisingly, Hades said little, and actually made an attempt to explain what it was I was seeing. There were two lower decks, which astonished me. The Vixen only had one. We had the cargo stored on one end and the berthing on the other. On the Reliance, the top below deck was given over to cannons, gear, and hammocks. Below that was where all the stores were kept, as well as any treasure they looted.

Those words hit home to me again. This was a pirate ship. They stole from people, usually honest sailors. Even if the sailors were less than honest, their lives could be ruined. And these pirates weren't above murder, either. I saw Tanner die, after all.

And I just signed on to be one of them.

I couldn't conceal my relief when the boy came to find us and announced the quartermaster and captain were ready with the articles, whatever those were. That had yet to be explained to me, and I wasn't inclined to actually ask Hades anything.

We followed the boy back up to the main deck, where someone had set up a table and laid a stack sheaf of papers on it. The same three men that had "interviewed" me on the Vixen were standing there now.

The captain nodded as we approached. "Joseph! Good man. Good to have you onboard. Now, we have a custom onboard this ship. Most pirate ships do, actually. In order to be an official crewmember and receive your share of the cargo, you have to sign the articles. They're simple rules, really. Normally Harry would read them out to you, but you say you can read, so go ahead."

Articles. I stepped to the table and picked up the stack sheaf of papers with some hesitation.

They seemed simple enough.

I. Every man shall obey civil command; the Captain shall have one full share and a half of all Prizes; the Quartermaster, Boatswain, Carpenter, and Gunner shall have one share and a quarter.

II. If any man shall offer to run away, or keep any secret from the company, he shall be marooned with one bottle of powder, one bottle of water, one small arm, and a single shot.

III. If any man shall steal anything in the company to the value of a piece of eight, he shall be marooned or shot.

IV. If any time we shall meet another ship, if any man signs articles without the consent of the company he shall receive such punishment as the Captain deems fit.

V. That man that shall strike another whilst these Articles are in force, shall receive 39 stripes on the bare Back. If there is a quarrel, the men will follow the proper conventions of a duel.

VI. That man that shall snap his arms, or smoke tobacco in the hold, without a cap to his pipe, or carry a candle lighted without a lantern, shall suffer the same punishment as in the former Article.

VII. That man who does not keep his arms clean and fit for an engagement shall be cut off from his share, and suffer such other punishment as the Captain and the Company shall think fit.

VIII. If any man shall lose a joint in time of an engagement, shall have 400 pieces of eight; if a limb, 800.

IX. If at any time you meet with a decent woman, that man that offers to meddle with her, without her consent, shall suffer present death.

The last one got me. But then again, what was a decent woman? Did I count as one, having disguised myself as a man and run away to sea?

Nevertheless, I didn't have much choice. I looked up from the stack of papers to meet the captain's eye.

"Any questions?" he asked.

I shook my head.

The captain nodded at the quartermaster, who handed me a quill and ink. "Just sign at the bottom then, along with the rest of the signatures."

I stared at the page for a moment before dipping the quill in the ink. There were a great deal of Xs and other symbols adorning the last page. Apparently, even on a pirate ship, literacy was not common.

I signed my name Joseph Crawford and handed the quill and ink back to the quartermaster. That was it. I committed myself now. Somehow it felt a great deal more official now that it was in writing.

The captain laughed, a deep-bellied laugh that was at the same time annoying and infectious. "Welcome aboard, Joseph!" he roared.

The quartermaster clapped me on the back, and I jumped in surprise. He laughed at my expression.

"We're a jolly bunch here. You'll get used to it."

I wasn't certain, but I declined to answer as the quartermaster turned to one of the other men. "Isaac, you'll put him on the watch schedule? Eli, will you issue him some weapons? None of those damned merchant ships ever have any."

Isaac and Eli nodded. Eli gave me a sharp look.

"Have you ever even held a gun?" he asked.

I hesitated, but it seemed like a bad idea to lie. After all, everyone would know the truth the first time I picked one up. I shook my head.

Eli didn't seem disappointed or surprised. He turned to speak to Hades.

"He'll have lessons with you every morning 'til you pronounce him fit. That fit with your schedule?"

I tried to hide my dismay. I wanted to stay as far away from Hades as possible.

Hades, of course, nodded. "Don't want untrained men in a firefight," he said, his voice affable again. "Course I'll train him. We'll get out the cutlasses, too."

This was sounding better and better. I gritted my teeth. One thing at a time.

"Good," Eli said. He looked at me. "Hades show you where the gunnery is? Find me this afternoon, and I'll issue you something."

"I'll have you on the watch by nightfall," Isaac said.

The captain laughed. "All business, aren't you! Well, you conduct that. I will be retiring to my cabin, where Harry and I will be counting out the value of our spoils. I'm sure the crew will be happy to hear the sum."

The other men shook their heads and laughed as the captain and quartermaster sauntered off in the direction of the cabin.

I stood there, rather at a loss.

"Go help the crew with the loading," Isaac ordered. "Extra hands are always welcome. Remember, slackers don't belong on a pirate ship."

So that rule was still the same. It was a good thing I wasn't a slacker.

I avoided Hades' gaze as I made my way back towards the gangplank, where the last of the goods were being brought onboard the Reliance. I was in for it now. What had I gotten myself into?

*****Chapter 12*****

The rest of the day passed in a blur. I went from one task to the next, being introduced to any number of men as I went, all of whose names I instantly forgot. Every one of them smiled when they saw me, however, and welcomed me. It made my guard go up. After seeing how "happy" the sailors on the Vixen were, I was disinclined to trust this show of happiness and goodwill.

There was one man whose name I did remember, however, and that was because he was another black man. His eyes brightened with interest when he saw me.

"Hey, you the man from the ship over there?"

Instinctively, I glanced over to where the captains were finishing their final negotiations. Apparently, there had been some talk of keeping the Vixen, but the notion was abandoned as too time consuming.

I nodded. "Joseph Crawford," I said, extending my hand.

The man smiled as he accepted it. "Kwaku," he said. His voice caught me off guard. It sounded vaguely familiar. "How did you come to be a sailor, Joseph? It's odd to find men of our skin tone sailing the seas willingly."

I shrugged, something urging me to be more open than normal with this man. "My father was white," I said. "Actually married Ma. So while I look dark, I was raised with his class."

Kwaku snorted. "That must've been interesting."

It hit me at that moment. It was his accent. It was the same accent my Nana had had, and the sound was sending me back in time to the days of my childhood.

I decided to turn the tables. "What about you?" I asked.

Kwaku shrugged. "I was captured and sold. Got lucky. My master," he spat the word, "went on a voyage, and took me along. Good ol' Captain Victor here attacked, and Hades convinced him I would prove to be a loyal sailor if they set me free. Can't say he was wrong." He grinned.

I shivered a little at the mention of Hades. "What's his story?" I asked.

Kwaku seemed surprised. "Hades?" he shrugged. "Won't talk about it. Must have been a slave at some point, 'cause Hades is a name those white bastards who own slaves give us. Don't know why he kept it, though. I went back to my own fast enough."

I wish I knew what my Nana's name had actually been. She died so long ago, and for years, the only name I had for her was Nana.

I didn't have much chance to talk to Kwaku after that, but I made a note to speak to him further when I had the chance. Maybe, just maybe, he would know something about the place Nana had come from. And if he did, maybe he would know about my gift. It would be great if someone other than Hades could explain to me how to use it.

The berthing arrangements on the pirate ship were quite different than on the Vixen. I was given the midday watch the next morning, so for the night, I was directed to unsling one of the hammocks tied to the rafters of the lower deck.

I had never slept in a hammock before, but I dozed right off, lulled by the rocking of the ship. It was much more comfortable than the hard racks the Vixen had. I wondered why more merchant ships didn't use hammocks. It would probably give them more room for cargo.

Well, maybe they did. I had only ever been on one merchant ship, after all. And I doubted the Vixen should be used as an example for anything.

I woke up the next morning refreshed, but with a sense of dread I couldn't deny. I was supposed to have weaponry lessons with Hades this morning. Yesterday, the ship's gunner, Eli, had issued me two pistols and a cutlass, with stern directions that I was now responsible for them. I had to clean and care for them and no one would do it for me. If I didn't, I was likely to be punished according to the articles I signed.

I suppose I understood the significance of that. If we were to attack and I wasn't armed, that meant we were one man short. If we were attacked... we were pirates, after all. There were probably Navy ships of various countries who would be pleased to see all of us hang.

God damn it. Just when I got comfortable, I had to be reminded of that fact again.

I swung out of my hammock and nearly jumped out of my skin when I saw the boy, Derry, standing next to me. He laughed, his expression full of impish mischief.

I glared at the boy. "What, Derry?" I put my hands on my hips. I couldn't let this boy know I had been startled.

"Bos'n's waiting for you on the main deck!" Derry exclaimed. "Right in front of the helm. Says you're not to be late."

I muttered a curse under my breath before I remembered the boy's presence. He grinned again, apparently having heard much worse before.

"I'll let him know you're coming!" he scampered off before I could say a word.

Well, I had no choice, really. I might as well see to what was about to happen.

Hades was waiting for me when I climbed the ladder to the main deck. He had a sword in his hand, and he lunged at me as soon as my feet were stable.

I didn't know what to do. I fell backwards, and ended up tripping over my own feet. Hades laughed and lunged again.

Belatedly, I remembered I did have a cutlass in a sheath at my hip. I had no idea if I could draw it in time to defend myself, much less if I could actually defend myself against Hades.

It was time for trickery. Hades was coming towards me again, this time with a wide grin and an overhand swing. I decided to try the trick I used against the drunken government official.

I ducked low and ran forward, avoiding the swing of his cutlass by a narrow margin. Adrenaline pounded through me as I heard it swish dangerously close to my ear.

I ran headlong into Hades' knees, and he actually toppled to the ground. I fell myself, rolling quickly to feet and looking around wildly. Hades was standing up, which gave me just enough time to draw my cutlass.

But Hades didn't seem inclined to attack me again. "Who taught you that trick?" His face was full of laughter.

It caught me completely off guard. This man was so changeable. One moment he was threatening me with torture and slavery, and the next he was acting like my best friend.

I didn't trust him. For all I knew, any attempt at friendship was a fake, to make me lower my guard so he could take advantage of my trust. All I had to do was remember how casually he stabbed Tanner, lying there on the ground.

"My brother," I said in answer to Hades' question. I didn't feel like answering any more. I didn't want him finding out too much about Miguel.

"You have a sibling, hmm?" Hades' tone was too friendly.

I said nothing, just nodded.

Hades waited, then sighed. "This would be much easier if you would start to trust me, Jo."

I barked out a short laugh. "You'll have to do more than act friendly if that's going to happen," I said. "I don't take threats lightly."

Hades' eyes darkened again, and I felt all my suspicions confirmed. I held myself from backing up.

"You need to get used to threats in this line of work," he said. "Now, why didn't you draw your cutlass first thing? You got to it eventually, but you were pathetically slow in doing so."

I felt my temper start to fire again.

"You know I've never used the damn thing before," I snapped. "I didn't know if I could draw it in time, much less use it!"

Instantly, Hades' face changed. He stepped closer to me; his eyes narrowed.

"Remember what I told you about your tone, Josephine?"

I swallowed.

"Do you need a reminder?" he asked. "I could have you called up for insubordination and whipped within an inch of your life. I could reveal your identity to the entire crew. Do you want that?"

I shook my head.

"Good." His face was all smiles again. He held out his hand. "You're holding it wrong. Let me show you."

Hades led me through a series of exercises that left me sweating, and I wasn't entirely sure of their purpose. He was irritating to work with. I nearly lost my temper at least fifteen times, and the way he switched suddenly from friendly to threatening had me constantly off-balance.

I did learn things from him, however. When he finally told me to sheath my cutlass, I knew a great deal more about how to stab and dismember someone. I desperately hoped I would never have to use that knowledge, though I knew that hope was pointless.

The mood shifted when he told me to draw my pistols. When he saw they weren't loaded, he nearly gave me clout on the head. Or he would have, if I hadn't seen it coming and dodged.

"Idiot!" he scolded. "What if we were ambushed? Do you think you'd have time to load your guns in the middle of a firefight? And not knowing how to shoot is no excuse!"

My temper was flaring again, but he rode right over me, berating me. Apparently, shooting was so easy, a child would be able to figure it out. I may not have been able to hit the broad side of a barn, but that wasn't the point.

Somehow I managed to hold my temper during that lecture. Finally, I stalked away from him and started loading the two pistols. My hands were shaking with rage, which made the task more difficult, but I succeeded, even while Hades' angry words kept passing over me.

I turned to stare at him once I was done. "Satisfied?" I snapped.

Hades stopped, and his demeanor changed once again. I was getting awfully tired of his sudden mood shifts.

"Good," he said. "Now, I'm going to throw a target into the ocean, and you're going to shoot it. And you're going to mask the sound of you doing so."

I stared at him, completely taken aback. I was not expecting the sudden change of topic as well as mood.

Hades shook his head at me. "I told you I would teach you a bit of this as well," he said, his voice low and mocking. "Did you forget that so easily?"

I bit my lip. As angry and as frightened as I was, here was the chance I needed. If he wanted me to use my gift, he had to show me how to use it more effectively. Maybe I could learn enough to escape him somehow.

Hades chuckled, his voice insufferably calm. "Or are you too scared of me to even try?"

I cursed him, and Hades' eyes immediately darkened.

"Never curse me again. Do you know what that can do to a man?" he asked.

He stepped towards me, and I had to step back a pace. His tone was now deadly serious.

"What the hell are you talking about?" The anger in his eyes was enough to make me want to jump overboard.

He shook his head. "Ignorant," he muttered.

I couldn't take it. "Is that my fault?"

Hades didn't answer directly. "You have a power, Jo. Maybe you've only ever used it to mess with people and disguise yourself. But you can do so much more. Cursing is something all of us can do. It takes the right emotions and the right rituals, but those rituals are incredibly easy to discover. You need to watch who you're cursing, Jo. You might ruin their life."

At the moment, I couldn't see that as being a bad thing. But something else in his words had caught my attention.

"Rituals?" I asked.

Hades' eyes narrowed. "Mask your gunshot," he said. "Make sure you do. I don't want the lookouts in a panic."

I couldn't tell what was going on through his mind. Angrily, I reached for the power I could always feel, lurking underneath the water. I drew on it, focusing on the feeling of silence as I pulled the trigger on my pistol.

Instantly, Hades was on top of me, staring down at me with his arms crossed. "You really don't know what you're doing, do you?"

I shoved my pistol back in its holster. I couldn't take this anymore.

"Look, if you're going to teach me, teach me. But for the love of God, stop insulting me!" I was yelling by the end of the sentence.

Hades' eyes flared, but I was too angry and frightened to back down. I had been dealing with him for over two hours at this point, and I was ready to kill him.

"You may have threatened me to get me onboard this ship because you want to use my talents for your own selfish gain, but don't insult me at the same time! Teach me if you want to, but don't insult me!"

I didn't see Hades' blow coming until it was too late. He struck me square across the cheek, and for a moment I saw stars as my head reeled.

"Don't forget what those threats were, Jo. Remember your orders. Today I'll be giving you a free pass. If you show any temper tomorrow, you'll be facing the cat," he said, his voice low.

He straightened. "I think it's time to end today's lesson. You're free until your watch. Be here tomorrow morning. Maybe I'll show you some of those rituals you were curious about earlier."

I bit down on the rest of my angry words and spun around on my heel before storming off.

Hades was an insufferable, arrogant man, and he frightened me to the core. If I was honest with myself, that was what I was most angry about. It wasn't the fact that he threatened me; it was the fact that those threats scared me.

I looked down at my clenched fists. There was something I could do, though. I could learn as much as Hades was willing to teach me. He was the first person I ever met who even knew a little about how my gift worked. If he could teach me, maybe one day I could use that knowledge to escape this ship.

It would mean dealing with his temper and his threats, though. God damn it. Why couldn't Kwaku have been the one who knew how this worked? And why did Hades have to be the one teaching me weapons as well as how to use my gift?

I knew they were rhetorical questions the second they crossed my mind. Whatever was happening to me now, there was no point in asking why. The only thing I could do was deal with it.

I cursed under my breath. Deal with it. I always hated that phrase. It implied an acceptance of events that I hated.

I had to learn from him. It was the only way through that I could see. I had to suffer his teaching, and then I could turn the tables on him.

I had no idea how it would work, but I would make more detailed plans as I learned. For now, just the idea would help me keep my temper through his "lessons."

I needed to cool off, and I needed food before watch. I decided finding the galley would be my next mission.

*****Chapter 13*****

I didn't have many opportunities to observe the captain of my new ship during the first few days, although I saw him much more often than I had ever seen the captain of the Vixen. The captain there never bothered to stir out of his cabin. Captain Victor was everywhere, supervising, critiquing, and ordering people about.

I couldn't decide whether I liked him or not. On the one hand, I had to admit he was quite handsome for a white man. On the other, he came across as a loud buffoon.

There was something wrong with that idea, however, because how in God's name would Victor have become captain of a pirate ship if he actually was a buffoon? From what I had learned, the captain of this ship was elected. Elections could only be held in port, but Victor had been captain of this ship for close to five years. There would have been plenty of chances to dispose of him if he weren't worthy of the position.

He came up and talked to me once, which caught me completely off guard. It was after lookout watch and, for the first time on this ship, I felt some measure of peace.

"Lookout suits you?"

I spun around, nearly jumping out of my skin when I saw the captain.

He grinned at me.

I nodded. There was an unfamiliar gleam in his eye, but it didn't seem threatening.

"I used to love it too. There's something about the sea, am I right?" He actually seemed to be waiting for an answer.

I nodded again. For some reason I couldn't think of a thing to say.

"You ever have any trouble with anyone, you find me. I bet I know why you're at sea, but not all of my sailors share my views, even with Kwaku and Hades onboard. For some reason, you have to prove yourself twice over. So find me if there's trouble." He turned and left me staring after him.

Was he serious? Did he truly mean that? He would help me if any of the crew gave me trouble because of the color of my skin?

I didn't know, but it wasn't going to help me. Hades was the bos'n. His word would always carry more sway with the captain than mine would.

And besides, the captain would hardly trust a woman who had lied about her identity over his trusted bos'n.

I sighed. Despite being a pirate, the captain seemed nice. I wish I could have trusted him. But I knew nothing about him.

In light of this, I kept my eyes peeled, but there wasn't much to learn. At least, not about the captain. On the other hand, I learned a great deal from Hades, although my lessons with him were extremely tense. I kept covering my fear with anger, but somehow I managed to swallow enough of it that he only threatened me occasionally, and only hit me twice more.

I met the navigator of the ship my second day onboard the Reliance. His name was David, and he was Jewish. He was not my image of a pirate. He was rather short and squat, and he wore round glasses that almost completely obscured his face. His grasp of navigation, literature, history, and mathematics was phenomenal.

He proved more than willing to continue my lessons in navigation, although the lessons were very different from the ones I shared with Nelson. Nelson was very focused. He would overload me with information, and expect me to study and remember it the next time we talked. David, on the other hand, was more likely to start talking about some other story or method only tangentially related to what we had originally been talking about. I found him almost as frustrating to deal with as Hades, but in a very different way. I felt safe around David.

I got to know the boy Derry as well. It turned out he had been aboard ships since almost the moment he could walk. His mother was a stowaway discovered when he was born. Unfortunately, she died in childbirth, and the sailors took it upon themselves to raise the boy. I didn't know how he came to be on the pirate ship, but he seemed incredibly cheerful.

It was Derry who I went to when I began trying to figure out what the captain was really like. Children have remarkable hearing, and people will say things in front of them they normally wouldn't in front of anyone else. If anyone on this ship knew something about the captain, Derry would know.

"Captain Victor?" Derry looked at me with curious eyes. "Why you want to know about him?"

I shrugged. "I know nothing about him," I said. "I'd like to know a bit more about the man I'm sailing under."

"Well, why you asking me?" The confusion in the poor boy's tone was apparent. It was true. By all rights, I should have been asking the bos'n or quartermaster these questions.

"Because I bet you know more than anyone else on this ship," I said seriously. "And Hades, Isaac, and Harry are always so busy. I wouldn't want to disturb them."

Actually, I didn't want them to know that I was asking questions. But I didn't need to tell Derry that.

Derry's face cleared immediately. "All right," he said. "Though I'm not sure how much there is to tell."

I spread my arms. "Well, I know nothing, so anything you tell me is more than I know already."

Derry nodded decisively. "Captain Victor's been on this ship for ten years now. He became a pirate when he was just a little older than me! Quartermaster says he was fifteen when he was recruited. He became captain five years ago. That was right after I came here." Derry grinned. "Everyone knew it was gonna happen. Old captain hadn't gotten much treasure in a while, and everyone was grumbling. Victor said he knew where some really good prizes were sailing, and old captain tells him that if he thinks he can do better, he can lead the ship for one voyage. Victor grabbed three Spanish treasure galleons that trip." Derry smiled. "Course, crew elected him captain soon as they pulled into port again."

This was all news to me. A pirate for ten years? I had no idea the life expectancy of a pirate's life was that long.

I didn't have much time to talk to Derry. Apparently, the boy's duties had him running everywhere on the ship, a task he took to with all the enthusiasm in the world. That left me free to go to the deck and study with David.

To my surprise, I found Kwaku in the navigator's office as well. Both he and David were hunched over a book. Kwaku glanced up, startled, when I came in.

David clapped his hands. "Joseph!" he said. "Good, this will do very nicely."

I looked from David to Kwaku, who had a baffled expression on his face. "What do you mean?" I asked.

"You can help teach Kwaku to read," David said, as if it were the most obvious thing in the world. "And this way, you can learn navigation from me at the same time, and everyone's learning something. That is the way God would have it."

Kwaku stared at me. "You can read?"

I shrugged self-consciously. "Planter's upbringing," I mumbled. It seemed unfair that I could, knowing about Kwaku's past. It wasn't that he was stupid. He just never had the chance to learn. The fact that he was in David's office proved he was willing to make an effort.

Kwaku smiled, and I went to sit down beside him. As I began teaching him, I found Kwaku could already understand many of the basic letters. I had to laugh, though, as I realized what book we were reading. It was one of the waggoneers, a book that taught navigation as well as including sailing directions to various ports. This one was based off of Europe instead of the New World, but the navigation tactics were the same.

I admired David at that point. He had seen a way to kill two birds with one stone, and had taken it. More, this left him free to do his own work!

"Sail ho!"

Kwaku and I both looked up from the book with a start. I looked at Kwaku. "What does that mean?" I asked.

Kwaku shrugged. "Be ready for battle," he said. "Unless it's a Navy ship too big for us. If it's a merchant, we have room in the hull for more cargo. If it's a small Navy ship, it's likely faster than us."

He said it with such casualness that I remained calm until the truth of the words sunk in. There was at least a two out of three chance I was about to be involved in a battle at sea, and I had no idea how to deal with that.

Kwaku must have seen my expression, because he laughed. "You'll do fine," he said. "Anyone who's had the benefit of Hades' instruction the past few days hardly counts as an amateur swordsman anymore."

I was learning more than that. Hades followed through on his promise, sort of. I now knew the basics of a number of African rituals designed to help harness the power that I could feel. I winced as I remembered his lecture.

Idiot. You may be using that power that you feel, but the strength to control it is coming from you. Do you realize how close you came to burning yourself out? You could have been dead, and it would have served you right.

It wasn't my fault; I hadn't known! It turned out I was right about the plants after all. Not only did they contain power, but when used in rituals, they helped give me the strength to control it.

I hadn't actually had a chance to try any of these rituals yet. I was going to have to, soon. Preferably sometime Hades wasn't around to watch me make a mistake.

I tried to return to the reading after that, but my concentration was broken. Kwaku was doing better than me, but then again, he had been in an attack before. He was a pirate. I wasn't really, at least not yet.

It wasn't long before we heard a cry echoing from the deck. "General quarters! Man your battle stations!"

Kwaku and I looked at each other, then turned to David. He shook his head at both of us. "Good luck out there," he said. "Don't break anything."

I had to suppress a laugh as we said our farewells and went out to the main deck. Kwaku walked unerringly towards the mainmast. As far as I knew, I had no assigned battle station yet, so I followed him.

I saw the ship we were following almost as soon as my feet touched the deck. It was a small schooner, light and fast, but it flew the Spanish flag, and it rode low in the water. Either it had a great many people onboard, or there was a great deal of cargo.

Kwaku grinned at me. "Rich prize," he said. "The Spanish ships are almost always worth taking."

I smiled back, but my insides were churning. We were about to attack this ship. The men onboard hadn't done anything to have their livelihoods taken away from them, had they? Even if they were like the men of the Vixen.

All at once, I remembered who the men of the Vixen were likely to have sold me to. The Spanish in St. Augustine. The Spanish liked having Taino slaves, apparently.

My resolve hardened and I stared across the water at the ship. I was justifying the actions I was about to undertake, I knew that. But I didn't have any choice in the matter, so I might as well deal with the guilt now.

There were a few orders to adjust the rigging, but other than that, the pursuit was accomplished in relative silence. Oh, there were men talking and laughing, guessing how large the size of their take was likely to be. But there were no real battle cries, or threats to the Spanish ship.

That changed as we came into range. I wasn't a gunner, so I didn't hear the command for the guns to fire a warning shot. I jumped as the shot hit the water, then jumped again as the Spanish ship heeled around to present a brace of guns pointed at us.

Kwaku shook his head. "Idiots," he said. "They can't hope to outmatch us. All they can do is buy themselves a little time."

We weren't even about to give them that time, apparently. I heard the captain shout a helm command, and suddenly we were turning, facing the other ship broadside to broadside. There was a loud boom, and our guns tore into the Spanish ship.

The smell of gunpowder hung heavy in the air, and smoke obscured my view of the Spanish ship for a moment. When I could see again, I realized our gunners must have been extraordinarily skilled... Or lucky. One of the cannonballs had flown straight into the mast of the Spanish ship, which now teetered dangerously.

We started moving closer, and Kwaku smiled. "Now we see if they're as stupid in person as at a distance," he said.

I swallowed hard and double checked the weapons at my belt. Kwaku grinned at me. "You part of the boarding team?"

I shrugged. I honestly had no idea.

"You should be, your first time. Come on, I'll show you where we muster."

It really wasn't an official gathering, I realized. It was just a group of two dozen men gathered on the main deck, getting grappling hooks ready to throw to the other ship. Hades stood on the rail, waving his cutlass and shouting curses in Spanish.

It caught me off guard to hear Hades speak in a foreign language, but it shouldn't have. He may have been a slave to them at one point.

To my surprise, the captain was on the deck as well, the quartermaster and boatswain with him. His face was a wild grin. When he saw me looking at him, he saluted me with his cutlass. I started, and hesitantly returned the salute.

The approach to the Spanish ship seemed to take forever, and yet we were there way too fast for me.

I saw Kwaku draw one of his pistols, so I followed his example. He grinned at me. "We'll go across the gangplank," he said. "Don't want you swinging in the air during your first battle. Good way to get shot."

I didn't answer. Suddenly, the captain shouted, "Now!" and the air was filled with battle cries, gunfire, and screams. The two boats shuddered as the Reliance made contact with the Spanish ship, and Kwaku shouted in wild joy.

"Now!" he yelled at me, before leaping across to join the fray on the Spanish ship.

I couldn't think at that point. I followed, and what confronted me was a scene of chaos.

At least it was easy to tell who the Spanish were. All of them wore some kind of uniform, which made it easy to distinguish them. I could barely make out individuals, however. I saw Kwaku dive in to fight a Spaniard, his cutlass drawn, but then my view was distracted by Hades and another sailor dismembering another Spaniard.

I didn't have time to be sick. Suddenly, there was a Spaniard in front of me, a gun pointed at my head. I ducked instinctively, and squeezed the trigger on my own gun.

Somehow I got my shot off first. The Spaniard's bullet flew over my head, close enough to shave me. Mine hit him in the shoulder, and he let out a cry of anguish before falling back out of sight.

I jammed my gun back into its holster and reached for my cutlass. I didn't think there would be another opportunity for such a shot as that.

I made my way through the crowd, searching for someone I knew or something I could do. I had no idea what I was doing.

Suddenly, I saw the captain in front of me. He had been separated from the quartermaster and boatswain somehow, and was battling two Spaniards at once. He still seemed to have the upper hand, and the grin on his face was as fierce as ever. At least it was until he saw the third Spaniard pointing a gun at him.

I still don't know what possessed me. I threw myself at the gun-wielding Spaniard, sending both of us to the deck in a sprawl. His gun went off, and for a moment I froze, fearing I'd been shot. But I didn't feel any bleeding, so I writhed around, somehow slicing through his throat with my cutlass.

It was an awful feeling. The only other man I might have killed was the other Spaniard a few seconds earlier. This one was right next to me. I felt his body stiffen in shock, then go limp. His blood flowed all over my hands and shirt. I could feel his labored breathing right next to my ear.

I pushed away from him in horror. I couldn't quite believe what I had just done.

A hand clapped me on the shoulder. "My thanks, Joseph!" the captain said. "Now, back to the fray!"

The captain leapt away, and I scrambled to my feet, suddenly fearful another Spaniard might be coming up behind me to ambush me.

But the fight was pretty much over. The only Spaniards I saw left standing were holding their hands up in surrender, their weapons at their feet. The pirates were starting to shout and dance, making threats and yelling celebratory toasts.

I couldn't tear my eyes away from the blood and gore on the deck. The stench was incredible. I couldn't believe the entire battle had maybe taken five minutes. It seemed like it had been an eternity. My shirt was soaked in the blood of the sailor I had killed.

I felt myself retch, and I ran for the side of the ship. I couldn't let any of the pirates see me throw up. That would be a sign of weakness that they would pounce on.

I barely made it out of sight before my stomach revolted. I saw the battle again in fresh detail. The surprise and agony in the Spaniard's face as I shot him. The blood spilling over my hands as I cut the Spaniard's throat. His lifeless body falling almost on top of mine.

I felt a hand on my shoulder, and I wanted to run and hide again. But the hand was comforting, and so I let my stomach finish emptying itself into the sea.

"First battle, hmm?"

I turned at the sound of the captain's voice. Damn it all. It would be him.

I nodded jerkily. The captain handed me a cloth to wipe my mouth with.

"I did the same," he said. "Most sailors do. Don't let anyone tell you otherwise."

I stared at him without answering. Somehow, his presence seemed at the same time both a comfort and a threat, and I couldn't begin to figure out why I felt that way.

"You saved my life," the captain said. "I couldn't have gotten away from those two long enough to dodge a bullet. I owe you, Joseph."

I swallowed. Of all things, I hadn't expected that.

"I... You're welcome?" I managed. Oh, God damn my twisted tongue.

The captain laughed. "You'll be rewarded," he said. "Mark my words. I'll make sure to let Harry know to change your share for this cargo. And next time we make port, I'll be treating you to a night that you'll scarcely remember."

He moved away at that point, for which I was extremely grateful. I couldn't even make sense of most of his words with him standing so near to me.

"Take as much time as you need to steady yourself, Joseph," the captain said. "But be sure to be back onboard the Reliance when we set sail! I would hate to lose a man such as yourself, especially now that you've saved my life."

He strode off, whistling a merry tune.

I stared after him. Now that he was gone, I was able to examine my reaction more, and I did not like what I found.

I was an idiot. I had allowed a man's presence to interfere with my thought process. Just because his presence was so powerful was no reason to allow him to intimidate me.

I shook myself. I had to get back to the Reliance. The memory of the gore was a dim one, now, gone with both the contents of my stomach and the captain's hand on my shoulder. I bit my lip angrily. What had come over me?

My lips were dry, so I licked them to bring some moisture back. I straightened from the rail and started making my way back to the gangway to the Reliance.

I nearly bolted when I saw Hades making his way towards me. I couldn't deal with him at that moment in time. I just couldn't. But I wasn't going to be given a choice.

"Jo!" He yelled. "How'd you enjoy your first battle? Was it everything you've ever dreamed of?"

How the hell was I supposed to answer that?

"No," I snapped, "it wasn't." I pushed my way past him and made my way towards the gangway as quickly as I could without running.

I saw Kwaku give me a curious glance, but I ignored him. My stomach twisted again when I saw Derry waving merrily at all the pirates as they came back on the Reliance loaded with whatever had been in the hold.

What kind of people were these men, anyway?

*****Chapter 14*****

I woke the next morning in no better frame of mind. I still felt sick every time I thought of the battle, and even more so when I thought of the man I killed. I had killed a man. There was no way around that. I saved the captain's life by doing so, but it was a life he himself had put at risk. I was under no obligation to save him. I liked him, but there was no reason to almost take a bullet for him. I didn't trust him, after all.

Deep down, I knew the last part of that thought was a lie, but I didn't stop to examine it.

My reaction to him after the battle seemed even more silly now. My thoughts had been completely halted when he put his hand on my shoulder. No one ever had that effect on me before, not even Hades when he was threatening me. Why in God's name had Victor's touch done that to me?

I didn't want to think about it, so I swung myself out of my hammock and made my way to the deck. Hades had told me that he would be too busy for lessons this morning, for which I was eternally grateful. In this state of mind, I was likely to snap at the slightest provocation, and I didn't think Hades would take that very well.

I decided instead to go to the navigator's office. My watch wasn't until late afternoon today, so I had plenty of time to go over charts and navigation.

I didn't realize this was the time of morning that the captain, quartermaster, boatswain, and navigator all had their morning meeting. The door to the navigator's cabin was open, but every one of them was clearly visible as they bent over some charts on the table. I hesitated.

David saw me and waved. I cursed silently as the captain looked up to see what had caught David's attention. His eyes met mine, and he smiled.

"Joseph! What are you doing here?"

David answered before I could. "I've been teaching him navigation, Captain," he said. He looked at me. "I have some books if you'd like to study while we have our meeting. We can go over practical aspects once the meeting's done."

I had no graceful way to back out of that, so I entered the cabin and took the book David handed me. He gestured to a stool in the back of the cabin, and I took a seat.

I attempted to read, truly I did. But between the captain's presence and the conversation going on, I was far too distracted.

"Where was the La Coraje last sighted, again?" Harry, the quartermaster, was bending over the chart, his brow furrowed in concentration. "That would be a fine prize, if we could lay our hands on it. And if it doesn't have an escort."

Victor tapped his fingers on the table. "Last I heard, they were travelling from St. Augustine to Hispaniola. They were supposed to leave three days ago, so if we chart their most likely route." He tuned to look at David.

"Oh, certainly." David took out a compass and pencil and started making marks on the chart, muttering under his breath as he did so. "If they're a galleon, they're travelling slow, which means..." his voice trailed off into a murmur.

Victor, Harry, and Isaac all watched with varying degrees of patience as David completed his work. He looked up in triumph.

"If I'm correct, they'll likely be just around the shoals here." He pointed. "That's where they are now. By the time we reach the shoals, they'll be here." He pointed again. I wished I could see the chart from where I sat. So this was how pirate ships went a hunting.

The captain pursed his lips. "Anyway to get ahead of them?" he asked.

David's brow furrowed, and he bent over the chart again. "Possibly," he allowed. "The winds being favorable. If we go this way," he traced a line, "we'd end up ahead of their most likely track. The only difficulty with it is we'd be travelling directly through Spanish waters."

Victor cocked his head, considering.

"We need to make port soon, Captain," Harry said. "We have enough supplies for maybe another week, at most."

The captain nodded. "And the men deserve a few nights on the town." He looked at the chart again. "If we go through here," he said, "then we may encounter La Coraje around here. If not, then St. John's is only a day's transit. Does that suit everyone?"

Everyone seemed to be in perfect agreement with the captain's plan. He nodded. "Then the meeting is adjourned."

He glanced over at me, and I nearly froze. "Good luck in your studies, Joseph," he said.

It took until the captain, quartermaster, and boatswain had left the cabin for me to regain my composure enough to speak.

David chuckled. "No need to be so intimidated by him, Joseph," he said. "True, he's the captain, but he really is quite friendly. I heard you saved his life yesterday. He should be awed by you, not the other way around."

I snapped a glare onto David, but he just laughed. "Now, did you get anything out of that book, or were you too distracted by the planning?"

I flushed a little, and David's look became knowing. "Well, then it's time for practical lessons. Here, I'll show you how to plot a most likely course for a ship to take. For instance, in the La Coraje's case."

The next two hours passed in an enjoyable way. David managed to keep his tangents to a minimum, and I learned so much from him. I wondered if I could actually become a navigator one day. It did seem to be the sort of job I would enjoy doing.

I was a pirate now, though. How in God's name would I ever be able to sign aboard another ship as a navigator? Didn't being a pirate automatically make me not welcome aboard any merchant ship I encountered? Assuming they knew I had been a pirate.

I could hide that, though. It wouldn't even take using my gift, which would mean even people with other gifts wouldn't be able to tell.

That thought brought up Hades and Reddings, and my mood darkened. Aside from the attacking ships part, being on this pirate ship wasn't bad. Except for Hades and his threats. Even with how much he was teaching me, I wasn't sure if I could be around him much more.

Maybe I would try to leave the ship when we reached St. John's. I could disguise myself, and sign aboard another ship going somewhere else. Maybe I could even cross the Atlantic and see Europe. Wouldn't that be a sight! All I would have to do was stay out of Hades' way when we were in port.

I could do that. I nodded to myself as David went over our current course and bearing. It would be a shame to leave Kwaku and David, of course, but I was certain I could find other friends on different ships.

A heavy knock on the cabin door jolted me out of my thoughts. David looked up in annoyance. "Who is it?" he asked.

"Is Jo in there with you?" Hades' voice came through the door.

David glanced at me, and I rolled my eyes. "What do you want, Hades?" I called back. "I'm learning."

"Time for you to learn some other things," Hades said. "Come with me."

I was half hoping David would interfere, but he sighed and waved me away. "Come back tomorrow, if you feel like it," he said.

Reluctantly, I made my way to the door and opened it. The glare on Hades' face almost made me take a step back. What had I done now?

"Come with me." He turned and stalked off towards the stern of the ship.

I followed warily. What was going on? I hadn't done anything I knew of to annoy Hades.

He stopped within sight of the ship's wheel. He turned towards me. "I hear you saved the captain's life, and now he's giving you a larger share of the bounty," he said, his voice hard.

I stiffened. "So?" I asked. "What does that have to do with you?"

Hades' glare deepened, if that were even possible. "I was the one who brought you onboard this ship," he said. "It seemed to me that I should be partly responsible for saving the captain, considering you would never have come willingly. What do you think of that?"

Anger boiled up in me. "You weren't the one who killed that Spanish sailor," I said heatedly. "I think I deserve whatever the captain decides to give me, thank you very much."

"And if for some reason the captain finds out who he's really giving it to?" he smiled smugly.

I stared at him, my mouth dropping open. Had I really just heard what he meant to say?

I laughed shortly. "How much are you asking for your share of the rescue?" I knew my voice was dripping with sarcasm, but I couldn't help it. He was trying to blackmail me out of money, now. What was he going to do next?

"Half of what the captain gives you."

I couldn't help but laugh. At that moment, I decided it didn't matter. No matter what, I was leaving in St. John's. Somehow I would find a way to sign aboard another ship. Whatever Hades had to teach me wasn't worth this.

"Fine," I said. "I'll give it to you in St. John's. Satisfied?"

Hades grinned. "Very," he said. He gave me a mock salute before he disappeared.

I stared after him, hatred roiling within me. He was no better than Reddings.

*****Chapter 15*****

I had reason to remember that sentiment two days later, when the La Coraje came into view. Before we even sighted it, Hades confronted me during one of our daily lessons.

"Jo, I want you to do something for me," he said, his voice so casual that I knew something was up.

I narrowed my eyes. "What's that?" I was hardly making any effort to be civil to him at this point. Hades knew how much I hated him, but he didn't care. I was doing what he wanted, after all.

"You remember the ritual I taught you?"

I jerked at the mention. The last ritual Hades had taught me was one that could be modified to fit almost any circumstance, as long as I had the right herbs. Hades had confirmed to me that the herbs I felt most drawn to were in fact the ones designed for my power. He even showed me the basics of what to do with them.

But it was more than just using herbs. What Hades showed me last time was nothing less than pure witchcraft.

"We're going to run into La Coraje this afternoon," Hades said calmly. "I want you to disguise the ship as a Spanish galleon in distress."

I gaped at him. Such a seeming was beyond anything I had ever attempted before. Something of that size and with that many eyes watching it would be exhausting.

"You're mad," I said flatly.

Hades laughed. "On the contrary, this is an excellent plan," he said. "The Spanish will suspect nothing, and they'll even come towards us to help. Their guard will be completely down when it is time to strike."

"That wasn't what I meant," I snapped, impatient with him. "I've never held a seeming of that size before. The last one I tried was a dolphin, and that nearly exhausted me!"

"Did you use the ritual?"

Reluctantly, I shook my head. I had no idea how much more power Hades' ritual would allow me to hold. Nevertheless, in the middle of a battle did not seem like the time to experiment.

Hades shrugged as if the matter was settled. "Then there's nothing to argue about," he said. "I'll tell you when it's time to start the ritual."

My temper snapped again. Remarkable how often that seemed to happen around Hades. "I didn't say I'd do it."

Hades' eyes flashed and I stepped back instinctively. Suddenly Hades was right on top of me, towering over me. I swallowed, but held my ground and glared back at him.

"Remember what I can do to you, Josephine," he whispered.

I could feel my body beginning to shake. I didn't want to remember. I didn't want to know how complete this man's power over me was, at least until we pulled into St. John's. I'd never been this helpless before, not even when Reddings was threatening to enslave me. I hated it, and I hated Hades for putting me in this situation.

I closed my eyes and took a deep breath, forcing Hades' scowling visage out of my mind. I could still feel him towering over me.

It was only two days to St. John's. That was what David and I plotted last night. No storms, no law enforcement, and we would be in St. John's in two days. David told me the crew always had liberty for at least three days, and sometimes as much as a week. St. John's was full of lawless scum, and the Reliance could feel fairly safe about docking there for a while. That would give me plenty of time to escape.

I opened my eyes and stared at Hades again. "Very well," I snapped. I turned around to stalk away.

Hades' hand clapped down on my shoulder, and I froze.

"Smart decision, Jo," Hades said. "Now, shall we continue with your lesson?"

I nearly threw myself at him in frustration. Instead, I brought up my cutlass, preparing to defend myself against his attacks.

"So, what do you think of being a pirate so far?" Hades' voice was far too conversational.

I warded off a few lazy strikes. "It's a bit barbaric," I said, trying to keep my tone similar to his.

Hades laughed. "Well, that should suit you. After all, aren't the Taino barbaric compared to Europeans?"

I felt my temper flare, and I thought I saw an opening in his guard. I attacked, but he fended me off easily.

"The Europeans are the ones running this ship," I said. "Who are the barbarians now?"

"You mean Victor?" Hades attacked with an overhead swing, and I brought my cutlass up just in time to block it. My arm jarred as I felt the power in his swing.

I didn't answer as Hades attacked again. I had successfully avoided thinking about the captain since the day of the attack on the Spanish merchant.

"I can see things, you know," Hades said. "And I see a good deal more than you when it comes to you and the captain."

"What?" I was puzzled. What in the hells did he mean by that?

Hades laughed. "You haven't even admitted it to yourself, have you?" he asked. "Do you even know what it feels like?"

I was completely flabbergasted. I had no idea what Hades was talking about. I decided he was trying to distract me, and focused completely on his sword. I had yet to defeat him, but I knew I was improving. One day, I would be good enough to kill him.

Hades attacked again. "You lust after him," he said. "Are you that much of a virgin that you don't know the feeling of lust?"

I had enough of his taunts. I attacked hard, trying to bring my cutlass up under his guard. He sidestepped, and suddenly I was beside him instead of in front of him. I tried to turn to block his attack, but his sword came in low, slapping at my knees. I jumped backwards and brought my cutlass up to attack his sword arm. Somehow, too fast for me to see, Hades dropped his sword and instead kicked me in the back of the knees.

I ended up lying flat on my back, staring up at the cutlass that Hades had somehow picked up and presented at my throat. I had a sudden memory of seeing Tanner lying in exactly the same position I was in now.

Hades laughed. "I do believe I've found a weakness," he said. "Do you deny your attraction for the captain?"

I shook my head, not in disagreement but in disbelief. I had no feelings for the captain. I had barely spoken ten words to him total. Besides, I was supposed to be a boy. Was Hades mad?

Hades chuckled, as if he heard my thoughts. "Just remember, Jo, I can see things," he said.

I furrowed my brow. "What does that mean?" I asked.

Hades' eyes widened in mock surprise. "You mean you hadn't guessed?"

I gritted my teeth rather than answer. His cutlass was still extremely close to my throat.

"You knew I had some gift, otherwise I wouldn't be able to see through yours. You never thought to wonder what it was?"

Much to my chagrin, I hadn't. Now he had mentioned it though, I knew. "Sight."

Hades nodded. "Sight," he said. "I can see anything I want. That's how I know we're going to meet with La Coraje this afternoon. That's how I saw your encounter with the captain after the battle. Remember that, Jo."

My temper flared. Didn't he have enough of a hold over me?

I stilled, though, as a thought occurred to me. My gift was useless against him. Shouldn't that mean that his was useless against me?

I cocked my head curiously, but decided not to ask. Hades was sheathing his cutlass, and I didn't want him to decide I needed to be taught another lesson.

"You have a few hours," Hades said. "I'd suggest getting the ritual ready. You'll be on watch when we sight La Coraje. Do the ritual from the crow's nest."

I concealed my anger by scrambling to my feet. "How will you signal me?"

Hades smiled. "You'll know," he said. "Now get out of here and get ready."

I didn't need him to tell me a second time. Without making it seem like I was rushing, I nearly bolted down below to my hammock.

I was fuming as I reached it. I found the small chest that held my belongings and threw it open, searching for the herbs I knew were in there. Even these came from Hades. I couldn't escape his hold on me.

I grabbed for the necklace at my throat as I started sorting through the herbs. My body stilled as I remembered what amulet I wore.

Anansi. The spider. The trickster. It was appropriate, considering my gift. But what if there was more to it than that? Nana had always maintained that Anansi was as real as Jesus. What if she was right?

I glanced at the herbs. There were symbols that went along with the ritual, symbols I had never seen before. What if I added a symbol? What if the spider medallion became part of the seeming I cast?

There was only one way to find out, and considering the fact that I was already doing this ritual against my will, I had no difficulty with this small rebellion. I would call upon Anansi while performing the ritual. If Hades found out, he could lecture me later. Hopefully, he wouldn't realize anything, and I could be safely gone once we reached St. John's.

After Hades' words, I really didn't want to run into the captain before my watch, but of course he found me.

"Jo! How are you?"

I froze as the sound of his voice behind me. I took a deep, silent breath to steady myself before I turned around.

He was quite handsome, I noted absently. Even his ridiculous hat seemed to suit him.

I realized he was waiting for an answer. "Fine," I said.

He smiled. It was a brilliant smile, and it flustered me completely. "We'll be doing better than fine if we can catch La Coraje," he said. "No one's been giving you any trouble, right?"

I shook my head. I still couldn't tell him about Hades.

He narrowed his eyes. "Are you sure?" he asked. "You know I do not tolerate threats among my crewmembers. If there's a disagreement, you have a duel and settle it. Otherwise you can always come to me."

I blinked at the mention of dueling. That sounded ominous.

He smiled again. "Just remember you can always find me if there's a problem," he said. He clapped me on the back before walking away.

I stared after him, dumbfounded. I had never met a man as confusing as him.

He seemed sincere in his words. He really wanted to make sure that I was at home on the ship. If only I could trust him.

Hades was wrong, though. There was no way I was lusting after the captain. He thought I was a boy.

Finally, it was my turn to go up to the crow's nest. Derry was up there, and he waved eagerly at me.

"Captain says we may get some treasure soon!" he exclaimed.

I shuddered at the eagerness of the child's words. I couldn't recall if he had actually been involved in the previous attack, but I knew he couldn't have been sheltered from it. He knew what we were going to do. How did a child come to treat death so casually?

I stared out at the horizon, trying to organize my thoughts better. There were a few flaws to Hades' plan that I hadn't thought of before. One was that I had never actually seen a Spanish galleon in person. I had seen pictures, but I wasn't sure if that would be enough to fool an actual Spanish galleon.

The other was more interesting, however. I was fairly certain that it would be bad if the crew of the Reliance suddenly saw their ship turn into a Spanish galleon. Someone would be shouting the words witchcraft.

I puzzled over this as I stared out over the horizon. The water was flat and calm, and the sun was high overhead. It was blazing hot, but at least there was a breeze. The sails didn't even flap as we cut through the water.

I froze as I saw the brief silhouette of a sail on the horizon. I swallowed, my throat suddenly dry.

I needed to report it. There were others on this ship who was just as sharp-eyed as me, and they would see it soon. There would be questions asked if I didn't see it. And Hades would know we were in range for me to see.

"Sail!" I finally managed to shout.

Immediately there was a swarm of activity on the deck below. I saw the captain and the quartermaster come out with their spyglasses, and my heart skipped a beat. It was not because of Hades' words. It was because I knew that the ship I had seen was La Coraje, and I was going to have to attempt a ritual of witchcraft soon.

"La Coraje!"

I sighed internally as the shout went up and down the decks. Everyone knew what treasure a galleon carried. Even the least important of them carried tons more gold and silver than a merchant ship was ever likely to see.

I watched the scurry of activity as the pirates prepared for the attack. Everyone was excited, and it showed in the way that they moved and greeted each other. I could hear their shouts echo on the wind.

I soon saw the pirates were more than capable of disguising the ship for themselves. Although there were cannons on deck, they were covered in large pieces of canvas that kind of made them look like cargo. It was the men that would never pass for Spanish sailors.

I watched for close to two hours as we inched closer to La Coraje. They were halfway to the horizon from us when I saw Hades come up on deck.

I cursed under my breath. I almost allowed myself to hope that he would forget to signal me.

There was nothing to his signal. He looked up at me and drew a hand across his throat like he was holding a knife. I felt my blood surge at the implied threat. One day soon I would be free of that man.

I reached into the pouch that held the herbs Hades gave me. He hadn't actually told me what they were, but I had a solid understanding in plant matter. There were some powders, which I was fairly certain were dogwood and cedar bark. The dried plants were harder to tell, as they had been crushed, but by the smell one of them had to be collie.

I mixed the herbs and powders together and scattered them in a circle around me. I started to chant as I did so, words that held no meaning for me, as they were in Hades' native African tongue. I started sketching symbols in the air.

I made sure to add the symbol of Anansi near the end, and sent a silent prayer to the heavens for him to guide me through this web of blackmail and treachery I found myself in. I finished the sketching and lowered my hands.

Immediately, I felt power surging through me, so much that I nearly fell to my knees. I didn't know if I could hold it. I gritted my teeth. I would not let anything overpower me!

I formed the image of a Spanish galleon in my mind. It came easily. I gasped as the power surged towards it.

I realized halfway through that I had failed to come up with a solution that allowed the crew of the Reliance to see what they were doing. Desperately, before the seeming could take hold, I decided to place the seeming of the galleon right in front of us instead of on top of us, and try to make it one way, so that only the approaching galleon could see it.

I nearly staggered as the new seeming took hold. Power surged through me from the ocean, but I was nothing more than a vessel for it at this point. It was all I could do to hold onto my strength.

I clenched the edge of the crow's nest as we sailed closer to La Coraje. I felt my hands shaking, and I gripped it tighter. The power was flowing through me like a river, but I had no control over it anymore. I was scared what would happen once I released it.

There was a haze over my vision as I watched the Reliance approach. The ruse Hades had devised seemed to be working. La Coraje seemed to believe we were friendly, and was even drawing closer to us to allow for communication.

I had to continue holding on. The entire plan would melt away if I lost control of the seeming now. Hades wanted to wait until we were broadside to them, at which point we would blast them with our guns before boarding. We all knew the Spanish wouldn't surrender without a fight. The galleons were perhaps one of the few ships with soldiers on them. Apparently the pirate crew had fought soldiers before, and had always come out the better.

Looking down at the deck below, I could see why. Most of the men were crouched behind the covered cannons to disguise their numbers. All of them had multiple pistols, cutlasses, and other weapons. To my dismay, I even saw Derry perched near the ship's wheel with two pistols in hand.

A shout from La Coraje caught my attention, and I looked over to see a richly dressed, aristocratic Spaniard hailing us. I couldn't understand his words, but apparently some of the men on deck could. There were mutterings as his words were translated, and the captain came forward to hush them.

"No answer." I heard him say.

The Spaniard shouted again as we drew closer to La Coraje. I trembled. The seeming was becoming much harder to hold onto the closer we came, and the more the distance between us decreased. I had much less space to place my seeming of a disabled Spanish galleon.

How was a disabled Spanish galleon sailing, anyhow?

I didn't have time to think about the question. We drew up alongside, and the captain shouted for the gunners to fire.

The sound of the gunfire combined with the river of power running through me did bring me to my knees. I fell to the ground, shaking like a leaf. Dimly, I realized I should release the power flowing through me, that I would probably regret it if I let it keep controlling me. But I couldn't find the strength to stop it. It kept flowing, and I started seeing spots dancing in front of my eyes.

I mustered up one last bit of defiance. I grabbed the edge of the crow's nest again and hauled myself to my feet. The seeming was clear to me, lingering right in the place where the pirate ship and the Spanish galleon faced each other. It didn't belong there. The fight was already well underway.

A jolt of pain crashed into me, and I heard an inarticulate cry ripped from my throat. I couldn't hold on anymore, and the seeming vanished as if it had never been. The shouts of dismay from the Spanish crew told their confusion.

I didn't care. I sank to my knees and let the darkness claim me.

Tuppence Van de Vaarst

*****Chapter 16*****

I came to my senses slowly. First came my sense of motion. I was swaying, rocking back and forth gently. There was nothing stable underneath me, but the sensation, instead of being frightening, was oddly comforting.

Next came my sense of hearing. I heard the creaking of wood first, right next to my ear. It was rhythmic, aligned with the motion I was feeling. After that, I heard sounds of feet walking somewhere nearby, followed by the sound of water splashing.

My eyes flickered open. I was lying in my hammock, gently swaying. Although it was difficult to tell from down here, the light and the absence of other people told me it had to be at least midday.

My mind flickered back to the attack. The last thing I remembered was sinking to my knees as the pirates boarded. I had successfully handled more power than ever before. But at what price? How long had I been unconscious?

I felt a brief moment of panic as I realized my own seeming might have failed me during my state of unconsciousness. Hastily, I reached for the power, only to sigh back in relief as I felt the pulse of it still steady over my body. Even the medallion of Anansi still held its pulse of energy.

"So, you're finally awake."

I blinked and attempted to sit up. Kwaku was standing next to my hammock, looking down, his expression unreadable.

"How long have I been out?" I asked.

"Almost a full day."

I swallowed. I had lost a full day, all because Hades wanted me to cast a ritual that powerful?

"Hades said you were sick at the sight of the blood," Kwaku continued, his voice calm and level. "Is that true?"

I felt a deep flare of buried anger. Hades couldn't even be bothered to make up a story that would save my dignity. Now everyone would believe me a coward and weakling. As if I didn't have problems enough.

"That bastard would say that," I snapped without thinking.

Kwaku blinked, and I saw surprise flicker across his face. I snapped my mouth shut. I couldn't reveal too much. Much as I liked Kwaku, I couldn't trust him. I couldn't trust anyone on this benighted ship.

"Why is that?" he asked.

I didn't answer him. I couldn't. The full answer would require far too much explaining. How did I explain something like my gift to anyone? Much less the fact that I was female, and that Hades was using that to blackmail me?

"I saw you save the captain's life," he said. "I know you're not afraid of blood. I'm fairly certain you were sick afterwards, but everyone is after their first battle. There is no logical reason for you to have passed out while you were on lookout."

Angrily, I swung my feet out of the hammock. My legs shook a little, but I was able to stand up and glare at Kwaku.

He didn't flinch. "I know there's something up," he said. "We should stick together, Joseph. Remember that."

I said nothing as he turned and walked away. His shoulders were stiff, and everything about his body language said this was a conversation that was far from finished.

I knew his last words were right. Even though I wasn't African, we should stick together. In any other situation, both of us would be treated as slaves, as property, as less than human. We should be able to trust each other.

Then again, Hades was the same, and he threatened to have me tortured and raped if I didn't do his bidding.

It didn't matter. I was going to escape once we reached St. John's. I had to get off. I didn't think I could stand waking up like this again. If Hades knew this would happen to me, I was going to bloody murder him.

****

I managed to avoid meeting anyone else before we reached St. John's. I stayed down below, only appearing on deck once we sighted land. I went to work alongside a sailor I only had a passing familiarity with. I didn't know his name, and he gave me no chance to ask. A stream of words flowed constantly from his mouth.

"You ever been to St. John's? You'll like it. Ale's great, wenches pretty and cheap. There's a neat tavern two blocks from the docks. Girl there I met last time, name of Rachel. God, I love that girl. The tricks she knows would keep any man satisfied forever."

He babbled on but I let most of his words flow over me, only offering a grunt in reply when he seemed to expect one. I was plotting my escape. If I was going to avoid anyone on the crew, I needed to get as far away from the docks as possible. They would be hanging around in the taverns and brothels. If I went further inland, I might have a better chance.

Land crept slowly into view. Gradually, I was able to make out the shape of ships tied up to docks. The town was small, at least the part of it I could see from here. As we drew closer, I began to hear the sounds of hundreds of people going about their daily lives. I drew in a short breath. Even from this far out, I could smell the heavy scent of fish on the air.

"Technically a French port, this is. Not much enforcement around, though. Pirate haven, through and through. Love it here. Never have to worry about the law being set on you. Only have to worry about the cutpurses and whores. Honest folk, those. At least you know what they're aiming for."

I nearly burst out laughing at the sailor's words. Cutpurses and whores as honest folk, and this coming from a pirate. Then again, cutpurses and whores were likely a lot more honest than Hades or Reddings.

After what seemed like forever, we finally made our way to the dock. The spontaneous cheer the pirate crew let out took me aback, before I realized it had likely been a few weeks before any of them had seen land. Then again, it had been a couple of weeks for me as well.

The captain appeared suddenly to my right, and my breath caught in my throat. He grinned at the crew.

"Go to Harry to collect your pay!" he shouted. "God knows you deserve it! A man couldn't ask for a better bunch of scoundrels than you!"

Another cheer was raised, and before I knew it the captain turned to me. He tossed a purse, and I caught it instinctively, my hand dropping from the weight.

"Figured I'd pay you in person," he said. "Considering you saved my life. I remember promising you a night to remember, as well. Didn't I?"

My throat was dry, and it took me a moment to realize that he asked a question. I swallowed to clear my throat. "I believe you did say something like that, yes," I managed. I didn't want a night out with the captain. I wanted to escape this damned ship. Never mind the fact that I had no idea where I would go. I just knew I couldn't stay here.

The captain, Victor, grinned at me. "Glad you remember," he said. "There's a tavern here you'd really enjoy. The Mermaid. Near the west end of the docks. Meet me there around nine, sound good? I know how to show you the best night you'll ever have."

I highly doubted that, but I nodded anyway. With any luck, I would be far away by the time the clock bells chimed nine.

My plans of escape were delayed, however, when I saw Hades approach me. The rest of the pirates already started running down the gangplanks to the pier, laughing and shouting at each other as they went. No one was looking back to see Hades coming my direction.

I dug in the purse that the captain had given me and drew out a handful of coins. I didn't care how much they were. I just hoped that it would be enough to get Hades off my back long enough for me to escape.

I thrust them at Hades before he had a chance to utter a word. "Is this what you want?" I demanded.

Hades laughed, but his hand clenched over mind. "You must think I'm incredibly single-minded," he said. "What if I was just coming over here for a friendly chat?"

I wrenched my hand free, leaving the coins in his. He pocketed them deftly.

"You're never friendly," I snapped. I spun around on my heel and fled for the pier, taking the chance that Hades wouldn't risk blackmailing me again with so many potential witnesses nearby.

I was right. I breathed a sigh of relief as I reached the pier and realized Hades hadn't followed me. For whatever reason, he had decided to let me go.

Which was fine by me. I started walking as fast as I could. I had no idea where I was going, but I had to get away from the docks.

I should have been watching where I was going, but then again, I had no idea where I was. It wasn't long before I was completely lost. My only guide was away from the ocean.

I watched the streets change from taverns, to residential, to commercial, and back to residential, but I didn't slow my pace. I was angry. I hated running. I hated having to run. I hated Hades and Reddings. I even hated Victor, for making me freeze up every time I saw him. I hated my father and mother, and the fact that they let themselves be charmed by Reddings.

I dimly realized I should be looking for an inn to stay at, but I was so angry the thought didn't truly penetrate the haze of emotion. If I let myself stop walking, I would start shaking.

I realized it was dark all of a sudden. I was so lost in my own thoughts the dimming light failed to register. Lights had gone on in buildings, blindingly bright in many cases. Despite the darkness, the amount of people on the street had not gone down. If anything, it had increased.

I decided I really did need to start searching for an inn. I couldn't spend the night on the streets, after all, and I needed some place to go while I figured out what my next move was going to be. Much as I hated the fact that I was running, I really had no choice. I had to come to terms with that, and out on the street was not the place to do it.

I stopped in front of the nearest man, causing him to look at me in irritation.

"What?"

He was far from polite, but I didn't let that stop me. "Can you tell me where a good inn is?"

The man looked me up and down. I realized he was much better dressed than I was, and so were most of the other people on the street. I had wandered into the rich part of town.

"You'd have better luck down near the docks," he said. "Not much for your kind up here." He walked off without another word.

I felt my temper boil within me, fueled by my hate and frustration. Before I could do anything I regretted, I turned and stalked away, not caring what direction I was going.

Would I ever be rid of the prejudice that people showed? It didn't seem likely at this point. Unless I managed to disguise myself as white and male, I would be looked down upon by almost everyone I came across.

I should have paid more attention to where I was going. Before I knew it, I was walking along a side street full of people. Lights were everywhere, making it almost as bright as day, and dozens of women were leaning out of windows or standing on street corners, scantily dressed and waving at male passersby. One of them blew a kiss to me, and I hurried my footsteps. This was not a good place to be. If this was where the brothels and whores were, sailors would gather here in abundance.

"Hey, sweetie, where you going?"

I nearly jumped out of my skin as a woman laid her hand on my shoulder. She was nearly as tall as me, and she had long, red, curly hair that ran down her back in waves. This close to me, I could see the dark circles under her eyes and the paste that was caked onto her cheeks. Her lips were bright red, much brighter than anything nature could have produced. Her dress was little better than a smock, and it drooped off her shoulders, leaving almost nothing to the imagination.

I tensed. I didn't need this. I didn't need to be propositioned by a whore. Even if I had the right equipment, she was honestly probably little better than a thief.

I tried to remove her hand from my shoulder, but her grip tightened. She smiled again. "A man like you has to have urges. You've been underway for far too long. I can help you relieve the tension."

To me, her voice sounded desperate. I felt my throat constrict. I couldn't afford to help her. Whatever happened to put her on the street was her problem, not mine.

But for some reason I couldn't turn away. I could see the pain and desperation in her eyes. She didn't want to be here, but for some reason she had no choice.

"Do you want to be here?" I asked.

I saw shock and surprise flicker over the woman's face. Apparently, that was not a question that she was used to being asked.

I cursed myself. I couldn't afford this. But I couldn't help it.

I reached into the purse that Victor had given me and fingered one of the smaller coins. I reached out and thrust the coin into her hand.

"You don't have to sleep with me," I said roughly. "Just spend the night somewhere safe."

The woman's mouth dropped open, and she stared at the coin, at me, and then back at the coin again. I took advantage of her distraction to remove her hand from my shoulder and turn back into the crowd. I was cursing myself. Who knew what kind of money I would need to escape this place? That woman was hardly the only desperate whore on the streets. I couldn't help them all.

"You there! Wait!"

I turned instinctively and flinched as I saw three men approaching me. Although their expressions were friendly, the way they moved was predatory. They had seen me give the woman money, and now figured me for easy prey.

I didn't think. I turned and ran, heading for one of the back alleys. There was no one on this street who was likely to help me if three men decided to rob me. Even though I was still carrying my cutlass, I didn't think I could take on three men at the same time.

Heading into the back alley was a mistake. The lights disappeared, and I had difficulty seeing where I was going. My foot caught on something on the ground, and I stumbled, wincing as my ankle twisted.

"This way!"

I spun around, knowing that they were too close for me to outrun. Belatedly, I realized I should have tried to use my gift to disguise myself. But the first of the men was already upon me.

I never thought I would be grateful to Hades, but at that moment, I was. My cutlass came out instinctively, and I dropped low, bringing my sword up high to block his overhand strike. Then I swept out, forcing my attacker to jump back.

I cursed as I realized that allowed him to line up with the other two men, both of whom had long daggers in their hand. One of them smiled evilly.

"You could have made this easy, boy," he said. "You could have just handed over the money you were so willing to give to that whore. Now we'll just have to take if off your corpse."

After everything that had happened, this was just the final straw. I couldn't think, I was so angry. "I'm not a boy!" I shouted. "I'm a girl, you bloody idiots!"

I dropped the seeming I held over myself. I was still boyish and slim, but there were curves that no male figure would have. Before the three men could collect themselves, I charged towards them, dropping at the last second and slamming into the first man's knees. He dropped, and I came up again, driving my cutlass into his leg as I did so. He screamed, and suddenly the other two men were on me.

I tried to fend them off as best as I could, but when it was two against one, there was only so much I could do. I lost my cutlass fairly quickly, but I didn't let that slow me down. When one of them came at me with his knife, I grabbed at it, letting it slice into my hand instead of my throat. I turned it towards him, and he yelled as it grazed his shoulder.

My advantage was short lived, however, as suddenly I felt a stabbing pain in my arm. I let loose a shriek as the knife dragged across my upper arm, leaving a trail of fire in its path. My grip on the other man's knife loosened, and he pulled it free from my hand, preparing to strike again.

"Joseph!"

I didn't know who was calling my name, but I took advantage of the sudden hesitation of my attackers. I backpedaled rapidly, clutching my right arm to my chest. My cutlass was on the ground, and I scooped it up in my left hand. My right hand was useless. I wasn't much of a fighter with my left hand, but it was better than nothing.

The two men standing up came towards me again, followed more slowly by the third one, who had managed to finally drag himself upright. Behind them, however, came a flying fury. A sword came flashing, cutting down the man who just dragged himself up, and stabbing into the back of one of my knife-wielding attackers.

The remaining knife-fighter charged towards me again. I managed to get my cutlass up just enough, but his knife still cut into my shoulder. I screamed, but before I could respond or the man could finish me, he dropped, a sword sticking through his back.

I found myself staring into the captain's face. The battle-lust was still clearly visible, but so was the concern.

"Joseph? Are you all right?"

I gasped in pain. I wasn't. My arm, hand, and shoulder were a mess. How had he found me? I didn't want to go back to the ship. I couldn't handle both him and Hades.

"Joseph?"

Victor reached towards me, and I flinched away as he touched my arm. Anger darkened his face. "Let's get you to a place where they can patch you up," he said. "I know of a good clinic here. Doctor's reputable, if you can pay him. Come on, I owe you one."

Reluctantly, I let Victor take my uninjured arm and guide me away from the alley. The pain was messing with my mind. I needed fixed before I could go anywhere. I could escape the Reliance later.

I couldn't tell where we were going. I focused on putting one step in front of the other. My arm was leaving a blood trail, despite my best attempt to bandage it with my shirt. Victor did not seem to notice, but I saw him quicken his footsteps, and I forced myself to keep pace.

Finally, we came to a little shack. It looked like it had seen better days many, many, years ago. I stared at it dubious, but Victor went right up and knocked on the door.

"George? Are you in there?"

The door opened, and a short, stocky man with spectacles stepped out. He glared at Victor. "What's this? Back again, Victor? What is it this time?"

"A friend." Victor gestured at me.

I wasn't sure I would have called the captain a friend, but if it was going to get my arm fixed, I wasn't going to argue. The doctor's eyes swept over me. He nodded. "Got the money?"

"When don't I?"

The doctor snorted. "Come on in, then."

I followed the doctor in, stumbling a little through the doorframe. He gestured for me to sit down on a low bed, and I did so gratefully. I was getting lightheaded.

"Swordfight?" he asked.

I nodded numbly.

"The others look worse than you, at least?"

I managed a ghost of a smile. "Captain killed them," I said.

The doctor looked at Victor again and shook his head. "Every time you're in St. John's, I swear I hear another story about you." He smeared some ointment on my cuts and started wrapping a bandage tightly around my arm. "What did this lass do to deserve being rescued?"

I froze. Hastily, I looked down at myself, and realized I never renewed my seeming after I dropped it in my anger during the fight. I glanced up at Victor, who was looking at the doctor with confusion.

"Lass?" he asked.

The doctor looked sharply at Victor. "What, you mean you didn't know?"

Victor stared at me. I caught my breath as his eyes met mine. He held them for a long moment, then looked up and down my body. I saw his eyes widen in surprise as they took in my chest and my hips.

I cursed under my breath. I should have cast a seeming. I should have pretended the doctor was mistaken. It was a bit late now.

"Lass." Victor's voice was measuring now, and I winced. "Well now, this is an interesting development."

My temper flared, and I glared at Victor. "You know nothing about it."

I saw anger appear in his eyes. I wasn't intimidated. Victor had nothing he could do to me at this point.

The doctor continued bandaging my wounds as Victor spoke again.

"What are you doing onboard my ship?"

I wanted to stand up and punch him in the face, but the doctor held me down. "Exactly what you've seen," I snapped. "Why, does it change now because I'm a woman? Do you want me to refund you the reward for saving your life? Is my ability in some way lessened now?"

I saw a smile quirk on Victor's lips, but he immediately concealed it. "It seems to me we're now even in the saving each other department," he said calmly.

I settled back as the doctor finished bandaging my arm. I nodded. "True. Thank you."

"You still didn't answer my question."

I felt my chest tighten. I wanted to tell him about Hades, but I couldn't. I still didn't know if he would value my word above his. I settled for half the truth.

"My old crew was plotting to sell me. Your attack came along at just the right time." I couldn't keep the bitterness out of my voice.

"And why was a woman aboard a ship?"

So many reasons.

But how to explain them all? "That's my business."

Victor's face darkened. "You should have told me. The anger built again in Victor's face. "You snuck aboard my ship!" he yelled. "Do you know what some of my sailors would think if they knew? They hold fast to the superstition that bringing a woman onboard is bad luck. They would have thrown you over the side!"

I laughed shortly. "What, they wouldn't have stripped me and raped me first?" I asked harshly. "That seems to be a common thing amongst sailors."

Victor's shook his head. "I would have killed any man who laid a finger on you," he said. "Didn't you read the articles before signing onboard?"

I had, and I remembered. I flushed and looked away. "I wasn't sure I was a decent woman anymore," I muttered.

I heard Victor's chuckle. "I consider you one," he said.

I snapped my gaze back to him, trying to discern the meaning I heard between his words. He continued.

"Now, you're coming back to the ship, and I'm putting you in my cabin so you can heal. I can see you're running on nothing but anger."

I glared at him again, but he was right. I had no strength to go find an inn or tavern on my own right now.

The doctor cleared his throat. "Victor, the coin?"

Victor laughed and handed him a handful of coins. "My thanks again, friend," he said. "When will he- she- be fully healed?"

The doctor pursed his lips. "At least a week of rest," he said. "If you're getting underway in that time, I wouldn't have her working the deck. Just don't reopen any of the cuts, and you'll be fine. Mind you don't get infected, now."

Victor nodded and took my uninjured arm, steering me towards the door.

My mind was blank as we walked back towards the Reliance. The captain knew. Hades knew. Somehow, the captain finding out I was a woman had not gone the way either Hades or I thought it would.

We boarded the ship, and Victor steered me towards his cabin. I didn't resist. I could feel my body start to tremble.

"Lie down."

I obeyed without really thinking about it. Victor pulled a sheet over me. "Sleep well," he said. "I'll be back in the morning to check on you."

There was something gentle about his voice, but I didn't have time to dwell on it. Darkness overtook me, and I drifted off to sleep.

*****Chapter 17*****

Waking up the next morning was an interesting experience to say the least.

I woke up feeling much better than I had the previous night. Most of my anger had faded away, leaving only dull pain in my arm, hand, and shoulder. I could move my right arm well enough, even with the cuts, but my shoulder screamed every time I tried to move it more than an inch.

I opened my eyes and remembered abruptly where I had spent the night. I was in the captain's cabin. Victor had left me here. Victor knew I was female.

What the hell was going to happen now? I was planning on leaving anyway, but would he now take the money he had given me and force me out on the streets of St. John's? I had no contacts here. What if I ended up a whore on the street like the poor woman I saw?

I couldn't let that happen to me. At least I had tools that she didn't. I fumbled around and found the purse still attached to my belt. I shoved it inside my shirt and drew on my power, making it look like part of my skin.

I thought for a moment. Victor already knew I was female. Was there any purpose to disguising myself as a man again?

After considering, I decided it wouldn't harm anything to look like a man again. I didn't want anyone else on the ship finding out. Victor said that most of the pirates would likely have thrown me overboard, so he wasn't going to tell anyone they had sheltered a woman for some time.

I just finished casting my seeming when there was a knock on the door. My head jerked up, and Victor entered before I had a chance to answer.

He grinned when he saw me. "Already awake, hmm?" he asked.

I glared at him. How dare he be so amused? I was injured, and I had no idea what was going on. The least he could do was show some sympathy.

"Good morning to you, too," I said. I attempted to relax back against the cushions on his bunk. They were comfortable. Victor's presence was not.

Of all things, his grin broadened. "Now you're comfortable around me," he said. "I was worried for a while you would always be tense. It always took a great deal of effort for me to draw words out of Joseph. What is your real name, anyway?"

There wasn't any point in concealing it. "Josephine," I said. "I wasn't really lying. Just shorting it."

"Josephine," Victor spoke my name slowly. "It's a pretty name. A bit long for you, though."

I couldn't tell what to make of his words. "I usually go by Jo," I said.

He nodded. "That suits you much better," he said. "Jo. I'll have to remember that. Although it will deflect suspicion if I continue to call you Joseph."

My eyes snapped to his. "What?" I asked. What in God's name did he mean by that?

His eyes widened. "Well, you're staying, aren't you?" he asked. "You didn't think I would throw you out on the streets of St. John's? I like to think of myself as a bit more of a gentleman than that."

I couldn't face this conversation sitting down. I swung my legs over and stood up, holding my left arm close to my side.

"I've hardly been left with a good impression of what might happen to me," I said. "You have to understand that."

Victor shrugged. "Well, your disguise is impeccable," he said. He cocked his head, noticing finally that I looked very masculine.

"You looked different last night."

I shrugged, trying to appear nonchalant. I didn't really want to have to explain this. "I have a good disguise."

Victor shook his head. "There were curves yesterday," he said. "I remember them quite clearly. I know you can bind your breasts, but curves are harder to disguise, and you're hardly in baggy enough clothing for that."

To my shock, he reached out and put his hands on my waist. I thrust him back instinctively, and he laughed.

"My apologies," he said. "I had no intention to harm or offend."

He continued looking at me curiously. I returned his stare with as firm a glare as I could muster, but it was growing difficult to maintain. He was standing so close to me. And he was so close to figuring it out.

"You've spent a great deal of time with Hades," he finally said, startling me. It seemed to be a complete change of topic.

I nodded warily. Where was he going with this?

"What has he been teaching you?"

"Sword fighting," I said sharply. "And guns. Just like Isaac told him to."

"What else?"

I shook my head, unwilling to say anything. I suppose it hardly mattered if Victor knew Hades had been blackmailing me at this point. My secret was already out and Hades really couldn't hold it over me anymore. He still scared me, however.

"I know Hades can do certain things," Victor said slowly. "I believe it has something to do with his heritage. Do you have some of the same abilities?"

My jaw dropped and I stared at him in shock. How the hell did Victor know about these things if he had none of the gift himself? He didn't, I was sure of that. Otherwise he would have seen through my disguise immediately.

He laughed at my expression. "Hit the nail on the head!" he exclaimed.

I felt anger flare in me again at his amusement. "Is it that funny?" I snapped at him.

Victor shook his head, still chuckling. "You should see your expression, Jo," he said. "I'm sorry if I offended you."

I was still mad. "You seem to like laughing at me," I said angrily. "You seem to like watching me make a fool out of myself. Why?"

"I'm not laughing at you," Victor said. His smile gave the lie to his words.

I turned away. "Yes, you are. Is it because I'm a woman doing a man's job?"

"Jo."

I shook my head. "You've laughed at me a great deal," I said. "And I don't even look like a woman right now."

I dropped my seeming and heard Victor's breath catch. I hardly cared. I didn't know what had come over me, but I couldn't seem to stop it. "This is who I am, Victor," I said. "Don't laugh at me. Don't laugh at what I've been through." "This is who I am, Victor!" I shouted. "Don't laugh at me because of it!"

"Josephine."

I hardly heard Victor begin his words. I realized I was shaking. I opened my mouth to continue, when his mouth covered mine.

I froze. Never before had a man kissed me, and certainly not like this.

I had no excuse for what I did next. A properly reared woman would certainly have never responded the way I did, and I was supposed to have been properly reared. But I was angry, frustrated, tired, confused, and hurt.

I reached around the back of his head, ignoring my arm's protests, and pulled him closer towards me. I heard his sound of surprise and then his tongue was invading my mouth.

I was lost in a sea of sensation. I now knew what Hades meant when he talked about me lusting after Victor. He was right, much as I hated to admit it. The feel of Victor's mouth on mine was like lightning.

It was also frying my brain, but I didn't care. I didn't care as Victor's hands moved to my neck and down my back. I even encouraged him, nipping at his lips when he hesitated too long.

"Jo," Victor's voice was a harsh whisper. "Do you even know what I'm going to do to you?"

I felt my temper flare a little. "I would have stopped you by now if I didn't want it," I snapped.

Victor laughed, and he moved his lips to my neck. "You'd hardly have a chance of that."

I wanted to argue with him, but he bit down, and I had to hold onto him to remain standing. My hands curled into claws and dug into his back. He gasped. I must have hurt him, but I didn't care.

What happened next was hardly surprising. I, at least, was fueled by frustration, anger, and desire, and Victor could hardly have been in better shape. Soon enough, we were stripping each other, with hardly a care of the condition of our clothes once we were done with them. The feeling of his skin on mine was even better than his lips. When his hand cupped my left breast, I couldn't help a soft moan.

He chuckled, and I immediately went to take my revenge. Remembering how his lips had felt on my throat, I bit at his neck.

His chuckle turned into a growl, and I was being pushed back and thrown on the bed. I had a brief moment to be grateful he had his own private cabin, and then he was on top of me.

It was like nothing I ever imagined. My mother told me nothing about sex. I had heard about it, certainly, but never that it could make me feel like this. I was out of control. I was biting and scratching him, and at the same time pulling him closer and deeper. My world was exploding in showers of sparks.

When it was over, we lay there for a long moment, Victor propping himself up on his elbows over me, gasping for breath. We stared at each other for a long while.

Victor swallowed. "I… Did not intend for that to just happen," he said.

I swallowed. I felt raw. I couldn't yet say what my reaction to this was going to be.

"Neither did I," I managed.

A wry smile found Victor's face. "At least we're both on the same page in that regard," he said. He began easing himself away from me and off the bed.

I was still in a slight state of shock, but when Victor handed me my clothes, I immediately began dressing. I didn't know what was going to happen from here, but I wanted to be dressed to confront it.

Victor dressed at the same pace I did. My breathing was still ragged when I finished. We stared at each other.

"I'll go make sure that you get some breakfast," Victor said finally. "You probably want to resume your disguise. I'll get Derry to deliver it."

Before I could answer, he was out the door.

I stared after him. What the hell did I just let happen? And what was going to happen now because of it? Of all the things that I imagined possible when I left home, being seduced by a pirate captain had not been at the top of the list.

I sat back down on the bed, trying to sort through my thoughts. This was going to take a lot of thinking.

****

I would like to say I thought very hard and seriously about what happened between Victor and me, but of course I didn't. Thinking had never been my strong suit, especially when my feelings became involved.

I had the presence of mind to cast my seeming again, so at least I was decent when Derry bounded through the door without bothering to knock. The food was simple stuff, but it wasn't what we had been eating underway. This was actually cooked.

"Captain says you got in a fight!" he exclaimed. "Three against one! And you killed them all!"

I was startled. Was that all he said? "I didn't kill all of them," I said warily. "The captain did a fair bit of the killing himself."

Derry waved his hand impatiently. "What was it like? Tell me!"

I couldn't believe the child's enthusiasm. Was he really that bloodthirsty, or was it from being raised amongst all these pirates?

I shook my head. "It was terrifying," I said. "I thought I was going to die. There are very few men who can hold off three at once, and I am definitely not one of them."

Derry looked a little disappointed. I pulled my shirt sleeve up to show him the bandages on my arm and hand.

"Derry, this is what they did to me," I said firmly. "It hurts like hell. I would have been perfectly happy to walk through St. John's without three thugs deciding it would be fun to mug me. I'm not sorry they're dead, but I really wish I didn't to have get hurt for that to happen."

He cocked his head. "So, if you hadn't gotten hurt, it would have been all right?"

I sighed. There was no distracting this child. "I don't like fighting," I said. "I'm not good at it. There are better and less dangerous ways to get what you want."

Derry still looked confused, but at least he stopped badgering me. I was surprised at my own words, and a little ashamed. Me, the person who stoutly defended herself from a government official who insulted her race, the person who killed sailors during a pirate attack, who felt the blood of one of them drip down her as she saved her captain's life, didn't like fighting?

Not to mention that my entire illusion during the attack on La Coraje had allowed a lot more fighting and killing to take place. I was being a hypocrite. But if it persuaded Derry to be different, then so be it.

"Oh, Captain said to tell you we're getting underway in a week," he said. "You're not to leave his cabin until he can get a surgeon's approval you're healed enough to work. He'll be by in a few hours."

My temper flared up, and I had to throttle it down before I took it out on Derry. The boy was only a messenger after all.

But really! Was Victor just assuming that because of what we shared I'd be willing to sail with him again? Granted, he didn't know I was trying to leave the ship, but he should at least have that conversation with me before assuming I was willing to stay.

And why did he want me to stay, anyway? He already mentioned the crew would likely have a fit over me being onboard if they knew I was a woman. Did he mean to keep me as his own personal whore? If that was the case, he could bid farewell to that idea. As pleasant as the experience was, I wasn't at all sure if I was ready to repeat it just yet.

"Where will the captain be for the next few hours?" I asked.

Derry shrugged. "No one knows," he said. "Everyone assumes he has some secret way of finding out where the best targets are. He always disappears for a good while our first day in port somewhere."

That was hardly helpful. I didn't want to wait for Victor to show up again to have this conversation. I needed to know what was going to happen to me.

I clenched my jaw. Once again, my future was dependent on other people's choices. I hated that feeling. Just for once, I wanted my future to be decided by me.

I absentmindedly said farewell to Derry and started pacing the length of the room. I needed to figure out my options. It would help if I knew what Victor's plans and ideas for me were, but I needed to know what I wanted to do first.

The first problem, I realized, was that I had no clear idea what I wanted to do. I had signed onboard a ship to learn how to use the power of the sea. Well, I had certainly found that, although in one of the most unlikely situations I could have imagined. I had a store of rituals that Hades had told me about that I hadn't had a chance to put into practice yet. I had no idea if they would exhaust me as much as casting the seeming of a ship, but there was no way to find out but to try.

I shook my head. That was why I originally signed onboard a ship. I had that now. What did I want from the Reliance?

I had no clue.

There wasn't anything quite as frustrating as having no idea what I wanted to do. I decided to take a different tactic. What did I not want to do?

Those answers rose up immediately. I didn't want to deal with Hades blackmailing me anymore. I didn't want to be Victor's whore. I didn't want to marry Reddings, or any other man, even Victor.

At least Reddings wasn't an issue anymore. I was safe from him at this point. There was no way for him to find out where I was.

Hades, on the other hand. My lips started to broaden into a smile. He no longer had a true hold over me for blackmail. Wouldn't it be amusing if the next time he tried, I simply was able to tell him no? The expression on his face would be priceless.

The only question then, was Victor. If he was willing to keep our relationship similar to what it was, staying here wouldn't be a bad decision. David would continue to teach me navigation. I could mentor Derry and try to steer him away from bloodthirstiness and violence. I could talk to Kwaku and maybe learn more about the culture my Nana had come from. I could confound Hades. Staying here wouldn't be bad. It would be better than drifting aimlessly in St. John's, anyway. If I decided against it again, I could always leave.

I didn't realize how long it took me to come to this decision until I heard a knock on the door. Victor entered, moving as quietly as a cat. For a large man, it was surprising how little sound he could make.

"Did Derry tell you we're leaving in a week?" he asked.

I nodded and folded my arms across my chest. I waited for him to make the next move.

Victor sighed. "I suppose there's a question I should have asked," he said. "Do you want to come, now that I know you're a woman?"

I couldn't quite believe my ears. Not because of what just happened between us, but because I was a woman.

"Is it a problem that I'm a woman?" I kept my tone level. It could be, considering the rest of the crew.

Victor shook his head. "I have no issue," he said. "Have you heard of Jacquotte Delahaye? Or Anne Dieu-le-Veut? Both female, and both wonderful pirates. I had the chance to meet Jacquotte earlier this year. She's frightening. As are you."

I wondered if that was intended to be a compliment or not. Either way, he hadn't answered the question I needed answered.

"And what will happen between us?" I asked, keeping my voice level. It was difficult. His presence was reminding my body of the way it felt when both of us were naked in his bed.

Victor stared at me. "What do you want to happen?" he asked.

What a question to turn back on me. "I won't be your whore while we're underway." I said. "I won't be your plaything. You won't threaten to reveal my gender to the rest of the crew if I displease you."

The shock in Victor's eyes had to be genuine. Those situations hadn't even crossed his mind.

He stepped forward to crowd against me. I stood firm, staring at him. I had too many men intimidate me, and I wasn't going to let Victor do it as well.

"Do you think so little of me, Jo?" he asked. "Have I proved nothing to you?"

"No one else has ever done anything trustworthy," I said, struggling to keep my voice steady. "Why should you?"

"Jo, listen." He caught my hand and I struggled to wrench it free. Suddenly, we were kissing again, and a whole host of feelings I buried this morning came surging forward again. I started clawing at his clothes and I felt his hands on my own.

What happened next was fairly inevitable. When it was over, we lay naked and panting in each other's arms. Victor propped himself up on an elbow to look at me.

"Does that mean you'll come along?" he asked.

I had to laugh. He hadn't answered my question in words, but he helped me answer the question as to what I wanted. I wanted to feel his hands on me again. I didn't know my body could feel the things he was awakening. It was a magic all of its own.

"I'll come," I said. "On one condition."

Victor nodded. "What's that?"

"You don't tell any of the crew I'm a woman. Any of them. Not Harry, not Isaac, not Hades. One day, while we're underway, I will tell them. And you will support me in whatever decision I make that day."

Victor nodded without hesitation, and I relaxed slightly. No matter what actually happened, at this point I had his word. I didn't know how much the word of a pirate was worth, but I was hoping it was worth something.

"Agreed," Victor said. He leaned down to kiss me. "Now, my navigator in training, would you mind showing me how to get to our destination again?"

*****Chapter 18*****

Surprisingly, very little changed over the next two days. I spent most of my time in Victor's cabin, recovering from my wounds. By the third day, however, I was bored enough that I ventured back out on deck.

It was nearly empty, except for the scattering of crew that had shore watch. The pirates didn't want anyone stealing their ship, after all.

"Jo!"

I turned and smiled as Kwaku approached me. "How'd you get shore watch?" I asked.

He shrugged. "Rotation." He grimaced in sympathy at the bandages on my shoulder and arm. "You're not the only one to run afoul of the low-life this port call," he said. "Looks like you got hurt the worst, though."

I had to suppress a smile at the idea of a pirate calling others low-life. I managed a nonchalant shrug instead. "You should see the other guys," I said instead.

Kwaku grinned and burst out into laughter. "You're in a fine mood," he observed. "Something change?"

I stilled, remembering our last conversation. Things hadn't really changed since then. Hades was still blackmailing me and lying about me, I was still on a pirate ship, and yet... everything had changed.

"Can we talk privately?" I asked slowly.

Kwaku's eyebrows narrowed, but he didn't say anything, just nodded. I looked around.

"Helm's pretty empty right now," Kwaku said. "Most of us are minding the gangway and stores."

I nodded and followed him to the helm. We were in broad view of anyone who cared to look, but we would also be able to see anyone who wanted to listen to us before they could hear what we were saying.

Kwaku leaned against the wheel and crossed his arms. "What is it?" he asked.

I sighed and looked away. This wasn't as easy as Victor just finding out. "I want to tell you something," I said. "But I'm not sure how you're going to take this."

I looked back to see his eyes widen slightly. "Go ahead," he said warily.

I cursed under my breath. "The captain already knows," I said shortly. "I'm a woman."

Kwaku stared at me blankly. "You're joking."

I couldn't help a smile from spreading across my face. I still wore my seeming, after all. I looked very masculine. I released my hold on it, letting Kwaku see my true body.

"I am not," I said, trying to keep my voice steady. "I am female."

I saw him staring hard at me, and I bit my lip to keep silent. I was cursing myself. I shouldn't have told him, I should have given him more warning, I should have...

He burst out laughing.

I glared at him. "Something funny?" I asked.

Kwaku was almost doubled over, he was laughing so hard. I bit down hard on my lip to avoid yelling at him. Me being a woman was hardly a laughing matter.

"Oh, this is great!" he finally exclaimed. "I can't wait to see how the rest react!"

"Don't tell anyone else!" I exclaimed.

He grinned. "Your secret's safe with me," he said. "The captain knows?"

I nodded.

"Then that's all I need to worry about," he said. "What a joke!"

I stared at him. "Why is this a joke?"

Kwaku shook his head. "We all have secrets," he said. "I knew you had one. I thought you'd been a slave somewhere, and you were hiding it. Thought you might have been the bastard of a plantation owner, maybe with a price on your head. Maybe you killed someone. This was the last thing I expected." He grinned. "Also, the last time a woman was on board this ship, six of the crew ended up in various duels over her. Wonder if any will be fought over you?"

I started to relax slightly. No matter why Kwaku found my situation funny, at least he wasn't raging because I'd deceived him in any way.

"So, how'd you end up here?"

I didn't end up telling him all of my story, but I told him enough. That I'd run away to avoid being married, and about the fight with the government official in Port Royal. How the crew of the Vixen had been ready to sell me into slavery. I didn't tell him about my gift, or about Hades. Those could wait.

We talked for a long time. It was almost noon when Victor came back and found the two of us talking.

Kwaku saluted him as he turned to leave. "Jo, if you're feeling up to it, want to get a few drinks tonight?" he asked. He grinned at Victor. "Shouldn't spent your first port call holed up onboard."

Victor raised his eyebrows, and I couldn't help grinning. "Absolutely."

Once Kwaku was out of earshot, Victor turned to him. "Sharing secrets?" he asked.

I shrugged. I supposed it was obvious from the fact that I wasn't wearing my seeming. "Kwaku's been a friend," was all I said.

Victor seemed to accept that. "Mind if I join this excursion tonight?"

I glanced at him, and he smiled. "I never did show you the night of your life for rescuing me," he pointed out.

I had to laugh at that. "I'd like that."

"Good," Victor grinned. "Pirates we may be, but we know how to spend gold just as well as any other man! Or woman." He frowned at me.

Reminded by his words, I drew on my power and cast my seeming again. I shouldn't have really let it down for so long.

"I like you better the other way."

I laughed at him. "Maybe you'll see me that way tonight," I said, then nearly bit my tongue. What was getting into me? Ma would have fainted to hear me talk like this.

Victor grinned. "Just maybe?"

A shiver went down my spine, and at that moment I didn't care what Ma thought of me. "Maybe," I said with a smile.

"I guess I'll just have to convince you," Victor said. "Tell me, Jo, have you ever had whiskey?"

*****Chapter 19*****

The rest of the week was fairly uneventful. I didn't help with the preparations for getting underway, due to my injuries. I did make it to the navigator's cabin, though, and helped David plot out our next course. We were making our way around a number of islands, sailing around trade routes, looking for rich ships to plunder. The thought didn't bother me as much as it had before.

I wasn't sure I liked the person I was becoming. My mother would have fainted dead away if she knew what my life was like right now. I was onboard a pirate ship, disguised as a man, and secret lovers with the captain. And I was planning on revealing my identity to the rest of the crew at some point. As soon as Hades tried to blackmail me again.

I spent a good deal of time with Kwaku during those days, talking about Africa. I still didn't tell him about Hades or my abilities, but we shared other things.

"My Nana sounded like you," I said.

Kwaku nodded. "Lots of my folk are over here. My village was easy pickings, being right on the coast. What was her name?"

I shrugged. "I don't remember. She died when I was very young."

He sighed. "That's too bad. It would have been good to know if someone else had made it out all right."

"Do you ever want to go back? To Africa, I mean?"

He shook his head. We were standing at the ship's wheel. Kwaku was technically on watch, and was holding fast to the tiller while we had our conversation.

"Much happier here than I was there," he said. "I didn't miss Africa while I was a slave. I missed freedom. Here, I have that."

I gazed out over the open stretch of water. I had to agree with him. There was nothing to hold me back, not anymore.

I smiled wryly as I saw Hades make his way across the deck. I hadn't had a lesson from him since we got underway. My injuries made a convenient excuse to avoid him. I knew he would corner me some time, but I was enjoying the cat and mouse game we were currently playing.

I really had no idea what I was doing. Once Hades decided to confront me, then my only solution was to reveal my gender to the entire crew and hope Victor would back me up. But I was enjoying the situation far too much to think. I imagined Hades must have felt like this when I first came aboard the ship. He must have been just as smug when he watched me, certain I would do exactly what he wanted me to.

Of course my illusions and smugness only lasted until the day he finally managed to corner me.

It had been a good day up until then. I spent the morning in the navigator's office, plotting the next part of our course. We had word of a few Dutch trading ships that were supposed to be well-loaded traveling down to Jamaica to trade with the English there. It felt odd to be plotting a course near Jamaica without actually planning on landing there.

My injuries were almost completely healed. I could move without pain, and all that remained were a few long, red lines where I had been cut. I even practiced a little with my cutlass in the captain's cabin before venturing out on deck.

I hadn't spent every night in the captain's cabin, but something generally happened between us every few days. Usually there was a shouting match involved, then the pair of us would end up naked on the bed. I was beginning to wonder about our pattern. Were we only capable of loving each other when we were angry?

My thoughts were distracted by this, which is why Hades managed to corner me. I was below deck, organizing my chest of belongings. Although I hadn't spent the previous night in my hammock, I still kept it for appearance's sake.

"Jo. Do you have a moment?"

I flew to my feet, taken entirely by surprise. I hadn't heard him approach, and every sense in my body stood in high alert, like a deer preparing to flee.

Hades smiled at me. "Good to see you again," he said. "Your wounds seem to be better. Ready to start your lessons again soon? You shouldn't be slacking on them."

I took a deep breath to steady myself. I had to remember he didn't have any power over me anymore. But it was hard.

"What do you want, Hades?" I asked. I tried to make my voice as hard as possible. I wasn't certain how well I succeeded.

From the smile in Hades' eyes, not very well. "Why, I was just checking up on you," he said. "I didn't want you to forget about your duties onboard the Reliance. I know you've been injured and recovering, but we have things we need to attend to."

That took me aback. "We?"

Hades took a step forward, trying to back me up against the wall. I stood firm and glared at him.

"I know what's been going on in the captain's cabin," he said softly. "I may not be able to see you, but I can see him just fine. If you don't want the rest of the crew to find out, then you'll share the same with me."

My jaw dropped.

"That's a fine way to proposition someone," I snapped. "Have you ever considered the answer might be no?"

Hades held fast to his calm demeanor. "You wouldn't dare gainsay me," he said. "Not when you have so much to lose. What would David, Kwaku, and Derry think when they found out you were posing as a woman? How would our good captain feel about having to explain to the crew why he was concealing you?"

I didn't care about his reasons. I could deal with everything except Victor's reaction, and his reaction worried me less than the thought of sleeping with this bastard.

"No," I snapped. "Go to hell, and take your third leg with you."

The rage that flared up in Hades' face took me aback, and I did back into the wall then. "You will not say no to me!" he shouted.

I felt my anger flaring, and I let it. "You will not force me, you bastard!" I screamed back. "Let everyone know! They can't touch me! I read the articles I signed!"

Black fury reigned in Hades' eyes. I ignored it and thrust him away from me. I ran past him before he could grab me, flying up the stairs to the main deck.

"Come back, you bitch!" Hades yelled. "You will be sorry for this!"

Dimly, I wondered if he was right, but I didn't care. I hated that man, and I wouldn't take any more nonsense from him.

I don't know what possessed me at the time. I climbed up on the deck and looked around. At least a dozen other pirates, including Kwaku, stood around, working on various projects and repairs. They looked surprised to see me flying up the ladder.

I waited until Hades came up behind me. Then I shouted in my loudest voice, "Hades! Bos'n of the Reliance! I challenge you to a duel!"

At my words, pandemonium reigned. Hades stared at me in shock. The other pirates were equally dumbfounded, but they immediately started filling the air with questions. I didn't answer any of them, just looked Hades straight in the eye.

"What's going on here?"

I didn't relax at the sound of Victor's voice. Now was the test of his promise to me. Would he remember and stand by it?

Hades spoke first. "Captain," he said, his voice biting hard, "This woman has had the gall to challenge me to a duel."

Victor's eyes widened as he looked at me. His face seemed calm, but I could tell he was wearing a mask.

"Have you now?" he said.

Victor may have focused on the part about the duel, but the other pirates heard the first part of Hades' sentence.

"What?" Derry exclaimed in his high pitched voice.

The echoing shouts of surprise rang through the air as the other pirates turned to each other. I steeled myself and dropped my seeming, letting them take closer looks at me to see Hades was speaking the truth.

"What is a woman doing onboard our ship?"

Victor's lips tightened. "Saving my life at least once, Isaac. Can you claim the same for yourself?"

The murmurs and grumblings of the crew did not die down. They were clearly not happy with the revelation of my true gender.

"She's a liar and a whore," Hades said, satisfaction coloring his voice. "Who else would sneak their way onboard a pirate ship?"

I raised my voice. "What kind of man would blackmail me to come onboard?" I demanded. "What kind of man would use threats of rape and torture to keep me in line? What kind of man would threaten to betray the articles he signed, just to threaten a woman? What kind of man are you, Hades?"

The roar of voices started again. If Hades' eyes were daggers, I would have been long dead by now.

"Silence!"

The sound of Victor's raised voice was possibly the only thing that could have quieted the growing mob. Victor turned to Harry, who moved up to stand next to him.

"Harry," Victor said, "What is the ship's policy when it comes to duels?"

Harry cleared his throat, obviously trying not to stare at me. I stared at him, though, letting my eyes bore into him. He shifted.

"The two combatants shall be dropped off at a deserted island with their choice of weapons and a second. They shall fight to first blood or to the death, whichever is agreed upon. If to first blood, the loser shall be deposited at the next port of call, and shall never sail with the Reliance again."

I should have been more scared at Harry's words. I knew I wasn't a match for Hades when it came to swordplay or guns. I had no hope of winning a duel against him. But I was so mad, any other emotion was simply drowned out.

Victor nodded. "David!" he yelled. "Plot us a course to the nearest island. I want this matter settled as quickly as possible. The rest of you, back to work. You," he pointed a finger at me, "come to my cabin. We need to discuss a few matters in private."

The rest of the crew trickled reluctantly back into doing whatever tasks they were assigned to. I saw Kwaku giving me a reassuring look. I steeled my shoulders and followed Victor to his cabin.

As soon as I closed the door behind me, he was on me. "What in God's name are you thinking, woman?" he yelled. "Why are you challenging Hades to a duel? Do you know what he could do to you? What is worth the possibility of dying on a deserted island?"

Anger boiled over in me. "You don't know what he's done!" I yelled back. "He was the one who forced me to sign aboard this god-forsaken ship. He was the one who blackmailed me into making sure I was doing his bidding at all times. He was the one who threatened me with rape and dismemberment! I have more than enough reasons to challenge him to a duel!"

"He'll kill you!" Victor shouted. "I've never seen Hades lose a fight, not once! You never even held a sword until he showed you. How do you expect to defeat him?"

"By killing him!" I wasn't in the mood for logical answers.

Victor lost it. He started shouting and calling me names, idiot and selfish being the least of them. I returned the favor, calling him a buffoon and a bastard, as well as much worse.

We were both ready to kill each other when Victor reached out to throttle me. I squirmed out of his grip and struck at him. His hands grasped my wrists, and suddenly we were kissing again.

We took a good deal of the anger we were both feeling out on each other. We left our clothes and the cabin a mess, to say the least. When Victor cried out, moving on top of me, I shuddered, feeling a warm sensation of peace drift over me.

The fight wasn't over, of course. Victor glared down at me. "You're still an idiot," he said.

I shrugged. I was done with the name-calling. "There's no backing out of it now," I said. "And you'll support me, remember? You promised me that."

Victor growled, and I suppressed a shiver of excitement. "I have so many names I could call you right now," he said.

I raised my eyebrows, daring him to voice any of those words.

He sighed and shook his head. "One condition," he said. "I train you until we reach the island. If you're going to fight Hades, you're going to go as well prepared as possible."

It was hardly an unreasonable request, so I agreed. After all, I hardly wanted to die, despite my admittedly idiotic actions. Hades would pay for what he had done to me, though, no matter what the cost.

*****Chapter 20*****

I had no plan. The deserted island was only a day away, and Victor had only had one chance to drill me. He tried to seem confident about my chances against Hades, but I could tell he didn't hold out much hope.

The rest of the crew had taken the news of my gender far better than I thought they would. Kwaku and Victor's defense had helped, of course. But even Harry and David were defending me. Of course, it might be because everyone expected Hades to kill me.

I decided I wouldn't let it bother me. I didn't have to beat Hades in a fair fight. All I had to do was cheat.

The question, of course, was how I would go about cheating. On any other opponent, the answer would have been easy. I would have used my gift to seem like I was somewhere I wasn't, and stabbed them in the back when they weren't looking. Hades, on the other hand, wouldn't be fooled by such a trick. That left me with slightly more unconventional methods.

To my surprise, it was Derry who gave me the answer. Derry had been following me around, awestruck, since I made the announcement of my sex. I didn't know precisely how to feel about that. It wasn't like I was that out of the ordinary, was I? Victor mentioned at least two other female pirates who made names for themselves.

"Jo?"

At the sound of his voice, I looked up from staring across the ocean. The rest of the crew had started calling me Jo instead of Joseph, following Victor's example. I felt more comfortable with it.

"What?" I asked Derry. He seemed anxious, like he was trying to decide whether or not to tell me something.

Derry shifted from foot to foot. "You're fighting Hades tomorrow, right?"

I nodded. Everyone knew that.

"Captain says he doesn't believe you'll win," Derry said. "He's upset."

I concealed a rueful smile. Of course Victor was upset. I had specifically used his promise against him. It was worth it, though.

"He says Hades is the best fighter he's seen."

I knew that was true. I hadn't truly figured out a way to get around that fact.

Derry looked down. "I have a secret."

I stared at Derry, drawing my eyebrows in. The boy was up to something. And from the sound of it, he wanted to help me.

"What's the secret?" I asked.

Derry held out a small, hollow tube. I took it curiously. It didn't look like anything I'd ever seen before.

He handed me a small leather pouch to go along with it. "Careful," he said. "Don't touch the darts."

At those words, I understood what the cylinder I held in my hand was. It was a blowgun. The darts must have poison coated on them. I stared at Derry. "Where'd you get this?"

Derry shrugged. "Captain said I always had to have a way to defend myself," he said. "This seemed like the best solution."

I shook my head in admiration. For once, I was not going to feel bad about the boy being raised in a violence-rich environment.

"Thank you," I said. "It will definitely come in useful."

Derry grinned. "I hope so!" he exclaimed, his voice suddenly cheerful. "Will you take me with you? I want to watch!"

I made a decision on impulse. I couldn't ask Victor to be my second, after all. he was the captain, and therefore supposed to be impartial. Kwaku would probably have been the better choice, but Derry was the one who had probably already saved my life.

"I'll do better than that," I said. "Derry, will you do me the great honor of being my second?"

Derry's eyes glowed. "You want me as your second?" he gasped. "Truly?"

I had to laugh. "I wouldn't have asked if I hadn't meant it," I said.

He laughed out loud, and to my surprise threw his arms around me and cheered. I returned the embrace hesitantly. I didn't quite know what to make of his enthusiasm.

He quickly released me and straightened. "We need a plan," he said, suddenly becoming serious. "Hades might also have a secret weapon. We need to find a way to neutralize it if he uses it."

I smiled and patted his shoulder. "We'll talk tomorrow morning," I said. "You think of things now, and tell me then. I need time to think right now."

Luckily, Derry was an understanding boy. He ran off eagerly, no doubt to share the news that I had chosen him as my second.

I returned my gaze back to the open water. My mind was already whirling. The most important thing I had to worry about was concealing the blowgun from Hades until the time came to use it. He could see things, except on me. I could hide the blowgun for now, but we would be searched before the duel.

But would Derry be searched?

I cocked my head as a solution occurred to me. Of course Derry would be armed. Hades likely knew about his blowgun. He wouldn't be surprised to see Derry carrying it if he was my second.

I smiled and felt my lips purse. I should have felt terrible. I was using a child's weapon to cheat in a duel to kill a man. I had no illusions as to what the poison on the darts probably did to a man. Even if they didn't kill him outright, I fully intended to finish the job with my cutlass.

I shuddered at the thought. I had come a long way from the woman who threw up after murdering a Spanish sailor to save Victor's life.

"Heavy thoughts, Jo?"

I turned to see Victor standing there, his arms crossed. I shrugged.

"Just waiting for tomorrow," I said.

Victor shook his head. "You are an idiot," he said. "But I've already told you that."

I smiled. I had a weapon he knew nothing about. "You may be surprised by the outcome."

I nearly laughed at the glare on Victor's face. I couldn't say what came over me. The anger was transformed into a strange recklessness I didn't know what to do with.

"You'll see," I promised. "Tomorrow we land. Derry's my second. He may have saved my life today."

The anger on Victor's face changed to confusion. "What's that supposed to mean?"

I turned away, still smiling. "You'll see."

*****Chapter 21*****

The next morning dawned bright and clear. The island hung in the water, a bright spot in the sea of blue. A few lonely palm trees lined the beach. It was the perfect spot to leave someone so they would never be found again.

Not that either Hades or I would be facing that fate. We both made it abundantly clear to the other one of us was not making it off that island alive.

My hysterical optimism had started to fade and I was starting to get nervous. I talked to Derry earlier, and he enthusiastically agreed to keep the blowgun until I needed it.

I hated being nervous. Hades held enough power over me. I was finished letting him control my emotions. I was going to kill him for daring to do so again.

I let my anger overtake me. I knew it probably wasn't the best course of action, but it was better than being scared.

There were six of us who went to the deserted island in a small rowboat. Victor and Harry, as witnesses. Hades and myself. Derry and another sailor named Seamus as our seconds. I never had a chance to talk to Seamus before this, and I observed him curiously as we rowed towards the shore. His hair was bright red and his face covered in freckles. When you combined that with his name, he had to be an Irishman, which was confirmed when he opened his mouth to speak.

"How much farther?" His brogue was heavy, so heavy I almost had to strain to understand him.

Hades, Victor, and I ignored him. Harry was the one who answered. "Not much," he said. "Come on, row harder. The sooner we get there the sooner we can get this over with."

I was in complete agreement with Harry on this point. I needed to finish this and the sooner the better.

We had agreed on one pistol each, followed by cutlasses. I figured I would take my chances with the bullets. Once the swords started clanging, Derry would find an opportunity to throw me the blowgun, and I would kill Hades once and for all.

I saw Hades double-checking his pistol out of the corner of my eye. I ignored him. Kwaku and Derry had already double checked my pistol before we left. I wasn't planning on being able to kill Hades with it, anyway.

Finally, finally, I felt the boat hit the shore. Derry and Seamus jumped overboard. Hades and I followed, pulling the boat up onto dry land. Victor and Harry got out. Harry started pacing a circle in the ground.

The circle wasn't for anything other than our starting positions. Hades and I would each start on one end, our backs towards each other. On Victor's command, we would both spin and fire, and then drop pistols and start slashing at each other with cutlasses, assuming either of us were still alive after that exchange.

Most duels I heard of had both participants shooting as fast as they could in hopes of getting their shot off before their opponent. I was hoping to try a different approach. All I had to do was dodge the first bullet.

Dodge the first bullet. Which was much easier said than done. And I couldn't use my gift to make Hades forget where I really was.

Nevertheless, I had no choice. I exchanged looks with Derry and he nodded solemnly.

I turned to Victor and took a deep breath. "Ready," I said.

Victor sighed. "Are the two of you still prepared to see this to the end?" he said.

Hades growled in agreement. I merely nodded without looking at him. The only time I would look him in the eye after this was when I killed him.

Victor nodded. "You both know the rules. One pistol, then cutlasses. Take your places in the circle."

The sun was low in the east, so I deliberately went and picked a spot at the northern edge of the circle. This way Hades couldn't claim I was trying to gain an advantage by making him face the light, and he couldn't do the same to me.

He had intended to; I saw that immediately from the angry glint in his eye. That was all I saw before Victor ordered the two of us to turn around.

I obeyed, my heart starting to pound in my chest. The world seemed to narrow. I had to avoid being killed. I had to kill Hades.

"Draw your pistols!"

I nearly fumbled as I drew the pistol out of its holster. I tried to calm down, but it wasn't working. Fear and anger were destroying any chance I might have.

"Begin!"

It was an instinctive reaction. Instead of spinning around, I dropped to the ground just as Hades' gun went off. It was so close I heard the shot whiz over my head.

Hades roared in outrage and I scrambled to my feet, pointing my gun in his general direction. My hands were shaking, but I managed to aim for center mass and fire.

I couldn't tell if I hit or not. Hades certainly didn't seem to slow any. I backed up a few steps and drew my cutlass. Hades came charging towards me, his cutlass held high in the air.

I sidestepped, barely parrying the swing of his sword as he ran past me. I managed to glance at Derry. I needed that blowgun now.

My eyes widened, and I felt my breath catch in my throat. Derry was deep in an argument with Seamus, who seemed intent on getting something from the boy. Harry was watching with concern, but not as if he was about to interfere.

I knew at that moment my plan had failed. Hades had seen the blowgun, despite my best efforts to keep him from suspecting. He knew Derry held it, but instead of calling me out, he had decided to let Seamus take it off the boy.

I backed away as Hades starting coming towards me again. The fight between the two of us had just taken on an added dimension. Despite myself, I knew Victor was right. I had no real hope of beating Hades in a cutlass fight. Especially not since Hades was the one to teach me almost everything I knew about fighting.

I blocked his strike again, but this time I was desperate. I fell back, and I saw the satisfaction in Hades' eyes.

Anger welled up inside me. I couldn't let this man take everything I gained. He held too much power over me, and now that I finally had regained it, he was stealing it again. He was going to kill me just to prove I had no power.

I attacked, but Hades blocked me easily and came in with a repose. I stifled a yelp as his cutlass scratched my arm, right in the same place I was hit in the fight in St. John's.

"Stop, you two! Stop!"

My head jerked around at the noise, and luckily Hades' did as well, otherwise I surely would have been dead. But the shout wasn't directed at the two of us. The argument between Derry and Seamus turned into a full-scale scuffle, with Seamus trying to throttle the boy and Derry trying to poke out Seamus's eyes. Victor and Harry were trying to break the two of them up.

I turned my gaze back to Hades who, at the moment, was still distracted. I took a chance and leapt forward, bringing my cutlass down in the same move he used so very often.

It nearly worked, but unfortunately Hades saw me coming at the last minute. He blocked me, and his teeth bared into a feral grin.

"Your secret weapon is useless, now!" he shouted. "You have no chance against me! You may as well accept that, Josephine!"

I ignored him and focused on parrying the numerous attacks. I tried to ignore the nagging feeling that he was right. I had no chance. And with Derry distracted, there was no way I could get my hands on the blowgun.

My arm wrenched as I tried to parry the next attack. Hades grinned and hit my sword again. Despite my best efforts, my cutlass went flying out of my hand, nearly tearing my arm out of its socket. I gasped and tried to stagger backwards, but Hades was advancing faster than I could retreat.

His grin was evil. "You're helpless now," he said. "Why don't you just admit you were always helpless? That you were a fool to try to escape me?"

I clenched my fists. "Would you let me live if I did?" I snapped. I was stalling. I needed a way to get back to my cutlass.

Hades laughed. "Of course not," he said. "But I'm not going to kill you until you admit it."

That could be my chance. I dove in the direction my cutlass lay, only to have Hades snatch it up from the ground before I could get near.

"No chance," he repeated. "Admit it."

I wasn't about to. I glared at him, fists clenched, waiting for him to make a move.

The grin didn't fade from his face as he started advancing, but suddenly he slowed. I watched warily as he took another step, then another, then slowly toppled to the ground.

I looked around in surprise and saw my answer. Harry and Victor finally succeeded in separating Derry and Seamus. Harry still had Seamus firmly pinned, and Victor had his sword to his throat, but Derry was standing free, and was slipping something back underneath his shirt.

The boy had killed Hades for me. I stared at Derry, trying to comprehend my emotions.

He grinned at me, obviously misreading my reaction, and shook his head. I nodded slightly in comprehension. He didn't want Victor or Harry realizing what he had just done.

"What in the hells." Harry released Seamus and started forward. I watched Seamus warily, but he just stood there. Maybe now that Hades was dead, there was no point in him trying to keep me from cheating.

Because I cheated. I stood over Hades as Victor checked him for a pulse. I was the one to challenge him to a duel, and I let someone else kill him for me. I knew I couldn't beat him in a fair fight, so I changed the rules. If that wasn't cowardly, I didn't know what was.

Victor shook his head. "He's dead," he said. "Can't tell why."

"Maybe he died of anger?" Derry suggested. "He was certainly mad enough at Jo."

Victor turned cool, calculating eyes on Derry. In that moment, I knew that Derry and I were in trouble. He knew Derry killed Hades. He knew I cheated in the duel.

"That's quite possible," he said. "I've heard of such things happening, though I've never seen it myself."

He turned towards me. "Well, congratulations, Jo. Since the duel and quarrel is now resolved, you are welcome again on the Reliance."

I swallowed and nodded. I took a step towards Hades, trying to convince myself to look at the body. I took my cutlass from his hand.

"You cheater!"

I turned just in time to see Seamus charging me. Without conscious thought, I pointed my cutlass at him.

He should have parried. He had his sword out and everything. Instead, he ran right onto my blade, his eyes widening in shock. My blade slid into his unresisting flesh, and I let go in horror. Seamus staggered back a step, his eyes widening.

"Cheater..." he whispered, before collapsing to the sand.

I stared at him, bile rising in my throat. I hadn't intended to kill him. I didn't even know him very well. What hurt worse, though, was that every word he said was true.

"God damn!" Harry rushed forward and turned Seamus over. Even I could see it was much too late to do anything to save him. The blood was everywhere, covering his clothes, his face, and my cutlass. I looked away, trying not to be sick.

"Well, that solves that problem."

I looked at Victor in shock, and he shrugged. "If you hadn't killed him, I would have had to figure out how to pay him to keep silent. Interfering in a duel is forbidden, and I would hate to punish Derry for that."

Derry crossed his arms indignantly, and Victor raised a hand. "Don't speak," he ordered. "As far as I'm concerned, Hades died of heart failure. Don't say anything that could make me think otherwise."

Derry snapped his mouth shut. I felt sick.

Victor turned to look at me. "Retrieve your cutlass, Jo," he said. "Let's head back to the Reliance. We have pirating to do, and you have just proven you are quite an able pirate."

His words struck me like a blow. Was that what I had just done? Was cheating the mark of a successful pirate?

I didn't have time to ponder now. I would have time back on the ship. I retrieved my sword and washed most of the blood off in the surf. I climbed uneasily back into the rowboat.

Victor, Harry, and Derry climbed in beside me. Apparently we were just going to leave the corpses on the beach.

"So, Harry, who do you think the new bos'n should be?"

I tried to ignore the conversation as I began to row. I was just a bit miserable.

Harry shrugged. "Why are you asking me?" he said. "You'll make your pick just as you please, whatever else I say."

Victor grinned. "But I value your opinion, old friend," he said. "Do you think the men would object if I named a woman to stand over them?"

My gaze snapped to Victor in shock. Had I really heard him right? He was thinking of naming me bos'n? It was laughable!

Instead of laughing, however, Harry seemed to be contemplating his answer very seriously. "Before today, I would have said no," he said. "Now, however, she has proven that she has a strong of heart as any of the men. She has no hesitations about killing and fighting. I think the men would accept her, especially after learning she killed Hades."

This couldn't be happening. I looked back and forth from Victor to Harry, my mouth dropping open.

Victor laughed at me. "Don't act so surprised, Jo," he said. "Nothing's official yet. Wait until we get back to the ship."

I snapped my mouth shut.

"I think it's great!" Derry piped up. "Jo would make an awesome bos'n! I like her!"

Victor laughed again. "You see, Jo? It's not such an unreasonable idea after all. You already have the loyalty of one of the most important members of my ship."

I shook my head numbly. Victor was teasing me. I had just cheated in a duel. He was getting back at me because of it. This was my way of repaying the cheating.

"You won't have a chance of being bos'n if we don't get back to the ship," Harry said.

With a start, I realized I had stopped rowing. I blocked out the rest of their words and focused on rowing. They weren't serious. I knew they weren't serious. We would get back to the Reliance and things would go back to normal.

*****Chapter 22*****

Of course I was wrong.

Everyone was waiting when we got back to the ship. Even though there was technically work to be done, everyone found an excuse to be on deck when our rowboat pulled alongside. I climbed up the rope Jacob's ladder and found myself staring at a sea of faces.

The murmurs that went through the pirates when I climbed onboard nearly made me flinch. They were full of disbelief and awe. No one expected me to come back from fighting Hades, apparently.

Victor climbed aboard after me, followed by Harry and Derry. There were more murmurs when people realized that Seamus was missing.

Victor stared at the crowd and laughed. "Well, apparently I don't need to call you all together!" he shouted. "Jo is the winner of the duel between herself and Hades. Any man who wishes to challenge the outcome must first come to me."

Murmurs swept the crowd again, but this time they were murmurs of satisfaction. I didn't know what to do or think, so I just stood still and stared.

Victor's smile turned wry. "This does mean, of course, that we are in need of a new bos'n," he said. "I don't think anyone will doubt my choice when I appoint Jo to the position. She has proved her mettle often enough, first by saving my life and now by killing one of the finest swordsmen I have ever known."

There was a brief moment of silence, and then Derry let out a whoop. The cheer was followed by the rest of the pirates.

I stared at them in shock. They were cheering me becoming bos'n? Me, a woman, and a colored one at that?

They had every reason to be angry at me instead of happy for me. Any number of them probably had prior claims on the position. And yet, I couldn't find a single face in the crowd that wasn't genuinely pleased with what Victor said.

"Make a note of this in the logs, Harry," Victor said. "Bos'n, come to my cabin, and I will instruct you on your new duties."

It took me a moment before I fully comprehended he was talking to me. I followed him to his cabin in a daze, still trying to realize what had just happened.

As soon as the door closed behind me, Victor pressed me up against it. "You are an idiot and a genius," he hissed. "What in God's name did you think you were doing?"

I flushed. "Winning," I snapped. "I wasn't about to let him kill me."

"You could have gone about it in a smarter way," Victor growled. "You nearly died so many times out there. If you just wanted to kill him, there were much better ways to go about it."

I stared at him in confusion. I thought he was annoyed because I cheated. He seemed more annoyed about the fact I almost died a number of times.

"I cheated," I said slowly, trying to gauge his reaction.

He snorted. "Everyone cheats," he said. "You were smart too. You knew Hades would kill you in a fair fight, so you changed the rules. That's how we survive out here. Nothing wrong with that."

In fact, I could see a great many things wrong with that, but I held my tongue. Victor was continuing to speak.

"I was about to interfere in the fight, if that bastard Seamus hadn't started the scuffle with Derry," he continued. "Did you really think I would have let you die?"

I stared at him. I hadn't even thought about it.

"Why did you call for a duel?" Victor demanded. "You could have used Derry's blowgun and killed him at any time aboard the ship. I don't know why I let the boy have that, except it's proven invaluable on a number of occasions. But why wait until we got to the island to use it?"

He was being serious, I realized. He honestly wanted to know the answer.

I took a deep breath, trying to decide how to say it. "Because Hades would have seen it," I said. "He did, actually. That's why Derry and Seamus were fighting. He knew what my plan was. He had seen Derry and I talking, and deduced the reason."

Victor's brows furrowed. "Everyone has seen you and Derry talking," he said. "There's nothing odd about that."

I shook my head. "You knew there was something odd about Hades," I said. "You mentioned it to me when you found out I was a woman. Hades could see things others couldn't. That's why he knew I was going to kill him."

Victor's eyes narrowed. "He saw through your disguise," he said.

I hadn't expected him to come to the conclusion so quickly, but I nodded. "I told you he was blackmailing me," I said.

Victor nodded, his demeanor changing. "You still should have killed him outright. Or told me about the blackmail."

I lost my temper. "Why should I have done that?" I demanded. "How in God's name was I to know if you would support Hades or me? He'd been on the ship for a lot longer than I had, and I had already proven I was a liar by dressing up as a man!"

I saw anger flare in Victor's eyes, but I didn't care. I went to push him away from me, but he held me fast, drew me close, and kissed me.

I wondered a moment why all of our fights seemed to end in this position, but I hardly cared. I kissed him back with all the passion my anger stirred.

A while later, we lay on his bed, idly running our hands over each other. In a low voice, Victor started telling me what my duties would be now that I was bos'n. I listened closely.

There wasn't much different from my normal duties as a sailor. The most distinct difference was that now I would have to sit in on the officer's meetings, and I was in charge of directing the men to where they would work.

We lay silent for a while. "Why would you kill any man who lay a hand on me?" I finally asked.

Victor raised an eyebrow, but didn't seem surprised by the question. "Because it's in the articles."

I glared at him, though without any real heat. "And why is it in the articles?"

He sighed. "Do you really want to know?"

I nodded.

Victor paused, running his hands over my shoulders as he stared off into space. I let him think. Somehow I had the feeling this was more serious than I had originally anticipated.

"I had a sister, once."

His words startled me, and I turned to stare at him. His eyes were still staring off into space.

"She was a decent girl. Always was. The good one of the two of us. The one who was a credit to society." He laughed shortly. "The one to whom nothing bad should have ever happened."

I bit my lip. I could already tell where this was going.

"She was sailing from St. Kitts to Port Royal. Pirates attacked. They did not treat anyone on that crew, or any of the passengers, gently. My sister died a few weeks after her arrival in Port Royal because of their actions."

I couldn't think of anything to say to that. Victor continued on.

"I wasn't captain yet, but a few months later I was. I found out the name of the ship that had attacked my sister. And I made them pay." His voice was hard.

I reached to where his hand was stroking my shoulder and squeezed it. His eyes met mine.

"I swore then that my crew would never be responsible for such an act. So it went in the articles."

It was on the tip of my tongue to ask what the difference was between rape and murder and piracy, but I stopped myself. Somehow, I knew there was a difference, even if I couldn't define it.

Victor smiled then, and the blankness I had seen in his eyes disappeared. He leaned down and kissed me. "So no one will lay a hand on you, bos'n."

Bos'n.

"You're sure men will obey me?" I asked again. Despite the crew's reaction, I still harbored severe doubts about the wisdom of this plan.

Victor laughed. "Of course they will," he said. "You'll see."

I shook my head. I couldn't dissuade him, but I still doubted him. I was a woman, and a dark-skinned one at that. Why would the men on board respect me?

But Victor did. And I had proven my worth by killing Hades, as horrible as that sounded. There wasn't a man on this ship who would currently challenge me. And by the time their awe faded away, I would have proven myself again. I would make sure of that.

*****Chapter 23*****

The next few months were like a perfect dream. Perfect if you were a pirate, at least. We attacked a number more ships and I started accumulating quite a fortune in gold. Not that I cared. Everyone else would go get drunk the first minute we were in port and I would watch them. I saved a great deal of money that way, and it was amusing as well.

Victor became a large part of my life onboard the Reliance as well. We still couldn't have an argument without us ending up in bed with each other. I didn't mind. I was enjoying our time together far too much.

The men came to respect me, as well. For myself, and not just for my actions. Even once people started realizing I was sleeping with the captain, their respect for me didn't fade. Kwaku became my right hand man, and Derry my eternal admirer.

Other than that, I studied my gift. I experimented with several of the rituals Hades told me about before I killed him. Most of them worked. Not as well as he said they would, but they did work. I started changing them a little, trying to figure out if the rituals should be changed because of the difference between our gifts. I made a few realizations, but nothing that could be counted as a breakthrough.

I hardly cared anymore. I was happy, odd as it was to say. I was a pirate. The law would catch up to us sooner or later, I knew that. Even so, I wished for this time to last forever.

Of course it didn't. It couldn't. But I didn't expect it to end the way it did.

We were in Charleston that day, a small port town on the coast. I had never been this far north before. The feel in the air was odd. I was used to a lot more humidity.

I was wandering the streets that night with Victor, Harry, and Kwaku. We were searching for a good pub, one that would let us spend the money we just "liberated" from a wealthy French merchant. Technically, the English were allies with the French at this time. I thought. Their allegiances kept switching. Anyway, even if they knew, we doubted the English in Charleston would object to us spending money stolen from the French.

"There we are!" Victor roared, pointing at a sign above a door. It had a rooster sitting on top of a brick.

I furrowed my brow. "What's the name of that place?" I asked.

Harry started laughing. We all already had a few drinks, even me.

I waited for someone to answer, but they were all laughing too hard. I put my hands on my hips. "I'm waiting."

Kwaku was the one who finally regained enough control to answer me. "The cockblock!" he wheezed, before falling back into laughter again.

I had to admit, it was funny. I didn't think it was as funny as the other three seemed to, but I chuckled anyway. "Do you guys want more drink, or are you just going to stand here?" I asked.

Laughing, the other three followed me into the bar.

At first glance, it seemed like any of the other places we had spent our nights in. The innkeeper was even friendly, seeing that we had plenty of gold to spend. A few lovely ladies fell in step alongside us. One of them even tried to flirt with me. I hadn't used my disguise in months, but I still kept to men's clothes. Apparently that was enough to fool a lot of people.

I ignored the woman and sat down at the table Victor had claimed for the four of us. Harry pulled out a deck of cards. "Anyone for a game?" he asked.

Of course we were all for a game. Harry began dealing, while I tried to steady my spinning head in order to concentrate.

We were a few hands in when I sensed something was wrong. I looked up towards the door and froze at the sight of a face I thought was long banished from my life.

Washed-out brown eyes framed by slicked back hair met my gaze as I sat there. He didn't seem to see me, and instead walked up towards the bartender.

I slammed my cards down on the table. "I have to go," I said. "I'll see you back at the ship."

I ignored the startled protests of the others as I nearly raced for the door, my heart beating in my chest, praying the man at the bar wouldn't decide to turn around.

I made it out onto the street, but I didn't slow down. I ran all the way back to the docks. It was only when my feet set foot on the Reliance that I allowed myself to breathe.

Reddings. What the hell was he doing here? And in a low-class tavern, at that? Last I knew, rich, white plantation owners didn't spend their time at sailor's pubs. It was one of the reasons I felt so safe going to them.

I shivered, unreasonable fear welling up in me. I prayed to the gods he hadn't seen me. He gave no sign of recognition, and I did look quite a bit different from the plantation daughter he had pretended to court. He was an actor and a charmer, though. How would I have been able to tell if he recognized me?

I was scared, and I hated myself for it. Angrily, I tried to talk some sense into myself. There was no way Reddings would search for me onboard a pirate ship. I was safe. If nothing else, we were due to sail in the morning. There was no way Reddings would be able to track our movements. Even if he recognized me, I was out of his reach.

I couldn't convince myself of that, however. I shivered again, my hands clutching at the rail. I thought I was free. I thought killing Hades set me free from being pursued and blackmailed. Apparently, I wasn't.

"Jo?"

I whirled, not expecting the sound. It was Victor, of course. He was standing behind me, his arms crossed over his chest. "Would you mind explaining to me what just happened there?"

I stared at Victor for a long moment. His eyes darkened.

"Answer me, Jo," he said. "If something is threatening you, I need to know about it."

I took a deep breath, and my entire body shuddered. Instantly, Victor came forward and clasped his hands around mine.

"Who was it who came through that door?" he demanded.

I took another deep breath. "A man," I whispered. "A man called Mr. Edward Reddings."

Victor's eyes narrowed. "And what is this Mr. Reddings to you?" he asked.

I shuddered again. I hated myself at that moment. To know Reddings could still have so much power over me long after I should be free of him was infuriating.

"I was supposed to marry him," I said. "At least, that's what everyone around me said I should do. That's what Reddings said he wanted. But I could tell." I sucked in another breath.

Victor waited, uncharacteristically patient.

Finally, I drew myself together and looked Victor in the eye. "He would have kept me as his slave, rather than his wife," I said shortly. "And I would have been helpless to do anything about it."

Victor cocked his head. "Even with your abilities?"

I bit my lip and nodded. "Mr. Reddings has abilities of his own." My voice cracked. "He can charm anyone he wants to. And he can see right through anything I do."

Victor's breath hissed in understanding. He released my hands, only to fold his arms around me.

I huddled in his arms, hardly wondering at the oddness of my situation. There was no way Victor loved me, but yet he was comforting me in the only way he knew how. And what was even odder was that it was working.

I took one final shuddering breath and straightened. "We sail tomorrow, right?" I asked.

He nodded.

"Then I shouldn't worry," I said. "There's no way he'll be able to trace us, if he even realized I was in the tavern. I look rather different dressed as a man than as a plantation daughter."

Victor laughed. "You, dressed as a plantation daughter? Now there's a sight I would like to see someday."

I glared at him, but there was too much relief for me to be truly angry. "It was what I was for seventeen years," I snapped.

He put his arms around me again, and I didn't resist. "I don't think it suited you," he said. "This is where you belong."

I narrowed my eyes, but Victor couldn't see my expression. This was where I belonged? It was where I ended up, certainly, but I hadn't given any thought to it being permanent. Everyone knew the life of a pirate usually ended well before old age.

Whatever I might have said to that vanished as Victor kissed me. I let myself surrender to his embrace as he dragged me back towards his cabin. Whatever he might mean by those words, it didn't matter in the long run.

****

We left the next morning as planned. Although I was antsy and irritable, there was no sign of anything out of the ordinary. No one was watching our ship with any kind of suspicion. And there was no sign of Mr. Reddings.

It was with great relief I watched the shore slip out of sight, however. I sighed in relief as land vanished from view.

"That grateful to be back at sea?"

I laughed at Kwaku's surprised expression. "Aren't you?" I was giddy with relief.

Kwaku shook his head. "Of course, but not like you," he said. "You couldn't wait to see the last of that place."

I shrugged, unwilling to admit to anyone else what had shaken me so bad. "It's all sorted," was all I said. "Shall we see to the daily running of the ship? It will likely fall apart if we're not there to supervise."

Kwaku nodded and dropped the subject. I started walking down the deck towards the ship's wheel.

I was joking about the daily running of the ship. At this point, it mostly ran itself. All I had to do was be present, which left me free to continue my lessons, both from David, and now from Victor.

Victor was waiting for me at the helm. "Jo!" he called. "Time for some practical navigation!"

It was his word for steering. I shook my head, laughing, as I took over the helm. "What's our course, captain?"

"Zero eight zero," Victor replied. "Heading south again. Port Royal sounds like a fine place to dock next."

I nearly choked. "Port Royal?" I asked.

Victor looked at me curiously. "Something wrong?" he asked.

I thought for a moment. There wasn't actually anyone who would be a danger to me in Port Royal. Reddings was in Charleston. Anyone else wasn't likely to remember me.

"No," I said slowly. "There's nothing wrong with Port Royal."

Victor crossed his arms. "Jo," he said warningly.

I glared at him. "I'm from Jamaica, is all. I haven't been home since I first ran away."

Victor seemed wary, but he accepted my explanation. I felt my temper bubbling. It was the truth!

"We're hoping to liberate a few ships along the way," Victor said. "Coffers are full, but there could always be more, right? The crew will be happy."

I nodded. I honestly couldn't care less about how full our coffers were, but I had begun to enjoy attacking other ships, much as it pained me to admit it. There was an adrenaline rush that came from nowhere else. It had been months since an attack made me sick.

"So, if Reddings wanted to make a slave out of you, why was your family willing to see you married?"

I nearly jumped at the change of topic. I glared at Victor. "Can we not talk about him?" I asked.

Victor shook his head. "You've got to face it," he said. "I can see it eating you alive, now that I know it's there."

I glared at him for a long while, but he remained unmoved. Finally, I sighed. "He can charm anyone," I said. "Anyone without a gift of their own. My parents adored him. They thought he was the most wonderful man to grace this planet. And to top it off, he was willing to marry me. Not many men were."

Victor raised an eyebrow at that. "That seems unlikely to me," he said.

I laughed. "What man who met my parent's approval would want a half-breed tomboy who's more likely to lash at him with her tongue than behave in a proper womanly fashion?" I demanded. "There aren't many of those out there, Victor."

He shrugged. "I'm sure there had to be a few."

I shook my head. "Mr. Reddings was the first one to make an offer for my hand," I said. "And even he didn't actually want me. He was courting another woman at the same time, a rich, white one. She would have been his wife. I would have been his slave."

"That's the thing that frightens you most," Victor said. "Slavery?"

I tightened my grip on the helm. "I am not frightened," I said. My voice was shaking so badly I knew it gave away my lie. I stared straight ahead.

"He has too much power over you from this far away," Victor said. "And none of it is physical. Get over your fear, Jo. He can't come after you anymore."

I knew Victor was right. Truly, I knew. But I couldn't convince myself of it.

*****Chapter 24*****

We went for over a week without seeing the slightest trace of another sail. I didn't mind, but I could tell the crew was starting to get restless. We were almost to Jamaica, and some of the crew spent all the ready cash they had back in Charleston. If we didn't attack another ship and gain a good bounty, they would be penniless in Port Royal.

I shook my head at the folly of the men. All they spent their money on was whores and alcohol. There were better things to waste your money on.

Derry was on lookout watch when the sail was finally spotted. He was so excited he nearly fell out of the crow's nest proclaiming the news.

I joined Victor and Harry on the deck as they stared out towards the ship. "What kind of ship is it?" I demanded.

Victor shrugged. "Large one," he said. "But there's very few people on deck, and they're all moving fast. They can't have very many extra guards."

I raised an eyebrow. "Is it worth it to take it?"

A grin spread over Victor's face. "The crew would kill me if we didn't," he said. "They've been spoiling for a good fight. So have you."

I glared at Victor, but he had already turned his attention back to the ship. "What do you think, Harry? Good cargo onboard?"

Harry shrugged. "Guess we'll find out," he said.

Victor nodded. "Lads! Prepare for attack!"

The preparations for attack were so ingrained in the crew's memory I didn't need to issue any additional orders. I walked through the main deck and below deck anyway, checking to make sure that the cannons were concealed, and that every cannon had their crew of gunners. Kwaku was manning one of the guns on the port side, and he gave me a cocky salute as I passed.

Now came the worst part of attacking another ship. The waiting.

I decided to take a chance. I wasn't going to disguise our entire ship like Hades made me do, but disguising the colors couldn't be such a bad idea.

"What colors does she fly?" I called to Victor.

"English," Victor said shortly. "Probably heading the same place we are."

I nodded in satisfaction and drew on my power, muttering a short ritual under my breath. This ritual wasn't very powerful, but I shouldn't need much from it.

I heard Derry's shout of surprise as the colors changed to English, and I grinned in satisfaction. Victor looked from me, to the colors, and back again.

"Nice work," he said. "That will let us get much closer."

I shrugged. "Should have done it earlier," I said. "It's a good trick, assuming they don't have anyone who can see through it."

Victor shrugged. "One day I'll get a collection of every country's flag," he said. "Allow us to sail with impunity. That would be the goal, at least."

I laughed. "Or you can just keep me around."

Victor smiled and said nothing. I returned to watching the ship as it drew near.

I hated how long it seemed to take for us to approach another ship. It could take hours, depending on the winds, tides, and currents. I was learning all the reasons from David, but knowing why didn't help when you were staring at a wide gap that was only slowly closing.

Finally, the ship sailed into a range where we could actually see the people on deck without use of a spyglass.

I narrowed my eyes. There were a lot fewer people than there should have been for this size of ship.

"Looks like easy prey!"

I nodded absently at the sailor's words. Something felt off about this, and I didn't know why.

"Jo, tell the men below to be ready at the cannons," Victor said. "We'll give them a full broadside first, then see how they react before we swing around to board."

I nodded and ran down below.

"Everyone ready?" I shouted. "Be ready for a broadside!"

I was answered with a chorus of shouts. Kwaku gave me a thumb's up before I ran back to the top deck.

I stared at Victor, waiting for his signal. I was the one who was going to relay his orders to down below. That was the bos'n's job, at least until we boarded. Then I was one of the boarding party.

"Fire!" Victor roared.

"Fire!" I screamed down below.

Immediately, the air was full of the sound of cannon fire and cracking wood. The smell of fire and smoke filled the air, and my eyes started to water.

I scrambled back above deck in case Victor had any more commands to pass on, but he didn't even turn towards me. There was chaos on the deck of the other ship, but a few sailors were rallying, obviously ready to fight.

"Stay ready!" I shouted to the men manning the cannons. I didn't know what Victor was planning, but it never hurt to be prepared.

I watched as Victor calmly ordered the helmsman to bring the Reliance around. We were going for another broadside, then.

"Prepare for another volley, boys!" I shouted. "Captain's bringing us around!"

A chorus of voices answered me, all in the affirmative. For a brief second, I allowed myself to be amazed they obeyed me without question. Me, a dark-skinned woman. And most of them were white men.

"Ready, Jo?"

I turned to see Victor looking at me. I glanced down below. "Kwaku! Are we ready?"

His answering shout was loud and strong. "Aye, Bos'n!"

I turned back to Victor. "Aye, Captain!"

"Then fire again!"

"Fire!" I shouted down to Kwaku.

Once again, the air filled with shouts, screams, and the roar of cannon fire. I flinched involuntarily as I saw one of our cannonballs hit the mast of the other ship, causing it to wobble dangerously.

"She's crippled, captain!" Harry's voice was joyous.

"Bring her around, helmsman!" Victor shouted. "Prepare to board!"

I shouted down to the men below that they were free to secure and board, then raced to my own spot on deck, drawing my cutlass as I did so. My pistol was ready in my left hand.

I found myself standing beside Victor as we pulled up alongside the other ship. "Ready, Jo?" he asked, grinning at me.

I couldn't stop myself from grinning back. "Ready," I answered.

Victor gave me a salute, then grabbed a line hanging down from the mast. "Grappling hooks!" he called. "Gunners, give them something to think about!"

Immediately, the air was filled with the sound of gunfire. Screams from the deck of the other ship were illustrative of how effective our gunners were. I couldn't stop a surge of pride.

"Let's go, boys!"

With shouts and whoops and battle cries, the pirates started swinging themselves over to the other ship.

I was right behind Victor. I waited until the distance had closed, and then I leaped over, pistol and cutlass ready at hand. I saw Kwaku engaging two swordsmen at once, and decided to even his odds by leaping into the fray.

They didn't see me coming, and by the time I got there, it was too late for them to rally. One of them turned to face me, but that left him wide open for Kwaku's strike. The other tried to turn and run, but my cutlass found his gut.

I tore it free and looked around, searching for another target.

"Jo! With me!"

I ran to join Victor, who stood with Harry and Isaac. "We're going down below, he said. "Captain's not out here. We need to find him."

I nodded. Only the captain had the authority to surrender the ship, after all.

Isaac turned to open a hatch in the deck. "Be ready," he said. "They could be waiting."

In answer, I switched my pistol to my right hand. Isaac nodded in approval and swung the hatch open.

No one was waiting for us, and we charged ahead, Victor and me in the lead.

It was dark below decks, much darker than it should have been. I felt tension building inside of me. On the Reliance there were lights everywhere, even during the day. Light made for good morale, after all. We were adamant about fire safety and no open flames ever burned below decks, but a small, closed lantern hung in every passageway. Even the Vixen had been the same.

Victor growled until his breath. "Bad captain," he said. "Can't be a happy crew."

I had to agree. It was dark, dank, and uncomfortable down here. Morale had to be low.

I was distracted from my thoughts by the sound of steel being pulled out of a sheath. I turned just in time to see three men charging us, swords in hand.

I fired my pistol, hitting one of them in the shoulder. He dropped behind, and I slammed my pistol back into its holster before switching my cutlass to my right hand.

My cutlass turned out to be unnecessary. Both Victor and Isaac had also gotten shots off, and the other two men dropped with various injuries. Victor hauled one of them up by the neck, groaning.

"Where's your captain?" he demanded. "Where is the coward who won't come out to fight? You should have no loyalty to a man like that."

Weakly, the man pointed down the passageway. A door was at the end, barely visible.

Victor dropped the man onto the deck. "Get ready," he snapped.

I had a second pistol, and I took it out of its holster and made sure it was ready. I held it in my left hand, though. The quarters down here were far too close for safe gunfire.

The four of us lined up at the door. A sound from behind distracted us, but it was only Kwaku and one of our gunners running up.

"Deck's secure, Captain," the gunner gasped. "No sign of the captain, though."

"He's through here," Victor growled.

The gunner nodded and lined up next to Kwaku.

Victor looked at Harry. "Now!" he hissed.

Harry kicked the door, and it broke open, smashing into the room beyond.

Shouts of terror were the first thing I registered, then I saw a white, plump, man holding a sword and shaking. Four men stood around him, obviously guarding him. They looked to be much better fighters than the one in the center.

I waited a split second, and with good reason. The gunner, Harry, and Kwaku all fired, dropping two of the guards. I charged forward, ignoring my pistol.

I knew the man I engaged was good, but he was no match for Victor, Kwaku, and me all at once. Harry, Isaac, and the gunner swarmed the other guard. Victor and I both managed killing blows on our guard at the same time.

Victor turned towards the man. "Are you the captain of this benighted ship, you coward?"

The man started to stammer something out, but I ignored him. I looked beyond into the cabin and gasped.

It was a huge room. It must have taken up at least half of the below-decks. There were no furnishings, and no storage. It was all lined with rows and rows of people. They were chained together hand and foot, and were looking at us with wide eyes.

I had heard of slave ships before. But seeing this was more than I had ever imagined.

Victor followed my gaze, then turned his eyes back to the captain. "You'd better answer," he said. "Otherwise my bos'n may have something to say to you. She has a dim opinion of your type of ship, you see."

Abruptly, I realized what Victor was trying to do. I turned blazing eyes towards the captain. He shrank back under my gaze.

"Well, are you the captain?"

"Y-y-yes!" the captain babbled. "Please, mercy, good sir, mercy!"

Victor laughed, his voice cold. "If you wanted mercy, you shouldn't have fought, idiot," he snapped. "Harry, Isaac, take him above deck. I want to deal with him in the light."

Harry and Isaac stepped forward to grab the captain's arms and drag him away.

I returned my gaze to the rows of people. Not one of them had moved, but they all stared at us, eyes wide.

Victor took my arm. "Leave them for now, Jo," he said. "We'll come to a decision amongst the crew. I promise it will be for the better."

I turned my glare on him. "You want to leave them down here, chained and helpless?" I snapped.

Victor grabbed my arm tighter. "Think, Jo," he snapped. "It will cause far too much confusion if we release them right now. Wait until we have the ship secured. Then we can figure out what to do."

I wasn't satisfied, but Kwaku unexpectedly chimed in. "He's right," he said. The tone in his voice caught me by surprise. There was a catch that was entirely unlike him.

I looked at Kwaku, surprised. Of all the people, I wouldn't have expected him to agree with leaving them chained.

"I've been here, Jo," Kwaku snapped. "Victor's right. It won't hurt them to be down here a few more hours."

I looked back at the rows of people. If Kwaku agreed...

I let Victor drag me out of the room and back towards the main deck. I was in a state of shock, I knew. I never expected to actually see a slave ship.

Victor made sure I stayed with him as we approached the captain, who was trembling, surrounded by our officers and a good handful of the crew. Only a few of the sailors of the slave ship remained alive and unwounded, and they were surrounded by the remainder of the pirates.

"Now, Captain," Victor said, his voice pleasant. "Suppose you tell me what your course and mission was."

The captain trembled and nearly collapsed into a puddle. I stared at him in disgust. Who would put a coward like this in charge of a ship?

"D-d-delivering slaves, good sir," the captain stammered.

Victor rolled his eyes. "I can see that," he said. "To where? And for whom? Or are you just working for yourself? I find that hard to believe, you worthless scumbag coward."

I had to admire Victor's tactics. My desire to tear the man's eyes out had to be written on my face. Victor was maintaining just an edge of civility, but with enough impatience to let the captain know that he would deal with me if he couldn't deal with Victor.

"To- to Port Royal," the captain stammered. "D-delivering slaves to Port Royal."

Victor took an obvious breath. "For whom?" he demanded.

Something stiffened the captain's spine, and I narrowed my eyes. This was not in character for the man.

"For the most illustrious plantation owner to exist on the island of Jamaica," the captain said. "Mr. Edward Reddings."

I nearly flew at the man right there. Kwaku was the one who grabbed my arm this time. I held myself back with a supreme answer of will.

"Jo," Victor said calmly. "Would you mind dealing with the rest of the sailors on this benighted ship? See if there are any likely recruits. If there aren't, I'm of a mind to teach these sailors a lesson about resisting our attacks."

I nodded shortly. Even if there were sailors who wanted to join us, I was not of a mind to let them. Victor's words let me know there was no need.

Kwaku followed me as I made my way towards the group of sailors. "You all right?" he asked softly.

I nodded shortly. I couldn't speak. I was so angry that anything I said would be a yell or an insult.

The circle of pirates parted to let me through. There were around ten of their men left alive, a good half of them injured in a small way. I could see a smaller group of men sitting on the ground, obviously severely injured. I wasn't worried about them.

"Who's in charge here?" I demanded.

The group of men turned, and one of them stepped forward, obviously bracing himself. I had a brief memory of myself standing on the Vixen, Tanner stepping forward. Now I was in Hades' shoes.

"What's your name, sailor?" I asked.

The man swallowed, then actually looked at me. "A woman?" he said, his voice incredulous. "You men let a woman be in charge?"

That was too much for me. I drew my cutlass and slashed the man across the face. He stumbled back, his eyes wide.

"Answer the question, scum," I said.

Defiance brimmed in the man's eyes. "Not to a woman," he said.

I couldn't take it anymore. Before the man could react, I drove my cutlass through his throat.

The gurgle he made as he went down was entirely too satisfying to me. I stared at the rest of the sailors.

"Anyone else care to answer that question without mocking me?" I demanded.

A long silence was the only answer I got.

My anger boiled up in me. I pointed at the first man I saw. "What's your name?" I demanded.

The man stared at me, then the man on the ground. He looked around, obviously considering the crowd of pirates around him.

"Do you want to share his fate?" I asked, getting impatient. "I was planning on just cutting off a finger, but if you really want to die."

The man jumped. "Quinn," he said. "Nate Quinn."

I allowed myself to smile, a cruel smile. "Good, Mr. Quinn," I said. "Now perhaps you can tell me about the man I just killed."

Quinn stared at the man lying on the deck, blood pouring out of his throat. "He was the boatswain," he said. "Frank Michaels."

"He was an idiot," I said. "Do I make myself clear?"

Quinn swallowed and nodded.

I turned away, disgusted. "Our captain has decided you need an example of why it is a bad idea to resist us," I said. "Since I see no brave souls who I would be willing to save, I believe it is time to continue with that example."

I turned to Kwaku. "Have them brought to me one at a time," I said. "They're each going to lose a finger. The man who brings them to me can make the choice of which one."

I saw bloodthirsty grins on the faces of my fellow pirates. For myself, I was so full of anger I was cold.

Kwaku nodded and pointed at Quinn. "You first."

I sheathed my cutlass and drew out my knife. I knew it was sharp enough for the task I had just set. I had spent the entire previous evening sharpening it.

I looked at the man who dragged Quinn to me. "What finger shall I cut off?" I asked. "Do keep in mind he did at least answer my questions. Eventually."

The man grinned at me. "If you want to be truly merciful, take the pinky," he said. "But the ring finger would do just as well. Can still work without those."

I smiled at him. "Your choice, my friend," I said. "Please tell me what hand, as well."

I couldn't stop myself from being satisfied at the way Quinn's body started to shake.

The pirate smiled a wide grin. "Left ring finger," he said. "He's got a ring."

He was right. It was a small silver ring, probably a marriage token.

I nodded. "You can take the ring," I told the pirate. He grinned in satisfaction and held Quinn's hand down. In one smooth motion, I brought my knife down on his finger.

Quinn screamed, one of the more bloodcurdling screams I'd ever heard. His finger dropped to the deck, to be scooped up eagerly by the pirate, who took the ring and slipped it onto his own finger.

I should have been disgusted. Instead, I was cold.

"Next," I said.

We went through the rest of the sailors in short order. I decided to leave the wounded ones alone. They were injured enough, and most of them would probably never recover fully anyway. They learned enough of a lesson.

I just finished when Victor came to find me.

"Are you done with these men, bos'n?" he asked.

I stared at the group of bleeding sailors. Some of them remained brave through the ordeal, but most were in various degrees of agony.

I nodded.

"Then come with me," Victor said. "We need to hold a vote."

I didn't know what Victor meant by that, but I followed him anyway.

I ended up in the captain's cabin with the rest of the Reliance's officers. It was an opulent cabin, much more richly furnished than Victor's. He sighed.

"I should have a cabin like this, shouldn't I?" he said.

Harry and Isaac laughed obligingly. I stared at them.

Victor cleared his throat. "We need to make a decision," he said. "The plunder we expected to seize from this ship has turned out to be human, rather than gold. We need to decide what happens to them."

The gunner, Eli, cleared his throat and looked at me. "Not to be cruel, but we could sell them," he suggested. "It's what they were bound for, anyway."

My jaw dropped open. "Are you seriously suggesting that?" I demanded.

Eli shrugged. "It's business," he said. "We want to get a profit. This is one way of doing so."

I wasn't going to stand for it. Victor laid a hand on my arm. "Are there any other options?" he asked. "And before we decide to sell them, how would we go about doing so?"

I couldn't believe my ears. I turned my gaze to Victor.

"We could have the captain here sell them, then turn the profits over to us," Harry suggested. "He's coward enough that he would do that."

Victor shrugged. "Any other options?"

I couldn't take it. "We could set them free," I said. "They aren't property, you idiots. Those are people down there. Humans, like you and me."

Eli shrugged. "That may be," he said. "But we need a profit from this enterprise."

I laughed, and the gunner stepped back, his eyes widening. I must have sounded crazy.

"Is profit all you bastards ever think about?" I demanded. "I saw women and children down in that hold. Are you seriously suggesting giving them to a cruel master, who will beat them and chain them for the rest of their lives? Ask Kwaku how that would feel. You could have asked Hades."

Victor held up his hand for silence, and I subsided. I still couldn't believe they were seriously considering selling those people for profit.

"Quartermaster," Victor said. "What else was there in that hold?"

Harry looked at a pile of notes. "Plenty of foodstuffs," he said. "Gold, too. Might have been pay for all the sailors. Not much, though."

"How much would it be if divided amongst the crew?" Victor said, his voice level.

Harry furrowed his brow as he tried to do the calculations. David looked over his shoulder and said, "Twenty shillings each."

Eli snorted. Victor quelled him with a look.

"Our options, as far as I can tell, are two," he said. "Sell them in the marketplace, and risk the wrath of whoever was supposed to buy them in the first place. Or, set them free, and give each man twenty shillings on top of what he would receive anyway."

Harry shifted in his seat. "Selling them sounds like a lot of trouble," he said.

Eli still looked rebellious, but the other officers were agreeing with Harry.

"Then let's vote," Victor said. "All in favor of selling them?"

Only Eli raised his hand.

"Of releasing them?"

Everyone else, with the exception of Victor himself, raised their hand. I let out my breath in a long sigh.

Victor nodded. "It's decided then," he said. "We'll release them. Jo, am I correct in the rumors of escaped slaves known as maroons on Jamaica?"

I blinked. I had heard rumors, but never anything substantial. "I think so."

"Then that's where we'll let them go. We'll make our way around the coast, to the east of Port Royal. They'll have to find their own way from there, but it will be a better life than they would have had."

I had to be satisfied with that. It was the most these people were going to receive.

"Dismissed," Victor said. "Jo, take Kwaku and two others and go down to unchain them. Tell them they are not to come above deck, though, not until we reach Jamaica. Tell them anything else they ask."

I nodded and nearly ran out the door.

Tuppence Van de Vaarst

*****Chapter 25*****

The rest of the day passed in something of a blur. I remember the rest of the crew conceding to the captain's plan rather reluctantly. It wasn't a rich haul we were getting, but, in my opinion, it was far better than selling anyone into slavery.

I had more vivid memories of the people below decks. They greeted my news with silence, but when Kwaku and I started unlocking their chains, movement and noise finally started to happen. Some wept with relief. Others curled up on themselves. The one that surprised me, however, was the woman who stood up and embraced me.

"Thank you," she said, her accent thick and heavy. "I will tell the others. Many do not speak English."

I returned her embrace hesitantly. She clung to me with a fierceness I had never experienced.

Finally, she pulled back and looked me straight in the eyes. Her hair was cropped short, like mine now was. Her skin was dark, of course, and her eyes were as black as midnight. She smiled. "I am Ria," she said.

I nodded. "Josephine," I said. I didn't know why I gave my full name. Everyone knew me as Jo. But for some reason, Ria seemed to deserve it.

Ria nodded. "Blessings to you, Josephine."

Not much after that, the meeting was clear. I finally ended up in my hammock on the Reliance, trying to manage some semblance of sleep.

I awoke the next morning feeling ill. My stomach was in revolt, and I barely managed to swing out of my hammock and stagger onto deck before throwing up. As soon as my stomach emptied itself of its contents, I felt better. Better and hungry.

I stared out at the flat sea, confused. I wasn't seasick. I knew what seasickness felt like, and this was not it. The hunger I felt gnawing at me was also completely different from any seasickness I had ever heard of. And who had ever gotten seasick on a flat sea? Not me.

I looked down at myself, considering. I shrugged. It must have been something I ate. Although that still didn't explain why I was hungry now.

I satisfied my hunger with a few biscuits before heading back up on deck. We were towing the slave ship behind us. It was reducing our speed drastically, but the mast was severely damaged, and there was no way it would be able to sail under its own power.

"We'll be at the coast this afternoon."

David came up behind me. I nodded absently.

"You can probably go over if you want to check on them," David said. "I heard there were some translation issues yesterday."

I shrugged. "They were fixed," I said. "One of the women spoke English."

David nodded. "Are you feeling well?" he asked.

I looked at him, startled.

"I heard about what you did yesterday, too."

Understanding suddenly dawned, and I flinched. I remembered what I had done to the sailors of the slave ship. It was entirely out of character for me. I couldn't bring myself to regret it, though. What I inflicted on the sailors was nothing compared to what the poor souls below decks would have suffered. Maybe they weren't directly involved in the sale, but they were certainly profiting off the trade.

Maybe one day I would feel worse about it. I certainly should.

I decided to follow David's suggestion and head over to the slave ship. I would feel better if I talked to Ria again and made sure she understood what was going to happen.

The former slaves were staying in the hold of the slave ship, so as to not arouse any undue suspicion if another ship saw us and there were hundreds of Africans on deck. In theory, I understood Victor's reasoning. But when I walked into the dark hold, I shuddered.

Ria was there almost immediately. She smiled a welcome at me.

I took her hand. "Are you all right down here?" I asked. "It seems so dark and unfriendly."

Ria shrugged. "It's only for one more day," she said. "Not even that. We've been here for almost a month. And now, we do not have chains."

There was that. Since Ria seemed to be handling herself fine, I let the subject drop. "Do you know what you will do when you reach Jamaica?"

Ria shrugged again and gave a little laugh. "It will be an adventure, to be sure," she said. Her accent was still thick and heavy, but her English was very good.

We sat down together against one of the walls. Other people looked at us, but decided to leave us alone. I wondered a little at that, but decided it was a good thing.

"There's a group on Jamaica that I've heard about," I said. "They call themselves the Maroons. They're mostly escaped slaves, and they're starting to frighten the English plantation owners. Everyone here would most likely be welcomed."

Ria's eyes brightened. "Do you know where we could find them?" she asked.

Regretfully, I shook my head. "I was on one of the white plantations," I said. "If I knew, they would hardly be safe."

Ria shrugged in resignation. "It is a clue, at least," she said. "We will search for them. Maybe you will join us, once your child is born."

It took me almost a full minute to process her last words. "What?"

Ria glanced at me in surprise. "You mean you do not know?" she asked.

"Know what?" I could hear the tension in my own voice.

She put her hands on my shoulders. "Josephine, you are with child."

I couldn't breathe. I stared at her in disbelief. I couldn't be pregnant. It was impossible.

But it wasn't. Victor and I had been together for many nights. I never thought about the possibility, but I should have. I was carrying Victor's child.

"Are you alright, Josephine?"

I swallowed hard and stared at Ria again. "You're certain?" I asked, my voice barely above a whisper.

She nodded. "The signs are unmistakable, even so early," she said. "I am sorry you did not know already. This was not planned?"

I shook my head numbly. I was pregnant with Victor's child. What in God's name was I going to do?

Nothing, for the moment. It wouldn't change what needed to be done. Ria and the others needed to make it safely to Jamaica so they could join the Maroons. I would deal with my pregnancy later.

I knew I was being an idiot. My pregnancy would not just magically go away. Sooner or later, I was going to have to deal with it, and I had no idea how.

Ria squeezed my shoulders again. "You will be fine," she said. "Having a child is not so bad a thing. You are certain to love him dearly."

I pushed that thought to the back of my mind. The fact that a child would come from this, that there would be someone to raise and look after, hadn't fully registered yet.

"We'll be at Jamaica in a few hours," I said. "I should go make certain everything is prepared."

Ria nodded and stood up next to me. "God go with you, Josephine."

I nodded and fled the hold. I needed sunlight. I needed time to think.

Tuppence Van de Vaarst

*****Chapter 26*****

I didn't get time to think, of course. Jamaica was already in sight when I came up on deck. I was immediately pressed into service: handling lines, directing work groups, and shouting at sailors. The island quickly came into view, but not quickly enough for me.

Some of the sailors were giving me dirty looks as I directed them. Apparently they heard I was mostly responsible for releasing the former slaves, rather than selling them. I hardly cared. I would use my gift to make their world spin if they thought to try anything against me.

I realized as we came closer, I hadn't even asked what was to become of the sailors from the slave ship. I already dealt a good deal of vengeance, but I wondered what Victor planned.

As my luck had it, I met Victor on the deck of the Reliance. We were almost in too shallow water for us to navigate, and were about to anchor. The rowboats would bring the former slaves to shore.

"What are you planning on doing with the sailors from the slave ship?" I asked. I didn't even know the name of the ship.

Victor shrugged. "We'll let them drift after we release the former slaves," he said. "You've already crippled most of them. We'll let them find their own way to shore."

There was no censure in his voice, but I flinched. I crippled the sailors without authorization from him. He should have been the one issuing that order, not me.

"Sorry," I mumbled.

Victor looked at me in surprise, then smiled. "You did nothing wrong," he said. Heedless of the other pirates, he put his arm around me. "I would have done the same thing. You just read my mind."

I looked at him in surprise. It was on the tip of my tongue to tell him what Ria just told me, but he turned away before the words made it to my mouth.

"Prepare the anchor!" he shouted. "Let's get these people ashore!"

I started helping organize the rowboats. Luckily, the slave ship had a lot of them. The former slaves would be able to row themselves to shore without any help from the pirates. There was even one rowboat left over, but I fully intended to just let that one drift, leaving the sailors on the slave ship stranded.

Ria came up to me just before she got into her rowboat. "God bless you, Josephine," she said. "You will always be welcome amongst us."

Before I could answer, she got into her rowboat. As it was lowered into the water, she blew me a kiss.

I stared after her, my thoughts in turmoil. But for once in my life, I had done the right thing.

****

We started towards Port Royal as soon as all the former slaves started rowing for Jamaica. It was already late afternoon. Technically, we could have docked, but Victor decided we would spend one more night at sea before pulling into harbor.

I spent the night in Victor's cabin. For once, we didn't argue or fight, but that was only because he was being so gentle with me. I wanted to rant and scream, I wanted to punch something, but he was obviously trying to make me feel better about the events of the day.

I wanted to tell him. How couldn't I? It was his child I was carrying. Surely he deserved to know about it just as much as I did.

I didn't tell him, though. I needed to come to terms with it myself, and that hadn't happened yet.

I woke up sick again the next morning. I slipped out of the cabin without waking Victor and threw up over the rail. I knew what this was, now. I had heard enough about pregnancy to know I could expect this for quite some time.

I stood staring out over the rail and looking towards Jamaica. What would my parents say if I came home to them in this state?

It was a silly question. My father would disown me. He'd have no choice. Either that, or he would lock me away until my child was born, then hide him from me and pretend my pregnancy never happened. Ma would burst into tears, and probably try to force me into a convent.

I wanted to curse Victor at that moment. This was just as much my fault as his, but I couldn't help blaming him. I never wanted to have a child.

My child.

My hand found its way to my belly, and I pressed gently. Although I couldn't feel anything yet, I could almost imagine I felt the tiny spark of life inside me.

I swallowed, feeling overwhelmed by emotions I had no control over. I was going to have a child. My child. I felt a fierce surge of protectiveness and love that shook me so hard I clutched at the rail.

"Sail! Two of them!"

I jerked around at the shout. It was barely sunrise. Most of the pirates hadn't woken up yet. Victor himself came stumbling out of his cabin at the shout, rubbing sleep from his eyes.

I saw the ships that the lookout had spotted. They were schooners, sleek, slim, and fast. Neither of them looked like merchant ships.

I looked at Victor questioningly. In my months of sailing with the pirates, we had very rarely come across ships that were not merchant vessels. The few we had, we merely avoided. With us flying the colors of whatever country we wanted, they left us alone, and we left them alone. These ships, however, were coming straight towards us, even with us flying the British flag.

"What do they want?" I asked Victor.

Victor looked at Harry, who had come up to stand next to him. Harry shook his head, and Victor shrugged.

"I guess we'll find out," he said. "Probably want to hail us, and make sure that we're not going to cause any trouble for Port Royal."

There was something more to it than that. Somehow, deep in my bones, I knew.

Luckily, Victor seemed to feel it as well. "Maintain course," he ordered the helmsman. "The rest of you, move down below. Get the cannons ready. We may need to make a hasty retreat."

The pirates followed Victor's word without grumbling. I went down below to direct the men. I had barely been there for ten minutes when Derry came to get me.

"Captain wants you, Jo," he said. His eyes were dark with worry. "He says there's something you need to see."

I didn't know what to make of Derry's words, so I took the steps two at a time as I climbed the ladder to the main deck. Victor was standing at the rail, staring at the schooners approaching us with his spyglass.

"What is it?" I demanded. "What do I need to see?"

Victor lowered the spyglass and looked at me. The expression on his face made me even more scared than before.

"What?"

Victor handed me the spyglass. "Look at the first schooner," he said. "On deck. Tell me if that's who I think it is."

I looked warily at him, but his eyes gave me no hint as to what I might see. I raised the spyglass to find the first schooner.

I nearly dropped it in shock. There, next to the helmsman, stood a familiar face. Twice I thought I had escaped him. Apparently, he was after me a third time.

I stared at Victor. He nodded, not needing anything other than my reaction to confirm his thoughts.

"Come about!" he shouted. "Harry, get the men to man the sails!"

Harry burst into action, and the men scrambled about, tightening some lines, loosening others. The boom swung across deck, and we spun around to face the complete opposite direction.

"We need to build speed," Victor said. "They have the advantage, currently. We have no true momentum anymore."

I stared back to where the schooners were still heading towards us. Reddings was still following me. How long would it be before I could truly escape him?

I looked at Victor. "We can't fight two ships at once, can we?" I asked.

Victor shrugged. "With good tactics," he said. "We need to find a shoal, and trap the two together so we're only fighting one at a time."

It seemed like a solid plan to me. "Do you want me to help David find one?"

Victor nodded. "Excellent suggestion," he said. "There have to be plenty around Jamaica."

I raced towards the navigator's cabin as if there were wings on my feet. David was already dragging his charts across the table.

"Shoal, right?" he asked.

I nodded, breathless. I threw myself towards the charts, my eyes skimming across the drawings.

There was only one shoal that was in easy striking distance that I could see. David saw it the same time that I did.

"There," he said, jabbing a finger at the chart. "I'll chart the course. Tell the captain to steer-" he paused, tilting his head around, "Two eight five for now. Send Derry down, I'll send him to tell you when the course changes."

I was out the door the instant David finished his sentence. I ran back towards the helm, shouting the new course to the helmsman as I went to stand beside Victor.

He was still standing at the railing, spyglass in his hand. The position of the other two ships didn't appear to have changed at all, but they were obviously pursuing us.

"Find one?" Victor asked, not turning his gaze away from the ships.

I nodded. "Course is already set. David will let us know when to change course."

Victor nodded and turned towards me. "How are you holding up?"

I paused. I was in a panic. I was in no shape for a fight. "I'll be fine," I said. I couldn't afford to be anything other than fine.

Victor nodded, taking me at my word. "Get ready for a fight, then," he said. "And hope we get to your shoal before either of the ships catch us."

I stared out at the ships. On one of them, Reddings was waiting for me. Somehow, he found out where I was. He was coming after me.

I felt my old, familiar anger boil up inside me again. After this encounter, one of us would never hunt the other again.

Tuppence Van de Vaarst

*****Chapter 27*****

We reached the shoal just in time. The first ship had just entered broadside range when we slipped behind the shoal.

We couldn't hope Reddings' ships didn't know about the shoal. They were from Jamaica, after all. This was their island.

At least we were only facing one ship, now. The entrance to the shoal wasn't big enough for both ships to chase us.

"Bring us about! I want a full broadside!" Victor's voice was harsh.

I relayed the orders, trying to keep my voice from cracking.

Our broadside was slightly short, and I cursed under my breath. It would take a few minutes for our gunners to reload.

"Jo, look at this."

I turned at the sound of Kwaku's voice. He was standing next to me, gazing across the sea.

I frowned. The second ship wasn't following the first. It was circling around, like it was trying to approach us from the other side of the shoal.

But they couldn't be. I had seen the chart. The water got far too shallow to allow a ship to cross that way. The only way out of the cove was the way we entered.

I couldn't risk it, though. "Kwaku, take over!" I shouted. I raced towards the navigator's cabin, feeling Victor's eyes on me as I passed him.

David was still bent over the charts. He looked up, startled, as I entered. "Jo?" he asked. "What's wrong?"

I stood over the chart and pointed. "There's no way a ship can get through there, right?" I asked.

David shook his head. "Not without withstanding some damage, no," he said. "Even a light schooner isn't going to make it without scraping her hull. She'd be in a bad position on the other side, if she didn't sink."

It was the answer I expected, but it didn't help. What the hell was Reddings up to?

Without explaining anything to David, I raced back to the helm. We fired another broadside during the time I was gone, but the other crew fired one as well, and I could see the damage in our sails.

I stared at the second ship. Victor saw it too, but he was focusing his attention on the first, no doubt trying to cripple it before the second ship did whatever it was trying to do.

It was heading for the other side of the shoal. There was no doubt of that in my mind. Reddings was going to trap us in a pincer. Somehow, he had a plan to get across, and then he would sink us.

It wasn't all to get to me, I realized. It could very well have been because we liberated the slaves that were bound for his plantation. That must have cost him a pretty penny.

I had no doubt he knew I was on board, however. Or if he didn't, he would find out as soon as he boarded us. And then he would enslave me, if he didn't kill me outright for all the trouble I caused him.

Unconsciously, my hand dropped to my stomach. I wanted to stand and fight. I wanted to make Reddings pay for all the pain and fear he had caused me. There was so much left undone. I still hadn't told Victor.

Wordlessly, I watched as the second ship made its way around. It was starting the crossing of the shoal now. I swallowed as a cannonball fell into the water dangerously close to our hull.

I made my way to Victor's side. "We're trapped," I said shortly.

Victor looked at me, then at the second ship making the crossing of the shoal. Somehow, despite all of David's reassurances, it was making it. I heard a few cries from the crew, but the ship wasn't slowing down any.

Victor clenched his teeth. "Then we'll go down fighting," he said. "Better that than to hang."

I couldn't die. I stared at Victor for a long moment. Should I tell him?

"Captain!" Kwaku's shout interrupted us. The first ship, the one Reddings was on, was closing fast.

Victor cursed. "All hands, another broadside, both directions!"

I looked and saw the second ship was also drawing closer. They were almost aligned so that if they were to fire at the same time, we would be destroyed from both sides.

Our guns rang out an instant later, flying into both ships. Almost simultaneously, Reddings' ship fired.

A cannonball ripped through the deck not ten feet from where Victor and I were standing. The Reliance shuddered, tilting dangerously to one side before righting itself. I clung desperately to the railing.

As I straightened, I managed to catch a glimpse of the second ship. Our gunners were accurate. Two large holes now exposed the below deck of the ship, and they had veered slightly away from us.

"Damage report!" Victor's voice cracked. I saw him climbing to his feet. He must have been knocked off balance.

"Mast's been hit, Captain!"

My heart sank, and I saw Victor's face darken. He glanced around quickly, then looked at me.

"Have everyone focus their fire on that ship." He pointed at the ship that crossed the shoals. "It has to have sustained damage crossing those shoals, and we've crippled it further. I want it out of commission. Now."

I turned and started running towards the ladder to the below deck. "Focus fire on larboard!"

Kwaku nodded at me grimly before turning to give the orders to the gunners. He knew what our situation was.

Our guns fired again, just as Reddings' ship fired another broadside into us. I staggered at the impact, falling to my knees on deck.

"Jo! Get everyone up here now! We're being boarded!"

I managed to relay Victor's orders in a hoarse yell. Soon the entire gun crew was up on deck, swords and pistols blazing in the sunlight. Reddings' ship was closing in fast, and I could see Reddings himself standing next to the helmsman. His eyes met mine, and I felt my stomach clench.

I turned away and saw the second ship veering even further away from us. At least we would only have to repel one ship at a time.

I drew both my pistols, leaving my cutlass in its sheath for now. I met Reddings' gaze again. He saw me and nodded, the slightest hint of a smile on his face.

My blood boiled. Here he was, taking my life away from me, and he had the gall to be smiling about it? I wasn't going to let him take anything from me. Or from my child.

"Board them, lads!"

"Stand ready to repel boarders!" Victor's voice was hard and clear over the din of combat.

I ran towards the rail as several of Reddings' sailors started swinging across on the rope attached to the mast. I fired one of my pistols at one, and he dropped into the water with a scream.

I couldn't believe how many of them there were. Reddings' ship got close enough for the sailors to jump across, it seemed like hundreds of them crossed onto the Reliance.

It was madness. I slashed at sailor after sailor, trying desperately to find Victor, Kwaku, Derry, anybody I knew. I couldn't see anyone. I was getting surrounded.

I felt the hands grab me from behind, and I jabbed behind me with my elbow. Another man grabbed me, and I was forced to the ground, a sword blade against my throat.

I couldn't breathe. Around me, the sounds of battle were fading, and someone, not Victor, was shouting orders to surrender.

We had lost. Reddings had taken our ship.

I couldn't give up. Not now. Not when I had so much to lose.

"Get them together."

The blade was removed from my neck, but I was given no chance to move by myself. I was hauled roughly to my feet and dragged over to where a handful of the pirates were kneeling on the deck. I was shoved down on my knees next to Kwaku.

"Don't move," the sailor ordered me.

I looked at Kwaku. He was kneeling, but he looked as if he would much rather collapse. Blood was leaking out of his leg in a slow, steady, stream, pooling beneath his knees.

I swallowed and looked around. Derry was being dragged over to us now, clearly dazed. He slumped next to me when the sailors dropped him, and I saw the blood caking on the side of his head.

"Sorry, Jo," he whispered. "I can't see straight."

I managed a smile for him. "You did your best, Derry. We'll get out of this, don't worry."

"Silence!" a hand slapped the back of my head.

I clamped down on my tongue. Despite my words to Derry, I couldn't see a way out of this. We were trapped and surrounded, and our weapons were being taken from us. I still couldn't find Victor.

As if my thought had summoned him, the next two sailors were dragging Victor. He had multiple wounds across his arms, and a streak of red glared where his face had been slashed, but his eyes still blazed. They blazed even brighter when he saw me.

He was alive. At least, for now.

One by one, the rest of the surviving pirates were brought to kneel beside us. Harry, Eli and David were missing. So were at least a third of the rest of the crew.

I swallowed as I saw Reddings stepping across the gangway between the two boats. He was as immaculately dressed as ever, as if the battle hadn't even grazed him.

The sailors all straightened, and the one who seemed to be in charge snapped a salute. "Mr. Reddings!"

Reddings nodded affably at the man. "Good work, Duncan. Have you isolated the captain?"

Duncan was about to speak when Victor struggled to his feet.

"Don't bother." His voice was hoarse. "I'm Captain Victor Abrams."

"Captain," Reddings' voice was cool. "Your ship put up quite a fight. You deserve some respect for that, at least. For a pirate and a thief."

Duncan gestured, and two other sailors moved to grab Victor's arms.

"Take him to the brig," Reddings ordered casually. "We'll hold him for trial in Port Royal."

The sailors hustled Victor off to the other ship. I stared after him. I should have told him sooner. Now I might never have a chance.

I stiffened as Reddings began to scan the rest of the pirates. I forced myself to meet his eyes as he found me.

Reddings said nothing, merely pointed. Two sailors grabbed my arms and hauled me upright, frog marching me in front of Reddings.

"Josephine Crawford." Reddings' voice was neutral. "You don't know how much trouble you've caused me."

I glared at him. "Not nearly as much as you've caused me."

Reddings' raised an eyebrow, but continued as if I said nothing. "Imagine my surprise when I see my erstwhile fiancé in a low-class bar in Charleston. In men's clothing, of all things. Imagine my further surprise when I find out the ship she flees to is a known pirate ship." He shook his head. "Josephine, Josephine. I thought you had better taste."

"I had enough taste not to marry you," I quipped. I was probably antagonizing him, but I couldn't help it.

His eyes darkened, but he continued still. "Imagine my further surprise when that same pirate ship is seen attacking one of my own slave ships not a fortnight later. Can you imagine what an opportunity this was? I had just arrived in Port Royal, too. I couldn't have been in a better position to pursue you. And possibly recover my slaves?" He looked expectantly at me. "My men are searching below decks. They'll have no hope of hiding."

In this, at least, I could disappoint him. "They're gone," I said with satisfaction. "They're not onboard. You'll never find them."

Reddings' composure dropped for an instant, and I saw the anger banked behind his mask. "Once again, you disappoint me, Josephine. You have been far more trouble than you would have been worth. You are going to have to make it up to me."

I spat in his face, and one of the sailors holding me gave me a clout on the side of the head.

Reddings shook his head. "Take her to my cabin and lock her in. I'll deal with her when we're done with this lot."

The two sailors began to lead me towards the other ship.

"You'll never get anything from me," I snapped. "You have nothing left to threaten me with. I'll take death over slavery."

The sailor's stopped at Reddings' hand signal. "Is that so?" he smiled. "Take her to the brig instead," he ordered. "Maybe with the prospect of death hanging over her, working for me won't seem like such a bad option."

The sailors laughed as they began leading me away again, but I felt a moment of relief. At least I wasn't going to Reddings' private cabin. And Victor would be down there.

*****Chapter 28*****

The brig was dark, damp, and cold, And the sailors guiding me down were none too gentle. They threw me down on the floor and locked the bars behind me, leaving me scrambling to my feet to shout curses after them.

There was a laugh behind me. "That's my Jo."

I turned to see Victor slumped on the floor in the corner of the brig. I fell to my knees beside him and slammed my fist onto the floor.

"God damn him."

Victor laughed again, but his voice was strained. "We're in for it now."

I shook my head. "We'll get out somehow. We have to."

Victor shook his head. "It took me over ten years to get here. That's a lot longer than most pirates. But I knew it would be the end. I'm sorry you didn't get longer."

He sounded resigned, and I felt panic rise in my throat. He couldn't be giving up. I needed him to help us escape!

He looked me in the eyes. "Jo, those weren't regular sailors. They were navy. I don't know how Reddings got them to sail on his ships after us, but he did. They're trained, and they outnumber us. We're only half a day at most from Port Royal. We're locked up with no weapons. What chance of escape do you see?"

I clenched my fists. "There has to be," I said stubbornly. I couldn't believe it would come to this.

Victor put a hand on my shoulder. "I'm sorry, Jo. I should have told you this life was usually one quick blaze of glory."

I stared at him, then slumped down to the floor. Victor was right. I couldn't see a way out of this.

I dropped my hand to my stomach. If I didn't tell him now, I might regret it forever.

"Victor, I need to tell you something."

Victor shook his head. "No, I need to tell you something."

I looked up, startled. His eyes were as serious as I'd ever seen them.

"I've been remarkably selfish these past few months," he said. "I know pirates are supposed to be, but I had it all. Gold, my ship, and a wonderful woman to share it with."

I swallowed. He couldn't be saying what I thought he was.

"Victor."

Victor put his finger over my lips. "Let me finish. I love you, Jo. I'm sorry I didn't do anything to prove it to you."

I stared at him, trying to fully comprehend what Victor was telling me. I never thought he loved me. Liked me and respected me, and certainly lusted after me. But love?

He took my hands, and I realized I was shaking.

"I'm sorry, Jo," he said again. "I shouldn't have been so selfish. When I realized I loved you, I should have thought about giving you a better life than the one we were living."

"It wasn't a bad life," I managed. My voice was shaking.

He laughed. "Threat of death every day? I found it exhilarating, but it didn't exactly end well."

"Victor," my voice cracked, and I swallowed and tried again. "I'm pregnant."

He froze, his hands still on mine. "What?" His voice was a harsh whisper.

I took one of his unmoving hands and placed it on my stomach. "I'm with child."

His eyes followed his hand, but he didn't seem to actually see. "No," he whispered. "No, oh God, Jo, no. I am so sorry."

I felt myself tensing all over. His distress was reminding me of my own.

"If I had known, if I'd even thought, Jo, I would never have-"

"Don't apologize," I cut him off and grabbed his shoulders. "I enjoyed every minute of it."

That broke Victor's tension, at least. "Even the part where you were blackmailed and cheated to win a duel?"

I glared at him. "Everything else, then."

He laughed shortly, then dropped his gaze back to my stomach. "A child," he whispered. "My God, Jo, I'm sorry. I should have thought about it, I should have..." his voice trailed off.

"Stop it," I snapped. "It's done. I'm pregnant. Should haves won't change a thing."

He met my eyes again. "I'm sorry, Jo."

I sighed. "It's not like it will change anything," I said. "We're still trapped."

Victor narrowed his eyes. "Didn't Reddings want you for himself?" he asked. "Why are you down here with me?"

I smiled. "I may have been annoying."

"That's my Jo," he said. "So is he still planning on keeping you as his personal slave?"

I shrugged, trying to cover my shaking. "I assume so. Though I may have told him I'd rather die."

"You- of course you did." Victor shook his head. "Do you think he'll try to force you into it again? Where are the rest of the crew?"

I shook my head. At least Victor seemed to have a little more energy. "Of course he'll try, and I'm not sure. I was the first one he saw."

Victor nodded. "We'll have to assume he'll want to hang the lot of us," he said. "He'll want the prestige. An entire crew of pirates."

I narrowed my eyes. "Do you have a plan?"

He shook his head. "No, but if you're with child, I am not going to just let them hang me," he said. "I am going to try and give you, and our child, a life."

I stilled for a moment. Our child. I liked those words, more than I thought I would.

Victor said he loved me, and I hadn't returned those words. I had been avoiding thinking about my feelings. I had assumed my life on the Reliance would be temporary, so I hadn't let myself realize how much I had fallen for him.

Father would have killed me if he knew I fell for a pirate. Reddings might kill me too, if he realized I let a pirate into my bed before he had his chance.

Reddings. He wanted me for my abilities. Abilities only he could see through.

I straightened. "I have an idea."

Victor started. "What?"

I grinned, feeling my belt pouch. They had taken my pistols and sword, but they hadn't taken the small stash of herbs. "Reddings won't come down here himself. When the next sailor comes, he won't see us."

His eyes widened in realization. "What will they see?"

I took a deep breath. "The wall."

It would drain me, I knew. I might be too tired to fight my way out, but I had to try. It was better than waiting for death here.

*****Chapter 29*****

It seemed like forever until the first sailor made their way back down to the brig. Victor and I hadn't said much else. Both of us were still trying to process what we had told each other.

I didn't know how Victor was handling what I told him. I still hadn't come to terms with it myself. I was having no luck comprehending his statement.

He loved me. How?

My thoughts were distracted by the clump of feet on the ladder leading to the brig. I scattered the herbs I prepared, then drew on the power of the sea beneath me.

I heard Victor's intake of breath, and I knew it must have worked. I could still see both of us, but no one else could. Except Reddings.

I nearly gasped myself as I saw the two sailors dragging a nearly unconscious Derry down the ladder. No one had done anything about his wounds, and I winced in sympathy as his head slammed against the wall, making him moan.

I glanced at Victor and saw him move into position next to the door. I put one hand on the iron bars to steady myself as I waited on the other side.

The two sailors stopped abruptly as they came to the bottom of the ladder. They dropped Derry and started coming towards the cell where Victor and I were, their voices raised.

"Prisoners escaped!"

I saw them scanning every inch of the cell, but if they didn't know about my abilities, then they had no reason to suspect it was anything other than empty.

They looked at each other. "Get the boy in there," one of them said.

I tensed as they started dragging Derry forward. One of them took a key from his pouch and started opening the door.

I had to wait for Victor's signal. I was the only one who could see what the other was doing.

The door opened slowly, and Victor nodded sharply. He pounced on the sailor closest to him, while I grabbed the cutlass hanging from the other sailor's belt and slashed his throat open.

It was over in an instant. The two sailors were dead, and I dropped to my knees beside Derry, dropping my seeming.

"Derry? Derry, are you all right?"

Derry's eyes flickered open, and he managed a feeble grin. "We escaping?"

Victor knelt down next to me. "Tell us quickly, Derry," he said. "What's going on out there? Where are the rest of the crew?"

"Crew's on this ship," Derry said. "On deck, mostly tied. They're towing the Reliance back to Port Royal. We're all to stand trial."

I glanced at Victor, a glimmer of hope forming. "Think we can get the Reliance back?" I asked.

"Depends on how much you can do," Victor said. "How many people can you hide?"

I shook my head. "Not all of us for long enough," I said regretfully.

Victor started to curse, and I shook my head. "I have a better idea. We can sneak up and cut everyone's bonds and give them weapons, and then attack all at once with the element of surprise."

Victor nodded. "How are you holding up, Derry?"

Derry waved a hand aimlessly. "I'll be fine, Captain."

"He can't fight," I said.

"I agree," Victor said before Derry could protest. "Derry, I have an important task for you. You know where my private stash is, right? Get back to the Reliance and gather as much as you can."

I stared at Victor, but I said nothing. It would keep Derry out of trouble.

Victor looked at me. "Ready, Jo?"

I nodded, drawing on the remaining power of the ritual and casting the seeming on the three of us this time. I let Victor and Derry go up the ladder first, then I followed.

I made it up just in time. Someone heard the sailor's warning about us escaping, and there were sailors running all over trying to find us. Two of them were coming towards the ladder down to the brig as I stepped out on deck.

We avoided them and headed towards the main deck. I saw Derry separate and head towards the stern, where the Reliance was being towed. Hopefully he would be safe enough.

Our escape being noticed wasn't a bad thing, I realized. The sailors guarding the remaining pirates were down to a mere handful while everyone else searched.

Quickly, Victor and I went up behind each pirate and cut their wrists free, ordering them to stay where they were. I saw a number of them flinch. Most of them had some idea of the abilities I had, but hadn't knowingly seen them in action yet.

As we untied everyone, I made it seem that they were still bound. It wouldn't do for the sailors to notice the pirates were free before we were ready.

Kwaku was the last one I came to. Someone had allowed him to bind his leg with his own shirt, so his wound had stopped bleeding, at least.

I pressed the sword I took into his hand. I could get another one when the attack started.

"Be ready," I whispered.

I made my way over to Victor. I was so tired. I couldn't hold onto the seeming for much longer if I was going to have the energy to fight.

I touched his arm lightly, and he jumped. I suppressed a smile.

"Ready, Jo?"

"Ready."

He nodded, and I grabbed a sword out of a nearby sailor's belt. Victor grabbed another, then yelled at the top of his lungs.

"Attack, pirates!"

Chaos erupted. I dropped my seeming on Victor and myself, keeping only enough of my concentration free to keep Derry hidden, wherever he was.

The surprise was working in our favor for now, at least. I kept close to Victor this time, the two of us working together to kill anyone who got in our way.

We didn't really have a plan besides getting back to the Reliance. I didn't even know if we could get the sails rigged in time.

There was a lull in the fighting, and I stopped, gasping for breath. Victor looked at me, concerned.

"Are you all right?"

I nodded, waving away his hand. We needed to get out of here. Most of the sailors hadn't arrived on deck to fight us yet.

Victor nodded. "Get us a lifeboat!" he shouted.

I glanced back at the Reliance and gaped. It was now several hundred yards or so behind us. Had Derry cut us loose from the tow?

As if my thought had summoned him, Derry appeared at my elbow, grinning. I dropped my seeming on him, and Victor jumped as Derry dropped a large pouch into his hand.

"Found it, Captain!" he said. His grin faded. "There's a lot of sailors on the Reliance. They were going to come over here and help. I stopped them."

Victor clapped him on the shoulder. "Good lad," he said. "Now get to the lifeboats. We're getting out of here."

He handed the pouch to me as Derry scampered away, much more agile than he should have been with his head injury.

"Hang onto this," Victor said.

I didn't stop to question him, just tied the pouch to my belt. It was heavy, and probably contained the best portions of whatever treasures Victor had looted over the past ten years.

We made our way towards the lifeboat the pirates were lowering to the water. I jumped at the sound of a pistol shot.

Reddings had decided to appear. He stood on the upper deck near the helm, and he was glaring directly at me.

"You will pay for this, Josephine!" he exclaimed. "You will not escape!"

I looked at Victor. "Run."

We ran to join the pirates lowering the lifeboat. More sailors were arriving on deck, and we didn't have much time.

"Drop it!" Victor exclaimed. "We'll jump!"

The boat landed in the water with a huge splash, saltwater soaking all of us as it sprayed up. The pirates started leaping into the ocean. Victor and I followed.

I gasped as the water enveloped me. The coolness was a shock after the heat of the air, and I struggled for the surface, gasping for breath.

I grabbed onto the side of the lifeboat and hauled myself in, nearly collapsing. Victor was already inside, helping to drag other pirates onboard. Derry was there, as was Kwaku. He looked as tired as I did.

"Get to the Reliance," Victor ordered. "We're not letting a bunch of navy take her, are we, lads?"

The pirates let loose a ragged cheer, and grabbed as many oars as were onboard and started rowing.

We were about halfway to the Reliance when the cannons started again. Reddings' ship had turned to face us and fired. Unfortunately, their cannons missed us and hit the Reliance instead.

I stared at the Reliance in dismay. The mast was cracking and about to fall. There was no way we were going to be able to sail out of here on it.

Victor cursed and grabbed an oar out of Derry's hands. "Get us there," he said.

"Captain, she's crippled!" one of the pirates exclaimed.

Victor nodded grimly. "Get us there," he said. "Jo and I will go aboard. The rest of you, head to the other ship. We wounded her, but she's in better shape than the Reliance."

I stared at the second navy ship. It was trailing behind the Reliance, moving slowly but steadily. It was small, a sloop, but it could be our only hope.

"What about you and Jo?" Derry's voice had never sounded more childlike to me than in that instant.

"We'll join you," Victor said. "Now row, damn you!"

We rowed. The cannons kept firing, but a small lifeboat is much harder to hit than a large ship. We made it to the side of the Reliance unscathed.

"Jo, do it again," Victor ordered.

I didn't know what he was planning, but I didn't question him. We jumped into the water, and I made us appear one with it.

"Head for the ship, lads!" Victor's voice rang. "Row for your lives!"

There were ropes trailing down from the side of the Reliance into the water, and Victor grabbed one of them. "Can you climb this?" he asked.

I didn't really have a choice. "Yes!" I shouted, treading water desperately. I wasn't that great of a swimmer, and my exhaustion from using my power was catching up with me.

"Good!" Victor started hauling himself out of the water and towards the deck of the Reliance.

My arms were burning as I hauled myself the first few feet up the rope. This wasn't like climbing up to the rigging. I had footholds to do that.

Desperately, I braced my feet against the Reliance's hull and tried to haul myself up that way. It was wet and slick, but I managed to scramble up to the rail. Somehow Victor found my arm to drag me onboard.

"Almost there, Jo," he said.

I coughed. "What's our plan?" I asked.

"We're sinking the ship." Victor's voice was grim. "She can still fire her cannons. We can't let that happen."

I felt my breath catch. The Reliance had been my home for the past few months. To abandon her felt wrong.

Victor was right, though. If we were going to escape on the navy sloop, we had no choice.

"Gunpowder magazine," Victor said shortly.

I followed him across the deck, dodging navy sailors. Derry had stranded a sizeable force behind, and they were desperately trying to make repairs.

We made it down to the gunpowder magazine without incident. It was all stacked neatly, and I swallowed at the image of it all exploding.

Victor began setting a fuse. "Be ready to run."

I nodded and stayed close to the exit. Victor paused as he finished laying out the fuse.

"Can I see you, Jo?" he asked. His voice was low.

Confused, I dropped my seeming, nearly staggering as the power left me. I didn't know if I could cast it again.

In two quick strides, Victor was at my side and kissing me. I kissed him back, wrapping my arms around him and holding on as tight as I could.

"I love you, Josephine Crawford," Victor said.

I swallowed. "Victor, I." I swallowed again. "I love you too."

He smiled. "I know." He glanced down at my stomach. "I'll give you both a good life. I promise."

I shook my head, not caring at the moment. "Let's just get out of here."

"Right." Victor nodded. "Ready?"

I nodded my agreement, and Victor crouched down to strike the fuse. "Run."

We ran up the ladder. I tried desperately to draw on more power to disguise us again, but it was hopeless. I could only hope we could make it out alive.

We almost made it. We were on the main deck before we were spotted racing for the side.

I grabbed Victor's hand as we ran. We were almost there. We had to make it.

A sailor ran straight into me from the side, and I fell to the deck. I shrieked as I poked as his eyes with my thumbs, trying to get him off of me. Victor was on top of him, dragging him off me and shoving him to one side.

There were more sailors coming. We weren't going to make it.

With a strength that seemed inhuman, Victor grabbed my arm and hauled me to my feet. I couldn't hold back a scream as he somehow picked me up and threw me towards the side.

"Swim, Jo!"

I hit the water hard, and I choked, trying desperately not to go under. "Victor!" I yelled, coughing as my mouth filled with water.

I managed to turn around. I could barely catch a glimpse of Victor on the deck of the Reliance, three sailors on top of him, him fighting desperately. "Swim!" he yelled again.

I couldn't leave him there. I started to try and swim back.

The explosion silenced all my hopes.

I screamed again as I was thrown backwards and sucked underwater, thrown and battered by waves. I couldn't tell which way was up. Pieces of wood and shrapnel slammed into me, ripping my hands to shreds as I fought desperately to stay alive.

Suddenly, my head broke the surface, and I managed to take a gasping breath before I was pulled under again. This time, I managed to keep my bearings, and I struggled to the surface again, grabbing onto the closest piece of wood I could see to try and help stay afloat.

There was carnage everywhere. The Reliance was gone. I was hanging onto a piece of her mast, but there were sails and pieces of hull littering the water around me. There were bodies, too. Several men in sailor's uniforms floated nearby.

"No," I whispered. Victor had to have survived. He couldn't have died in that explosion.

I looked around wildly and saw the two remaining ships. Reddings' ship was heading towards the carnage of the Reliance, while the second had turned around and was sailing in the opposite direction.

I stared after it in dismay. There was no way I was going to catch up with it.

I stared at the wreckage around me. Victor couldn't be dead.

"Victor!" I yelled.

There was no answer. I tried desperately to call again, to look around, but there was nothing moving. And Reddings' ship was getting closer.

I bit back a sob. This couldn't be happening. We had been so close to escaping.

I looked towards the shore. Jamaica rested there, seeming like a paradise right now. It was only a few hundred yards away. I could make it.

With one last look around, I let go of the mast and started swimming. My vision started blurring, but I kept my gaze fixed on the shoreline.

*****Chapter 30*****

I was weak and exhausted by the time I made it to the beach. I dropped to my knees, only grateful to be on dry land again. My tears were indistinguishable from the saltwater on my face as I turned back towards the sea. Reddings' ship was the only one in sight.

"I knew you'd be here."

Shocked, I spun around, trying to identify whether the voice was a threat or not. I still had the cutlass I stole, but I was in no shape to use it.

But it was Ria who sat on a rock watching me. I stared at her, trying to comprehend what I was seeing.

"Ria?" I stared at the girl I recently set afloat in a rowboat towards the shore. She was dressed better already.

Ria smiled at me. "It was a bit blurry, considering I can't actually tell anything about you, but I did know I had to be here today."

I stared at her. I was too weak to make sense of what she said.

She stepped off the rock and walked towards me. "That's my gift," she said. "I can tell when I'm supposed to be places, to nudge things forward. When I couldn't tell why, I knew it had to involve you."

I stared at her. "You have the power as well," I said. "Why can everyone tell I have it, but I can't tell who does?"

Ria laughed. "It's a simple enough trick," she said. "Someone never taught you. Even I, who had the weakest power of anyone my village knew, can manage it."

I shook my head. "That would be what Hades didn't teach me," I whispered.

Ria held out her hand. "You're supposed to come with me," she said.

I looked up. "Where?"

Ria smiled. "We found the Maroons. They welcomed us. And they'll welcome you too, especially with Anansi's gift."

"With- what?"

"Anansi's gift," Ria explained patiently. "You wear his symbol, you should know. Anansi gave you that power you have." I shook my head. I was too tired for this. I just lost everything I held dear. I couldn't comprehend anything Ria was telling me right now.

Ria put her hand on my shoulder. "Come with me and recover, at least," she said. "There will be plenty of time for thought later."

I couldn't help tears from leaking out of my eyes. But I followed her. It was my only option.

*****Chapter 31*****

Ria was right about the Maroons. They welcomed me enthusiastically, especially after Ria told them it was because of me they managed to escape. I stayed with them, mostly because I had nowhere else to go. I helped them improve their encampment over the next months, and even became involved in planning some of the raids on white plantations. After nine months passed, I gave birth to my son.

My son. I stared down at the infant in my arms, trying to decide what to call him. Should I follow English tradition, and name him after his father?

"Jo!"

I glanced up as Ria entered my cabin. I was given a space of my own for my childbirth, which was much preferred to the living quarters I'd been sharing with the rest of the Maroon women. I wasn't certain how I was going to raise a child in the longhouse. I didn't want every other woman breathing down my neck. Maybe I'd take up residence in a nearby cave.

"Jo, there's a message for you." Her eyes were dancing with excitement.

I straightened, shifting my hold on my son. He was fast asleep, but I knew he'd soon be awake and screaming.

I scanned the man who followed Ria into the cabin. Dark-skinned and tall, he was dressed in clothes typical of a sailor. I caught my breath in memory.

"This is Sheber," Ria said. "He has a message for you."

"A message?" I stared curiously at Sheber. "From who? And how did they know where to send it?"

"They didn't," Sheber answered. "He doesn't even know if you're alive."

I stared at him, realization dawning. "Who doesn't?"

"Captain Victor Abrams," Sheber said, a smile forming on his face. "He says to tell you he's alive. So are Derry and Kwaku. They've got a new ship now."

My breath caught in my throat. "He's alive?"

The last I had seen of Victor was the explosion of the Reliance. I had never expected to hear about him again.

"He said to tell you his ship is called the Josephine. And you're to use the gold he gave you to raise your child," Sheber said.

I swallowed hard. "Are you one of Victor's men?" my voice cracked.

Sheber shook his head. "He rescued me," he said. "I was a slave on a ship they attacked. He dropped me off in Port Royal to make my way here. His only price was bringing you his message. A duty which has now been discharged."

"Wait!" I exclaimed as he started for the door. "Where is he? How can I find him?"

"He was in Port Royal," Sheber said. "But he was planning to leave the day after I left them. He's probably at sea again."

I felt anger rising up in me. "He couldn't even wait for a reply? I want to join him!" I exclaimed as I started to my feet.

My movement jolted awake my son, who began wailing. My attention was distracted just long enough for Sheber to slip out the door.

"God damn him!" I exclaimed. "I want to find him, bastard that he is!"

Ria smiled as I turned towards my son, angrily trying to calm him. "Well, at least you have hope now," she said. "You know he's alive."

I glared at her, but my glare faded as I looked at my infant son's tiny face.

"Ria, what's the African word for hope?" I asked.

Ria blinked. "Well, it depends which language," she said. "There's hoop, matumaini, raza."

"Raza," I decided I liked the last one. "That's his name. Raza."

Ria looked at me, at my son, and smiled. "A good choice," she said.

I stared out the cabin door. I was going to raise Raza first. But one day, Victor would find me at his side. I would get back to sea again. Whether he liked it or not.

*****Epilogue*****

The boy ran down the forest path, carefully bouncing over the rocks. He laughed as he came to the entrance of the cave he called home.

"I did it, Ma!" he exclaimed. "I beat everyone!"

His mother came out of the cave, a smile on her face. She was slender and bony, her figure more like a boy's than a woman's, and she wore her hair cropped short. Like any boy, though, he thought his mother the most beautiful woman on earth.

"I had no doubt," she said. "Did you use your gift at all?"

The boy shook his head, proud of himself. "I didn't have to!" he boasted.

His mother smiled again. "Good," she said.

The boy walked over to his mother's side. "Do you think I'll make a good sailor one day, Ma?" he asked.

His mother's eyes darkened, as they always did when he mentioned his desire to set to sea.

"Certainly," she said.

"And will I find my father?" he asked.

His mother's eyes darkened even further, but the boy ignored it. He needed this answer.

"I'm sure you will," she said.

The boy smiled. "I know he's gone away," he said. "But we can find him again, right?"

His mother's face cleared. "Of course," she said. She smiled down at him.

The boy looked up at her again. "But you'll always be here, right, Ma?"

His mother's eyes softened. "I will always be here for you, son."

The boy smiled at her, but his gaze drifted towards the direction of the open water. Someday, when he was old enough, he would set sail. And he would find his father. Soon that day would come.

ACKNOWLEDGMENTS

Writing has always been my dream. There have been many people who have helped me finally make it reality. I'm sure I have forgotten people. Thank you all!

First, my parents, Jane and Jeff, have been the best and most supportive parents I could have ever had. Especially my father, who during the last few months of me trying to get this novel together started pushing me insistently. Thank you, Papa.

My grandmother, Marty Voght, was also a huge inspiration. As a published author herself, she was my role model.

My editor, Erin Foster, was a huge help during the editing process. Charlotte Hayes, my illustrator, gave me a wonderful cover that made me actually realize I had a book on my hands.

And last but certainly not least, thank you to Martin Wilsey and everyone at Tannerhauser Press for guiding me through the publishing process. This was the scariest part of writing, and I am very grateful for their assistance.

This book is my dream come true.

ABOUT THE AUTHOR

Tuppence Van de Vaarst has long been obsessed with history, writing, the ocean, and magic. She taught herself to read at the age of three and read every single book she could get her hands on. At the age of eleven, she started creating her own stories. As she grew, her passion for stories never faded.

When she was eighteen she decided to pursue her love of the ocean by enlisting in the United States Coast Guard. Although she decided military life did not suit her, she views it as a useful experience that she can now insert into her own writing.

She is currently studying for her Master's in Medieval Studies at the University College of Dublin.